IN HER SHADOW

Also by Emma Christie

The Silent Daughter
Find Her First

IN HER SHADOW

EMMA CHRISTIE

First published in 2024 by
Mountain Leopard Press
An imprint of HEADLINE PUBLISHING GROUP

1

Cataloguing in Publication Data is available from the British Library

Paperback ISBN: 978-1-80279-465-6
Ebook ISBN: 978-1-80279-466-3

Typeset in Sabon

Printed and bound in Great Britain by Clays Ltd, Elcograf S.p.A.

HEADLINE PUBLISHING GROUP
An Hachette UK Company
Carmelite House
50 Victoria Embankment
London EC4Y 0DZ

www.headline.co.uk
www.hachette.co.uk

To Sophie, a hero worth singing for.

CHAPTER 1

Sunday

Your bedroom carpet is itchy; warm against my back.

Inches above my face there's a snort and then your breathing changes rhythm. It's slower and deeper now, and even though I'm sure sleep has taken you, I stay where I am, press my palms softly against the underside of your mattress to see if I can feel your heartbeat. When I sense a pulse I close my eyes and focus, focus, focus on the rhythm of it, and just for a moment feel like I'm holding you instead.

Your body twitches as you fall into a deeper slumber, a series of tiny frights as the tightest parts of you start to loosen then tense up again. A reaction, maybe, to the images your brain throws at you once you stop trying to control it. The bed frame groans a little every time you move, and even though I'd be flattened if it broke, and even though the underside of the mattress is touching the tip of my nose, I smile because I'd die happy if the only thing between us was memory

1

foam and fitted sheets. I wonder if you'd be angry or sad when you woke up and found a flat and lifeless version of me among the mess.

Confession one: this was not part of my plan.

Confession two: I'm glad my plan failed.

And anyway, it's your fault. I'm only here, now, because you came home earlier than it says on the timetable that's stuck to your fridge. When you got back I was already up here, lying on your bed rather than under it. I moved quickly and quietly when you started climbing the stairs. And here I am, still. It's both a thrill and a terror to be in the same house as you after too many years spent too far apart. But I know I need to go now.

I gently roll out from underneath the bed frame, soundlessly stand up.

For years I've shared a room with someone I don't love, have learned how to get up and move around without fear of waking the sleeper. I'm an expert at the art, even if the beds are bunks.

Yours is a double. I bet you'd laugh at the idea of sleeping in beds made for children and sailors: one human stacked on top of the other to save space. There, I stood on my tiptoes to watch the sleeper, but here I have an open landscape: you, from head to toe. You've swaddled yourself in the bobbled white sheets with both legs curled in around your stomach and your arms pulled up to your chin. It makes you seem smaller than you are. I picture myself scooping you up and holding you to my chest. Our hearts, reunited.

And this time I won't let you go.

When I lean closer I can almost taste the bitter tang of old saliva on your tongue, but I don't mind because you're here, now, real, breathing; not just a photo that's long since curled in on itself.

I hunch down further, bring my face level to yours.

Your lips are dry but I want to touch them, just for a second, just because I can. My hands are an inch from your mouth when you twitch, suddenly, and my heart does the same. I'm close enough to see movement under your eyelids and try to remember what that means. Does it happen when sleep is deep or when waking is imminent? I wait with my breath held and my lungs bursting, and even though it hurts, all I can think of is this: you're even more beautiful asleep than I remember.

I reach out again, both hands stretched wide above your bed, head, mouth. Your breath is hot on my palms and there's a part of me that wants to capture it; to steal the most precious part of you and keep it for myself, forever.

I smile, then, and whisper: I'm here.

It's me, at last. Your happy ending.

CHAPTER 2

Monday

Dave Kellock's hands were so cold he could barely grip the sponge. He tossed it into the bucket then stood back, admired the gleaming windscreen of his bus. Not a splattered fly in sight. He'd almost lost a digit in the process but it was worth the suffering, always.

He rubbed his hands to warm them as he gazed out of the depot towards the beach and the pinkening sky above it. The day was waking up, and Portobello Promenade with it. There would be a few mad folk in swimming soon enough, boasting blue legs and woolly hats and the conviction that frigid water made them stronger, braver, purer, better.

He could do with some of that.

Dave turned back inside, flinching when he spotted the staff noticeboard. Crystal had pinned up the article from yesterday's newspaper. The headline read *Beloved Driver Bags City's Top Award*, and beneath it was a massive photo of his big baldy head next to the bus he usually drove. He'd been as shocked as anyone when the news came in. He'd been voted as Edinburgh's Outstanding Citizen Of The Year in recognition of all his voluntary work in and around the city, from beach litter collections to working the food bank to driving the big collection van for a local furniture charity. The award ceremony was this Thursday at the National Museum, and Crystal was making a right fuss. Said she'd be there with bells on, and he didn't doubt it. She'd even organised staff drinks afterwards with him and all the other drivers. He wished she hadn't. There were only so many pats on the back one man could take before it started bruising. To be fair, he'd lapped it up at first, agreed to an interview in the local press, despite the fact that alarm bells shrieked when he was asked.

The journalist brought with her a photographer and questions he didn't want to answer. *How do you feel? What inspires you to do so much for others?* He'd tried to halt the interview halfway through but the journalist had talked him round, said it would be good publicity for the charities he supported. So he'd gone ahead with it and, just like that, his face and name was printed on twenty thousand copies of the local daily. He'd momentarily enjoyed seeing himself in the paper and reading ego-swelling comments from lots of folk he didn't even know. They used words like *generous* and *reliable* and *cheerful*, and said he went out of his way to be helpful and was a local hero and that he was one of a kind.

Aye, he was one of a kind all right.

He plunged his hands back into the bucket of freezing water, and tried to rinse clean the dirty sponge. Most of the filth clung on. The majority of it was unidentifiable but some of it was easy to label, even out of context: the crisp complexity of an insect wing, a spindly black leg, bent at an invisible knee. Dave stared at the broken bits of tiny beings, daring himself to pick them off and ping them on to the floor with a flick of his middle finger. Instead he pushed the sponge under the surface and twisted it, hard. His guts echoed the movement of his hands.

His nerves were getting worse; always did at this time of year.

Too many birthdays and anniversaries; reminders.

He stood up, grimaced at himself in the windscreen. He'd been at it for almost an hour, face an inch from the surface as he scrubbed off the sticky splatters of tiny corpses. The cleaning staff had taken offence at first and other drivers took the piss, couldn't fathom why he'd come to work *early* to do a job others were paid to do. Dave had tried to laugh it off, told them he was a clean freak. As if *that* was the part of himself he most wanted to hide.

'Looking good, Dave.'

He turned, already smiling at the sound of Crystal's voice. 'Me or the bus?'

'What do you think?'

She winked on her way to the staff room and a few seconds later he heard the sound of a kettle boiling and two mugs being placed on the counter. Crystal always came in early as well, though Dave suspected that was more to do with escaping home than anything else.

He did a final revision of the windscreen; then, satisfied, poured the filthy water down the drain just outside the main door. He tossed the sponge into the bin, silently wishing the insects a better deal in the next life.

Back inside, the staff room smelled of coffee and microwave porridge. Crystal was flicking through the free newspaper but she closed it when he walked in. She smiled and handed over his mug then clinked hers against it. 'Here's to a quiet Monday.'

'May the wankers stay at home,' said Dave, taking a biscuit from the tin and pulling the paper towards him. The main story was a whinge about the city centre roadworks and down the side they'd squeezed in a report about a student being stabbed on the first day of Freshers' Week. Every day spawned a thousand private tragedies. Dave pushed the paper away and turned his back to the worktop, let his eyes blur as he stared instead at an enormous unused whiteboard. He wished his mind could be blank and empty, or at least wiped clean.

Crystal nudged him. 'You look lost.'

'Just tired.' Dave smiled, bringing his eyes back to hers.

Crystal wore make-up thick enough to write your name in, if you dared to reach over and drag a fingernail across her cheek. Dave knew why, wished he could save her from it. She'd married a dick, spent a decade regretting it and another one trying to walk away for good. Colin, a teacher, assumed they were all thick as tree trunks because they used their hands at work instead of their brains. Colin did the opposite, but clearly used his hands at home, fists pulled tight as a duck's arse. Dave had met him once at the pub, made sure he *accidentally* spilled a pint of beer down Colin's jeans so it looked like he'd pissed himself. Dave had been pretty pleased about it on the night but regretted it the next time he'd signed on for a shift, had seen the bruises on Crystal's arms when she'd tugged up her sleeve to check her watch. Colin's doing, but Dave's fault. He was a walking curse.

He took a sip of coffee and a bite of biscuit then realised he hadn't washed his hands after touching that sponge, that scraps of the dead were still on him. And now, in him. He gagged, turned, spat into the stainless steel sink.

'My coffee's not that bad, is it?' Crystal's voice was warm; but the bile in Dave's mouth was burning. He swallowed it down and closed his eyes, wishing for blackness. Instead his brain threw out the usual slow-motion replay.

Desperate eyes, an inch from his, as life leaked away. *Help us,* they said.

But Dave did not.

Crystal moved closer and put a hand on his back. He flinched, trying to ignore the part of himself that longed for any kind of human touch, for someone to reach out and tug him closer and tell him he was a good man after all.

'You OK?'

'Will be,' he said, spitting a few more times then turning on the tap, rinsing his mouth and the sink before he turned back to her. His face was flushed, his insides on fire.

'Heavy night on the beers?'

'As if,' he said. Almost twenty years since he'd touched one. 'Maybe something I ate.'

Lies came so naturally to him now that he rarely noticed them. They say that if you practise some-thing long enough it becomes automatic, something the body learns to do without any need for thought. Dave's specialist subject was mistruth.

'I should get started.'

'Before you go . . .' Crystal opened her handbag and pulled out an envelope. 'Happy birthday.'

'Bless you, Crystal. I'll keep it for my tea break,' he said, slipping it into his pocket and turning away from her before she noticed how easily kindness flattened him.

Ten minutes later he was sitting on the bus, adjusting the rear-view mirror and avoiding catching his own eye. Some folk were born looking as if they'd murder your family and he was one of them, didn't need a reminder. He tightened the fat knot on his company tie and turned to the first passenger who climbed on board, a crumpled woman carrying a battered Bag for Life in each hand. She smelled of fried onions.

'Good morning, sweetheart.' Dave gave her a smile big enough to share and, just like that, the daily charade began. If you're cheerful they'll love you and never look any deeper.

And we're off.

Behind him, most passengers sat with their heads hung over their phones, probably complaining to pals about their wives or work or weather – or the driver. You could never be too careful these days: one false move caught on camera could ruin a whole career.

Dave eased his foot on to the accelerator, enjoyed the familiar rumble and roar as the bus moved forward. This route had one hundred and ten stops and, in theory, took ninety-nine minutes to complete. Four times a day he drove from the depot in Portobello into the city centre and beyond; became a moving part in thousands of daily routines. He could set his clock by the habits of strangers, like the Spanish lad with the high-pitched voice who took the seven-thirty bus every single morning from Portobello High Street to Waverley Station. He'd pass the big sights of the city along the way – Arthur's Seat and the Scott Monument then the black crags topped with that great lump of a castle. From there the houses got bigger and the bus would be quieter, except on rugby days, when half the city would head for Murrayfield Stadium. They'd fill the bus with beery breath and stale farts, or stagger in noisy groups along the road while Dave trundled along behind. Animals, the lot of them. Dave would smile anyway, then whisk those who remained towards the zoo and the frigid pandas. When he reached the end of the route Dave turned and drove the same roads in reverse. But, as he closed in on the coast, his nerves would tighten, every time.

Portobello came first. Dave was born and bred five minutes from the beach and he'd moved back to his childhood home a couple of years ago. There, he felt fine. But the next town on his route was Musselburgh, a seaside community known as 'the Honest Toun'. Honest, my arse. It was home to Dave's greatest shame; the source of all his lies.

Driving through Musselburgh was Dave's daily flagellation. He could have requested a different route.

11

He could have looked the other way. Instead he slowed the bus when the town's harbour came into view and forced himself to look *there,* for as long as he could bear it. He told himself he was blessed in some ways; was one of few humans who could pinpoint with such precision the place where life went wrong.

From the harbour he drove on, shame trailing behind him like streamers on a wedding car. Then he pulled in to a stop on Musselburgh High Street.

The bus shelter was busy but only one person stepped forward, head down, hesitantly edging towards the open doors. Dave leaned forward. 'I don't bite, pal!'

And so she came closer, stepped on board.

Dave recognised the woman the moment their eyes met, even though she looked away almost immediately. In one hand she was clutching a bright blue leather purse. Her other hand was pulled into a fist so tight that the skin on her knuckles was creaseless and white. It wasn't raining but the hood of her dark green coat was pulled up, framing the face that had haunted him for decades.

She dropped a few coins into the box without looking at him again, asked for a single into Edinburgh then headed for a seat before the machine churned out her ticket. Usually he'd call passengers back if they forgot it, but instead he stared at that square of glossy paper, studying the smudged ink as if her name and address and reason for being on his bus would be written there in black and white. As if it would explain how the impossible could become the opposite of itself; how the woman he'd killed was here, now, sitting on his bus. Staring right at him.

CHAPTER 3

She sat in the row most folk avoided: that place where the floor curved up to house the wheel beneath it, forced knees towards chins. Heat and vibrations from the fat tyres would reverberate up through the floor and into your shoes and feet and would make their way to your arse via the burgundy-coloured carpet that covered every seat on the bus. Nobody ever chose that row if others were free, unless they enjoyed suffering.

'You wanting my money or not?' The question was followed immediately by an irritated *knock-knock* on the window that separated Dave from his passengers.

He dragged his eyes away from the woman, pushed a smile into place for the wee man with a big hairy mole on his chin. Brian, his name was. He was always pissed off about something; took the bus every Monday but never changed his shirt or his expression. The other drivers had no time for him but Dave knew anger was a bastard to carry around with you; that nobody in their right mind would actively choose it.

He blinked and held it for a few seconds, tried to use the momentary blackness to reset his mind.

Think logically, Dave. Focus on facts.

The woman on the bus could not be the person he thought it was for one startlingly simple reason. He'd killed her. End of story. It was his mind, playing nasty tricks.

The last time he'd seen her, those cheeks had been splattered with blood. As were his hands. They'd still been on her when heartbeats had stopped, and the child she'd been carrying had died with her.

Two lives, snuffed out. It's easier to lose control than to regain it.

Dave jumped and opened his eyes when Angry Brian rapped the glass, again. He felt another rush of bile in his throat. He needed to get off the bus; to unlock the cabin door and push past passengers and suck in the cold, damp air of an Edinburgh morning.

Take control, Dave. Use the mask. Hoist your shield.

'You hear me? I said you look like shite this morning.'

'Nice to see you too, Brian.'

'See me? Helps if you look, doesn't it? Instead of ogling the lassies.'

'I wasn't—'

'You were so.' Brian curled his top lip, exposed teeth with plaque so thick it looked like mashed potato. 'Lucky for you I'm a patient man.'

'And it's much appreciated,' said Dave, ending the conversation with a nod and a pointed glance over Brian's shoulder. Usually he'd chat for longer but he was worried that his thoughts would turn into words and tumble out of his mouth before he had time to stop them.

Brian harrumphed, then sat right next to a man reading the free paper, no doubt so he could complain about having elbows in his face. Next up was the ginger woman from the bakery, the one who winked every time she held up her bus card. *Smile and nod, Dave. Smile and nod.* Then came the blond lad with that mad spaniel that was a right pain in the arse but funny with it. 'I'll take whatever he's having,' said Dave. He'd made the same quip before but the boy laughed anyway then led the dog up the back; tried unsuccessfully to shoo it on to the floor when it leapt up on the seats and lay down. Dave called out to the folk still standing on the pavement but they smiled and waved him on. Doors closed, mirrors checked, foot down.

From the outside, an ordinary morning.

The next stop was only a short distance away but the traffic was moving at an inch per minute. He heard sighs from behind, swallowed his own. Somebody started muttering about roadworks and how useless the council was until someone else butted in and said it might be an accident that was causing the hold-ups on the road and they should be grateful it wasn't them that was in it. Nobody argued.

Dave pulled on the handbrake and searched for her in the rear-view mirror. The woman was looking right at him so he turned away, too fast, then cursed himself. He had to look, be sure. She might just be staring into space: body here and mind a million miles away. Your brain could take you anywhere you wanted: to the past or future, to somewhere imagined or real.

With the living, or with the dead.

He glanced in the mirror, met her eyes. She didn't flinch or blink or look away, and just before he turned back to the road he thought he saw her lips move, just a touch. Was she mouthing something to him? He flushed and looked away, anxiety creeping up his spine like cold fingers. It *could not* be her but it was, it was, it was, it was.

You're losing it, Dave. Again.

Ghosts don't pay in cash or leave a smudge on the window when they lean against it. Ghosts don't smile and pull their bag on to their lap when some old bastard with a gammy leg wants to sit on the seat next to them. Ghosts stare, scare, stalk. Ghosts settle old scores.

Stop it.

He'd been here before, knew it must be a trick of the light and mind and memory. He used to see her all the time, and not just on the buses. He could be at the depot or the supermarket or the football or the wee coffee shop on the corner of his road and he'd see her walk past the window and glance in his direction.

He'd once dared follow the figure he saw, reached for her arm while she waited for the supermarket doors to shudder open. She'd turned, shocked, shaken him off. He'd made excuses, said she looked like someone he used to know.

Didn't mention *he* was the reason she was a past tense.

The point was this: he was mistaken then and he was mistaken now. It could not be her.

But he'd check, once more. Just to be sure.

He glanced in the rear-view mirror, but instead of the woman, he caught the eye of some lad in a football top, bleached blond hair plastered to his scrawny wee face. He glared at Dave then burped. Dave shook his head. The rest of him was shaking already.

He shouldn't have fastened the top button, should have left the tie in the drawer same as everyone else. But he always had to go one better, didn't he? Cleanest bus, smartest driver, most outstanding citizen. What a joke. Well, he was choking here, properly choking, and it would serve him right. His breath sounded as though he'd been for a run. He tried to slow it, sucking in air through his nostrils in long, slow inhalations. His heart ignored his efforts but he kept at it until the skin on his knuckles was once again loose and wrinkled.

That's it, pal. Easy does it.

A bell rang and he realised he'd almost missed a stop. He pumped his foot against the brake pedal, trying to ease the bus to a halt without too many shudders. Made it. He let the air drain out of him and looked yet again in the rear-view mirror. The burping lad left and the space he'd stood in was filled by an old woman wearing a headscarf, a young mum with a double buggy, and two chattering cyclists, yellow neon splattered with mud. They obscured Dave's view of the woman but, as he pulled away from the stop, everyone swayed slightly with the movement. Again, their eyes met. Two humans, five metres apart. He held the woman's gaze this time; expected her to look away but she did not.

And then, it came; a thud.

Dave slammed on the brakes, too late.

Behind him, yelps of surprise and worried *what the fuck*s and the scrape of dumped drinks cans sliding under seats, along the plastic floor.

In front of him, a mountain bike; now scrap metal.

CHAPTER 4

Dave paused before he opened the door to the staff room at the depot, knew heads would turn with the hinges. Inside would be the smell of crap coffee and other people's sandwiches and the reek of gossip spreading faster than any virus ever could.

The golden boy, tarnished.

The good news? Nobody was hurt in the accident. There were shaking heads but everyone had walked away whole. The bad news? He'd rammed his bus into the back of a red campervan, bashed its arse to pieces and mangled the bike mounted on a back-door rack. The insurance company would pay for the damage to both vehicles but it would take more than paperwork to fix Dave, and his reputation.

He opened the door a few inches, heard chatter and the rumble of a boiling kettle. That was it, right there: ordinary life. For a moment he paused and soaked up the simplicity, enjoyed the illusion that he belonged there; that he was a man who deserved to be liked, praised, loved.

Few knew otherwise. And even fewer would believe what he saw when he closed his eyes.

That face, smudged with blood.

And Dave's hands on her.

He'd lost sight of the woman after the accident. He'd been busy with police and dealing with the pissed-off driver of the campervan. The passengers had been loaded on to another bus with another driver, were long gone by the time Dave was done with the formalities. He'd taken a taxi back to the depot, head in a mess. His brain had churned out theory after theory in the hope that one of them would seem logical. But the only one that made sense was this: he'd imagined the whole thing. He'd made a mistake. It was not her. If he'd had the opportunity to look at her properly, face to face, he'd have realised that.

And now? He should forget about it and move on. Easier said than done when the guilt stayed put; dug in its claws.

Sure enough, he decided to make himself feel even worse by typing her name into his phone – *Carmen Martinez* – then searching for it online. Nothing came up. He added his own name to the search box beside hers, was relieved when that search came back blank as well.

Thank Christ.

He wasn't surprised, though. Back then news came mainly in paper form, or on the TV. Instant internet news hadn't yet caught on, so most local newspaper stories were lost to bins and fires and chip shops. A few copies would be kept, of course, by libraries and archives and by the people whose stories they told.

Dave had kept dozens of cuttings, a sickening souvenir. The papers had used all the clichéd phrases bashed out whenever someone beautiful was killed at the hands of another. Add in the fact she was pregnant and you've got a story that grabs head-lines and hearts for weeks. He'd carefully cut arti-cles out of the paper with sharp scissors then folded them precisely to make sure the words and photos weren't lost in a greasy crease of newsprint. He'd hidden most of them in his mum's attic the day he fled Edinburgh almost two decades earlier and not looked at them since. But he'd read the articles so many times he could pretty much recite them word for word. They were an antidote of sorts: whenever he felt happy, he'd force himself to think of those articles and remember why he didn't deserve to feel good after all.

There was movement behind him. One of the drivers. 'You coming or going, pal?'

'Good question,' said Dave, then pushed open the staff room door. A few drivers were hunched over one of the tables, reading yesterday's paper by the looks of things. Crystal had been so chuffed, she'd bought about ten copies.

One of the drivers looked up. Jack, his name was. Built like a bull. Not to be messed with. But his hard face cracked into a smile when he saw Dave.

'Kept that one quiet,' he said, nodding to the paper. 'Well deserved, pal.'

'Just doing my bit.'

'More than most of us. Crystal says she's organised drinks on Thursday after the ceremony?'

'Don't feel like you have to—'

'Wouldn't miss it. We'll all raise a glass to you.'

Dave smiled, on the outside. It was embarrassing. He didn't do what he did for the praise. And all he wanted now was a cup of tea, a chat about what he'd had for his dinner last night.

He turned when he heard his name with a question mark attached. He scanned the tables and found Jimmy Jones staring right at him, chewing gum noisily with his fat mouth wide open. His was a face made for punching.

'I just hope the fame doesn't go to your head,' said Jimmy, nodding to the table with the newspaper. 'Good timing, by the way.'

'What is?'

'Smashing up your bus the minute you're named as the world's best driver, or whatever it is.'

'Fuck off, Jimmy.'

'Just saying.'

'Well, just don't, eh? And it's not *smashed up*. Just needs a bit of TLC.'

23

'What happened, anyway? Too busy daydreaming about your speech at the awards ceremony? Hope you've got a nice frock sorted.'

Dave turned his back on Jimmy, flipped the switch on the kettle even though it had just boiled. The noise of it would hopefully drown out whatever bullshit came next. Behind him, chatter resumed. Dave envied them. There was rarely a moment now when he was just there, just chatting, just having a cup of tea. Sometimes he could almost remember it: how easy life had felt without guilt embedded in every fibre of him.

'Making tea?' Jimmy appeared beside him. 'Gonnae make me a cup?'

'My pleasure,' he said, looking only at the kettle and the mug cupboard and the little brown jar that held shared staff teabags. 'No milk, right?'

'Good memory.'

'Aye.' Dave wished for a bad memory, for a faltering mind with gaping black holes where once there were stories. He envied folk with dementia. Even his very best moments were laced with shadows. He used to be able to stuff difficult days with rags of philosophy about living in the present moment and letting go of past sins. What he hadn't realised back then was that one bad deed *could* undo all the good ones; that memories of his best days served only to highlight how far he'd fallen. They were not a comfort at all, but a constant reminder of what he'd lost and could not recover.

Dave squeezed the teabag against the side of the mug with a spoon to release more of the flavour. When Dave had first met Carmen she was a self-declared tea-hating coffee-lover. It was the Spanish way, she'd said. But over the years he'd helped her learn to love it, told her she couldn't spend the rest of her days in Scotland politely refusing every cup she was offered – which in their social circle happened approximately every ten minutes. When she'd got pregnant he'd bought her a six-cup teapot as a gift. Big enough for all the family, he'd said. Carmen had cried, hugged him, then made tea for the first time in her life. *To family*, she'd said, and they'd laughed as they'd forced down tea as thick and strong as old beef gravy.

'Be nice to have that tea before Christmas.' Jimmy was peering impatiently into the mug, screwing up his hairy nose. Dave swallowed a sigh and handed it over, careful not to touch the rim. 'Too kind, Citizen Dave.' Jimmy found himself hilarious, was always making up crap nicknames for colleagues that he clearly hoped would stick and be credited to him but never did. Jimmy rested his mug on the mound of his beer belly, used the other hand to extract the chewing gum from the back of his mouth along with threads of sticky saliva. No wonder the man was single.

'By the way, you're wanted.' He took a noisy slurp after he'd said it.

'Where?'

'Crystal's office.' A yellow smile flashed. That man really needed to make pals with a dentist. 'And a wee birdie tells me it's not about the accident.'

'So what's it about?'

Jimmy shrugged dramatically. 'I'll tell you this much – it's not good.'

'Whatever.'

'I'd go now if I were you.'

Dave held up his mug. 'I'll drink this first.'

Jimmy's eyes twitched towards the window then back to Dave. He smiled again but there was a tremble to it this time. 'Don't say I didn't warn you,' he said, then left.

Dave stood, silent, sipping his tea and staring out of the window, trying to see what Jimmy had seen. A few of the drivers were leaning on the bonnet of a pale blue Volvo estate, laughing about something. The blonde lassie from the back office was inside her red Mini, mobile phone pressed against one ear and finger plugging the other. It was only when Dave stepped forward to the place where Jimmy had been standing that he saw it; a Skoda estate car parked next to the disabled bay, sitting squint as if the driver had been in a hurry.

If you'd been standing close to Dave and watching him carefully you might have noticed his face twitch slightly, despite his efforts to hold back the rush on the other side of his skin. He stared out of the window for a few more seconds then forced his feet towards the staff room door; didn't let his eyes or mind linger on the blue light, now dulled, or the word plastered over the side panels of that car. *Police*.

CHAPTER 5

Dave's nerves tightened when Crystal's office came into view. Usually he looked forward to that moment, would make sure he looked cheerful in case Crystal looked up from her desk as he was walking past. Today someone had lowered those dusty metal blinds over the little window that separated her office from the main hall. That was a first.

'Go on in, Dave.'

He jumped, turned. Crystal was standing in the corridor behind him, holding a steaming mug in each hand. Both these teas had milk added and they both drank theirs black. He looked from Crystal to the mugs and back; smiled. For once she didn't return it.

'Who—?'

'I said go on in.'

She nodded over his shoulder to the door that was half-open; half-shut if you were Dave in that moment. Two uniformed police officers filled the office, leaving little room for optimism. He nodded, turned, walked; did his best to keep his face bright as he stepped inside.

'David Kellock?'

'That's me.'

'Take a seat.' They nodded to Crystal's chair on the opposite side of the desk. She was right behind him, eased shut the door with her foot then sat the mugs down on the desk. One of them sloshed and spilled, bled beige on to a folded-over piece of printing paper Crystal was using as a coaster. The officers nodded thanks, then glanced at the shut door: a sign for her to leave. They had their tea. She was no longer of any use to them. 'If you can give us a few minutes?'

'Of course, of course.' Crystal's voice sounded different. Dave stared at her as she shrank into someone else and meekly retreated without looking at him. He half-expected her to curtsey on the way out. He'd never seen Crystal taking orders from anyone but wondered if that was what happened at home, if she became a bowed head and a string of whispered apologies; anything to avoid attack.

When the door clicked shut Dave walked around the desk and sat down on Crystal's seat, as instructed. He made sure he held himself in a way that suggested he was relaxed and happy to be there; the opposite to how he felt. If that kind of acting was an art form he was a master of it.

He felt odd, sitting in Crystal's chair.

The desktop was wide, sat atop three deep drawers on the left and Crystal's key cupboard on the right. Its door was open, exposing neat rows of metal hooks, each one holding a labelled key; mostly for the buses but some for the building, the lockers and the garage area. On the desktop, a big computer screen had yellow Post-it notes stuck down one side: handwritten notes with phone numbers and passwords and reminders about lost property and holiday requests and shift changes she had to enter into the system. Both the wooden desktop and the one on her computer were tidy. Everything had its place. Maybe she was naïve enough to believe that bad things wouldn't happen so long as she kept everything under strict control. But life always held surprises.

'So, how can I help?' Dave smiled as he said it, was pleased his voice sounded the same way as it did at work. Calm, confident – a man who was kind and could be trusted. 'Assume this has something to do with my . . . incident this morning?'

The female police officer shook her head. 'We need to ask about your whereabouts last night. We're hoping you can help us with . . . some enquiries. Shouldn't take long.'

'I was working until eight, then went home,' said Dave, shrugging for effect, relieved he didn't have to lie. He went to cross his arms then stopped himself; didn't want the officers to think he was on the defensive. Rarely did he make a move or say a word without considering its consequence and how it might be interpreted by others. It was exhausting, thinking that your every step was watched.

'You live alone, Mr Kellock?' The male officer's voice came out with phlegm attached, as if he needed to clear his throat. Was this going to be a *good cop, bad cop* routine like the ones on TV? Not that he watched that kind of thing any more. There was no room in his life for killings and death and police and bodies bundled into bags and zipped up with a noisy whirr.

'I do now, aye. In my mum's house. But she died just over a year ago.'

'Sorry for your loss.'

Dave nodded, was never sure how to respond to sympathy like that, born from good manners.

After almost two decades of working and travelling abroad Dave had moved back to his childhood home in Edinburgh two years ago for one simple reason: to help care for his mum. At first, she had been there with him. Her body, anyway; her mind was already gone. When she died Dave had planned to sell the house and once again leave the country. When he was on the road he could remake himself however and whenever he wanted; never had to pull too hard when he needed to uproot himself and go. But somehow, a year later, Portobello held him still. He'd lost his mum but was surprised to find he still felt at home there.

'So . . . you were in the house alone last night?'

'Aye.'

'And what time did you arrive?'

'Around half-eight, maybe nine?'

'Did you make any phone calls, specifically from your landline?'

Dave shook his head, confusion crinkling his face as the male officer leaned forward, elbows on the desk.

'Sure about that?'

'I rarely phone anyone.'

'We only care about last night.'

'The answer's the same,' said Dave, eyes flitting towards the dusty window blind and the shifting shadows that lay beyond it. 'Would you mind telling me what this is about?'

The male officer glanced at his colleague then leaned back in his chair, reached for his tea when she started talking. 'A call was made to the emergency line last night from *your* phone number, reporting a serious crime at an address in the city. Officers attending the scene found no evidence of the alleged incident.' She paused, studied Dave's face. 'My colleagues concluded it had been a hoax call of a particularly nasty nature. Made by a nuisance caller. From your landline.'

'What? I wouldn't—'

'If you'll let me finish? The victim claimed they'd also received several silent phone calls, earlier in the evening. We've already checked with the phone company and confirmed our suspicions. Those calls were made from your property as well.'

'That's impossible.'

'It's a fact.' Her stare had the impact of a heat lamp, pointing right at him. Dave cursed his warming blood as it raced to his cheeks. 'That's why we'd be delighted if you could help us with our enquiries. Given your insistence that you weren't at the property, perhaps you can tell us who *was* there? And why they might make calls of such an . . . upsetting nature.'

'I've already told you I live alone. And I've already told you I wouldn't make a hoax call. What did they claim had happened? Must be something serious if you lot are on the case.'

'I'm unable to share the details of the call.'

'Fair enough,' said Dave. 'I'm just sorry I can't be of any help.'

'Try harder.' That was phlegm boy, sitting back, enjoying the show.

'I don't need to try,' said Dave. 'I didn't make the call, end of story. Could there be a mistake with the number?'

The policewoman was shaking her head before he'd finished asking. 'Details of all emergency calls are automatically recorded by our system. The call was definitely made from your landline. Now, in case you're unaware: Section 127 of the Communications Act 2004 creates offences regarding improper use of the public electronic communications network for the purpose of causing annoyance, inconvenience or needless anxiety to another. Our records show that the vast majority of nuisance callers are suffering from *mental health issues*.'

She said those words slowly and stared at him as she slopped them out, eyes narrowed as if stress and depression and anxiety were mental limps, something that could be seen if you looked hard enough. Could she see the same *fragility* that the doctor had seen all those years ago? Maybe. Or most likely she'd done her homework before she'd come here, knew his history from old police reports. Dread roasted Dave's cheeks but he held his Mona Lisa smile and prayed the officer wouldn't notice. But her eyes were on him and weren't for shifting.

'Since you live alone, it seems the only possible caller is you, Mr Kellock.'

'It doesn't make any sense.'

The male officer slurped his tea then smiled before he spoke. 'Fair enough,' he said. 'Would you be kind enough to offer an alternative explanation?'

'Eh . . . there must have been someone in my house?'

A throat, cleared. But instead of phlegm, Dave imagined words like *bullshit*, *nonsense*, *aye fucking right*. The officer kept his mouth shut but moved his tongue around his mouth as though he was clearing the residue of all those words that, ultimately, all said the same thing. *Liar*.

'Any evidence of that, Mr Kellock? Broken locks, open windows and such like?'

'No, but . . .' Dave's eyes darted around the office, as if he'd find an explanation there. His gaze fell on that open cupboard, the rows of numbered keys. 'They must have had a key. I can ask my neighbour if she lost her set of spares?'

'Do that. Any other sets kept at the property? In the garden, for example?'

Dave shook his head. 'My mum used to keep keys for me in a plant pot, but that was years back. I'm sure I'd have noticed if they were still there. But I do leave an extra set here, in my locker. And it's not exactly high-security.' He pointed to Crystal's spare key collection. 'Someone could easily swipe whatever one they wanted. If they opened my locker they'd find my house keys. Easy. *And* they could put them back afterwards.'

The officers exchanged a look. 'So, in short, you're suggesting somebody accessed your keys and entered your property before you got home, made a nuisance call from your landline and then . . . left?'

'Exactly.'

Eyebrows, raised a fraction. 'Has anything been taken from your house?'

'Not that I've noticed. But I can check when I get home, let you know.'

'We'd very much appreciate that.' The female officer stood up and handed Dave a piece of paper with a handwritten number on one side. 'This is my direct line. Can you call us later, once you've had a chance to . . . check things over at home?'

'I'll update you as soon as I get there.'

'Good. Your boss here thinks very highly of you, told me you're getting some big award this week, for your voluntary work? So it'll be better for everyone if we can clear up this matter as quickly as possible. We wouldn't want this to damage your *outstanding* reputation.'

'Agreed,' said Dave, wishing the fierceness of a blush could be turned down using determination alone. No such luck. The policewoman stared at him with a strange smile on her face then turned and left. She knew how to touch a nerve, that one.

Dave stayed where he was, half-hoping Crystal would reappear with tea and a roll of the eyes and some comment about the woman's sour face. Instead he sensed movement at the window, was sure he heard the rattle of cheap plastic bangles moving down the corridor. Crystal, walking away.

He slipped out before she came back, kept his head down as he crossed the car park and headed for home. He kept checking over his shoulder but the only thing nipping his heels were questions. First he sees the woman he killed and crashes his bus. Secondly, he's accused of making nuisance calls to a stranger, and a vicious hoax call to the police. It was ludicrous, all of it. But he had to stay calm, keep his head. The only logical explanation was mistaken identity, twice in one single day. Unlikely? Yes. But possible.

Now all he had to do was prove it.

CHAPTER 6

*A*ll *of this started years ago, on the day I was forced into a car that smelled nothing like ours. They'd activated the child lock but I kept tugging the handle anyway in the hope I'd wear down the catch but all I wore down was the patience of the woman in the front seat. She twisted round and told me to give it a rest, as if I'd just sit there and be good as they ripped me away from the person and place I most loved. As the car turned out of the street I unclipped my belt and turned right round on my knees and held my face to the back window, holding my breath so I wouldn't steam up the glass. There was still time for you to save me. But then the driver accelerated and the woman in the passenger seat tutted and told me to sit, as though I were a dog waiting for a treat held in her hand. But all she was holding was me, captive. When I told her that, she sighed then looked at the man who was driving and both of them rolled their eyes.*

I turned to search for you again when we stopped at traffic lights I knew took forever to change. I pictured you sprinting up the street like someone in a film, shouting over and over that all of this had been a terrible misunderstanding. I imagined you leaping from pavement to road and drivers honking their horns and slamming on their brakes but you'd keep going anyway, zigging and zagging between hot metal and rubber until you reached me and all that would come between us was a pane of glass that could easily be broken.

But you did not come running and years came between us instead.

That night, and every night since, I've slept inches from someone I did not want to wake up with, and I've wondered, often, if your arms feel as empty as mine do. That's why I came straight here when, finally, they let me go.

I rang the doorbell of your house and, when nobody answered, I waited. Then I saw you walking up the street, gripping your key the way people do when they're anxious or paranoid. The serrated edge poked out between two of your fingers; became a weapon.

I could have stopped you there and then on your doorstep, shouted out the name that only I can call you. But nerves silenced me. That, and curiosity.

I wanted to see who you were, without me; see for myself the world I was born to be part of.

When you went inside I sneaked down the side path and climbed the fence at the bottom of your garden and stood in the small patch of woodland that's been there for much longer than either of us. I sat down and leaned back against a dead tree; noticed new shoots springing from the rot-softened trunk. From there, I watched you, hopeful.

What a novelty to have a back door and a garden that catches the sun and a step where you sit and drink coffee. You sighed between sips and even from my hiding place I could tell your sighs were long and hard and I imagined the whole of you, deflating; your head and face crumpling over a sagging chest. I pictured you, small and flat and floppy enough to fold over and over like a five-pound note; a fat wad that I could slip into my pocket and take with me wherever I go.

I smiled at the thought.

You, mine, at last.

CHAPTER 7

The walk home from work took twice as long as usual.

Dave kept stopping and checking over his shoulder, scanning the street for *that* face. Part of him thought the woman from the bus – or the ghost of her – would be waiting for him when he left the depot; or that she'd slip out from the shadows when he cut through the park.

Jesus Christ, what a day.

First he sees a ghost on his bus, then he crashes, and to top it off the police accuse him of being a nuisance caller – and not only that, one who's stupid enough to make the calls from their own landline. His mind wandered as he walked, imagining what crime had been reported. It must have been something pretty brutal if the police were following it up. Whatever it was, Dave didn't want his name anywhere near it.

It takes years to build a reputation, seconds to destroy it.

Hood up, head down, hands in pockets, Dave stepped off the pavement and on to cobbles that made his street look posher than it was. He loved it here, usually. Always had done.

But today his heart rate doubled when his house came into view.

The front gate was closed. His front door and windows were intact. He sighed and pulled out his keys. Part of him had hoped to find broken locks and smashed glass and some thug standing in his hall with his landline phone in their hand, just so he could call that arsehole officer and tell her the mystery was solved.

Instead, everything looked normal.

Deep breath, key turned, and he was in.

He noticed the smell right away: a perfume or after-shave that didn't belong in this house.

'Hello?'

His voice sounded as stupid as he felt. Intruders wouldn't return the greeting then pop their head over the banister and introduce themselves. His voice would be a warning to them, an alert that told them he was home, alone. He held his breath and listened, wondered if somewhere inside his home someone else was doing exactly the same thing. Watching, waiting, willing Dave to step inside and shut the door. Was this *it*? Karma, finally playing its cards? Maybe his vision of the woman on the bus had been a warning shot, a sign that the past had finally caught up with him after all these years.

His heartbeat made drums of his ears. If he were a brighter man, he'd turn around and run away. If he were an innocent man, he'd call the police. And if he were a braver man, he'd walk from room to room and face whatever menace stalked him. Instead he stood, silent and scared, as he scanned the doors that led off from the hall. They were all closed, exactly as they should be. But his eyes flipped from one handle to the next, half-expecting to see one of them turning, slowly, gripped by a hand on the other side. And what would the other hand hold? Dave pictured blunt objects and his own head, dented and bleeding. You reap what you sow.

Stop, Dave. Breathe. Be logical.

But every sound was a threat, the familiar creaks and clunks of the house transformed to something that could cause him harm. The doctor had taught him how to tug back those spiralling thoughts before they ran free, bring them to heel like a well-behaved dog. *Take action*, he'd said. *Work with facts instead of speculations. Transform panic into positive energy.* So, instead of staring uselessly at handles, Dave threw open the doors and switched on the lights and saw for himself the same truth, over and over. There was nobody there.

When the downstairs was clear he gazed upstairs to the gloomy, unlit landing; then forced his heavy feet forward. He paused halfway up and craned his neck so he could see into the landing and the rooms that led off it, eyes level with the carpet. All the doors were still closed but from here he could see a strip of light along the bottom of the bathroom door.

'Someone in there?'

Nothing.

Another step, eyes on the glow of gold beyond that door. He winced as he pushed it open using his foot, body tight and solid, ready for defence. But the bathroom was empty too and everything was exactly as he'd left it that morning, including the light above the sink, still switched on. He quickly checked the other rooms and was heading back downstairs when he noticed them: a few long-dead wasps sprinkled on the carpet underneath the glass hatch that led to the attic. They were always making nests up there, building homes and families in that dark, damp space that both protected and trapped them. They'd head for the only light source, crawl and buzz and die together on that frosted glass that they could see but not move through. Every time Dave opened the door it would rain crisp, dust-coated wings and legs and hollowed-out bodies that still held the trace of a stripe. That was the reason he kept that hand-held hoover in the landing cupboard. He'd open the attic door, let them fall, then suck them up, out of sight.

His eyes swung from the wasps to the attic door. When had he last been up there? He'd definitely have noticed those corpses on the carpet if they'd lain there for days. So how did they get there?

For a few moments he stood, staring up at the glass hatch.

Action, Dave. He grabbed the metal pole, hooked it into place and tugged. The door jerked open, offered him metal stairs and dust and the chance to prove he was a man of logic who would not be overcome by irrational fears and the terrors that his mind so enjoyed throwing at him.

The steps creaked under his weight as he climbed. He stopped and reached for the light switch when his top half was inside the attic, blinked as the naked bulb turned the darkness yellow. The attic was T-shaped, had an old green carpet running along the middle of each arm so he could crawl around without fear of impaling himself on a stray nail. He'd left the majority of his possessions here when he'd fled Edinburgh almost twenty years ago: a life packed into boxes and neatly labelled. Not that he'd kept much. A few pieces of furniture, boxes of novels, his record player and vinyl collection, the amp for an electric guitar long since sold. At the far end he kept boxes stuffed with paperwork that he couldn't be arsed filing, and behind those was a box of his mum's old crockery. Lining its base, hidden from sight, he kept *those* newspaper cuttings. Why, he wasn't sure. All the stories of the killings, wrapped up and stored away.

If only shame and guilt were as easy to deal with.

He wondered, often, if life would have felt *better* in jail; if paying a price for his actions would have somehow reduced his suffering. He felt guilty about the killings, aye, but even guiltier about the fact he'd evaded justice. Punishment would have done him good.

Now, staring at that box in the attic, he vowed to make a bonfire of the articles: sever the link between him and the faces on newsprint. But that was a job for another day. What he needed to do right now was check the far end of the attic then retreat. And to be honest, if somebody was lying in wait for him, he was fucked.

Deep breath and he inched forward. One, two and—

'Jesus!' His head smacked on the low ceiling.

Downstairs, someone was ringing the landline.

CHAPTER 8

Dave quickly peeked around the corner at the far end of the attic then eased himself round and crawled back to the hatch. And he was out. Nobody there. Nonsense over. He legged it back downstairs, towards the ringing landline phone that sat on his hall table. He rarely made or received calls, barely recognised the ringtone as his own.

It seemed too much of a coincidence that someone would opt for the landline today, less than an hour after he'd been interviewed by the police about a nuisance call made from this same phone. But who'd been holding the handset last night?

His hand hung in the air, fingers twitching, indecision swirling: to answer or not to answer. Logic told him to pick up, find out who was thinking of him right now, his name on their tongue as they waited for him to answer. But until he knew who'd last used this phone, he didn't want to touch it.

He switched on the lamp that sat next to the phone then hunched down and studied the handset, as if he'd be able to interpret the layers of greasy smudges coating the black plastic. If his life were a film the police would have sent in Forensics with white suits and rubber gloves and magic dust. But if you believed what you read in the tabloids they barely had sufficient resources to attend rapes and killings, never mind cases like this one: one man adamant he hadn't used his own telephone to make a hoax call to the police and silent calls to a stranger.

Hold that thought, Dave.

He went to the kitchen and the mountain of unopened letters by the bread bin that grew an inch every day. He would gather them up when he returned home from work, toss them on the pile to read later. They weighed a ton. He used both hands to shift the pile to the table and sifted through every size of glossy envelope until he found one from the phone company. The letter informed him of a new deal that was irrelevant to a man like him: *free calls to family and friends*. Pulling out his mobile, he dialled the customer service number, stood with his eyes closed and his teeth clenched when the hold music kicked off: an easy-listening version of 'Lovely Day' by Bill Withers. They'd murdered it. Not for the first time, Dave wondered about the lives of cover artists – singers and musicians who dedicated their lives to singing the songs of others, who knew their target audience was tourists in hotel lifts and pissed-off customers trying to get a better deal on their utilities. Hardly an adoring crowd.

But not everyone needed the adoration of others as desperately as he did.

The song had looped three times by the time a man's voice interrupted the chorus, asked him how he could help.

'I need to know the last numbers called from my landline,' said Dave, then answered a series of security questions to prove he was the person he claimed he was. Little did they know. But the man was satisfied that the date of birth matched the address and that he knew the first and fourth digit of the numerical pass-word he'd chosen when he first set up the account. A memorable date, they said. Most folk would choose a happy one, probably. Dave always chose *that day*: the moment his life was neatly sliced in two.

'Four and nine. Perfect. Just a moment and I'll get the information you need,' said the voice, then Dave was back on hold with 'Lovely Day', one hand press-ing the phone to his ear and the other gripping a pen. The only calls he remembered making were to an Indian takeaway. Any other numbers on the landline records had not been dialled by him.

The hold song was rising to its crescendo when the man came back on the line, silenced it. 'Got paper to hand?'

'Aye,' said Dave.

'Then here we go.'

The last call dialled from his landline was to the emergency services the previous night, made some time between the time he'd left work and the time he'd got home.

'Got that,' said Dave, underlining the time of the call. 'Anything else?'

Dave's skin warmed as the man read out a number he didn't recognise. He read it back to him, to be sure he'd got it right. It was an Edinburgh number, but not one he knew or remembered dialling. 'And when was that call made?' Dave tried to keep his voice casual and tried to swallow the gasp that came with the answer. The number had been dialled a few times the previous evening, not long before the emergency call.

He hung up and went back to the phone in the hall; pictured a stranger's fingers on the buttons, their voice in his hall. Who *was* it? And what crime had they reported to the police?

He felt sick at the thought of it: someone creeping around his home and touching his things. He glanced upstairs at the closed bedroom door, pictured someone standing on the other side of it with their ear to the wood and their breath held, waiting for him.

He reached for his mobile, wondered about calling the police. He was supposed to call that officer anyway. But what could he say? There was no sign of forced entry and he'd be digging himself a hole if he made claims he couldn't back up. Either the intruder had a key or they'd picked the lock or they'd slipped in via the tiny bathroom window upstairs. Or maybe it was the ghost that did it. The woman from the bus, haunting him all the way home.

Every explanation was absurd; impossible.

But the phone company said the calls had been made from here, and that meant someone *had* been inside.

First things first, he had to find out who, and how they'd got in. Secondly – who had they been calling? Dave pulled out his mobile, opened Google and typed in the number the phone company had given him. The search produced zero results. He then asked the internet how to trace an unknown phone number and dozens of potential solutions appeared on the screen, websites claiming they could identify any caller world-wide. He clicked one and followed the instructions until he hit a paywall. Card out, fee paid. This wasn't the time to be stingy. Now the screen switched back to a message that asked him to be patient as the site searched phone directories and social media profiles across the country. Dave was putting away his bank card when the screen flashed, and there it was.

A man's name: Jonathan Todd.

Meant nothing to Dave.

Below the name was an Edinburgh address he didn't recognise either, but this was the place. Whoever had been in Dave's house had called *this* man's home several times from the landline – then made a hoax call to the police.

So the name and address on Dave's screen belonged to the man who'd had police turn up at his door looking for evidence of some *serious* and *upsetting* crime, just hours after being targeted by silent calls.

Dave didn't yet know the why and how of the nuisance caller but at least he could pay Jonathan Todd a visit and reassure him it was a hoax; and nothing to do with him.

Decision made. He'd go there right now and talk to this Jonathan Todd face to face.

He called a taxi, was told he'd be quicker flagging one from Portobello High Street at this time of the evening. Jacket on, and he was halfway down the hall when the doorbell rang.

He jumped then stopped dead, studied the grey-black outline on the other side of the frosted glass, watched one of their arms rise to ring the bell again. He never got visitors, ever.

So who was here, now?

He stayed where he was, even though his mind and body were screaming at him to flee or to shout out and frighten away the approaching threat. He was all about the flight, not a scrap of fight left in him. Right now, he should still be at work. His home should be empty. And, right now, the person on the other side was reaching into their pocket. Dave watched, breathless, waiting for the sound he dreaded: a stranger pushing a key into his lock, then turning.

CHAPTER 9

No key came. Instead the person on the other side of
the frosted glass rang the doorbell again, pushed the
button a few times in quick succession, as if to prove it
was urgent. Dave stayed still. If *he* were breaking into
someone's house he'd ring the doorbell first, to be sure
the occupants weren't there.

The person rang the bell again and this time held
their finger on the button for longer than would ever
be necessary or considered even remotely polite.

'Come on, I know you're in there!'

'Crystal?'

'You going to invite me in, or what? Surely it's the
least you can do after standing me up. And there was
me ready to buy you a birthday drink.'

'What you talking about?'

When he pulled open the door her face was flushed;
hurt. 'Did you not open the card?'

Dave glanced to his backpack, dumped. 'I was . . .
keeping it, to open at home.'

'You're home now, are you not?'

'Come on, Crystal. There was the crash. And the police. And . . .' He sighed, held back the words on the tip of his tongue. A crash and a policeman he could deal with. A dead girl on his bus and a stranger in his home, he could not. *Happy fucking birthday, Dave.*

He reached down and pulled the card out of his backpack. She'd written his name in huge bubble letters on the front of a blue envelope. He opened the drawer by the door, pulled out the letter knife he'd bought years back in Spain. The handle was made of clear plastic encasing various euro coins. For luck, probably. He could do with some. He slit the envelope carefully, keeping his name intact, then pulled out a glossy card she'd made especially for him. There were three photos on the front: one of Dave cleaning his bus, another one showing him volunteering at a beach litter pick and, biggest of all, the two of them together at last year's Christmas party, standing side by side but an inch apart, his hands in his pockets, one of hers resting on his shoulder. They were the only two not drinking. He'd have talked to her all night if she hadn't been hauled up for karaoke and dancing with men far more entertaining than he was.

He opened it, not sure what to expect.

Let's do birthday drinks tonight. Meet 7pm at Pinyol? x

Dave stared at the single kiss, wondering if it had been automatic. Hopefully. There was no doubt

Crystal had been paying him significantly more attention since the award was announced; as though she suddenly saw his worth because others did. Och, that wasn't fair. She'd always been welcoming, friendly, the only person he felt a real connection with at the bus garage. But it was odd, this sensation that he was being pursued by someone. A novelty. Especially since it was a woman.

'Don't like it?'

He looked up, forced cheer into his voice. 'It's great, Crystal. Thank you, really. And I'm sorry I—'

'It's fine,' she said. 'But are you seriously going to leave me standing on your doorstep all night? You could maybe try inviting me in, offering me a coffee?'

'I'm . . . out of beans.'

'Is that really the best you can come up with?' Crystal laughed, loud and long enough that the neighbours would hear. 'I'll pop to the wee shop, then, will I? Buy some and bring them? Or we could have tea . . .'

'I'm in the middle of . . . something.'

'Then I won't stay long,' she said. He flinched when she placed a hand on his arm. 'I'm here as a pal, Dave. I'm not here to give you a lecture or pity or a philosophy lesson. I just want to check you're OK. Worry's a bit like cancer, isn't it? By the time your body starts showing obvious symptoms you're already riddled.'

Dave sucked his lips inside his mouth and bit down, hard. Was it really that obvious? He'd always tried so hard to present the image of a man at peace with the world, someone who loved their job and was naturally cheerful. He often conjured up images of his own funeral, tried to live up to the imagined niceties bellowed out by the minister before they burned him.

'Well?' Crystal edged even closer. 'Are you letting me in or not?'

She had a will made of steel girders, that one. But the confidence she oozed at work didn't seem to follow her home, did it? He couldn't imagine Crystal cowering; beaten, begging. But that was just it. The two of them were leading double lives, the reality of who they were trapped somewhere between their flawed idea of themselves and the image they presented to others.

'I appreciate you coming,' said Dave. 'But I'm fine, honestly.'

'Honestly, my arse. Has anyone ever told you you're a terrible liar?'

He could have laughed. All he did was lie. All of this, all of who he was, all of who he pretended to be, was a lie. She had no idea who she was talking to, the things he'd done.

'It's a cup of tea I'm asking for. Twenty minutes of your life. Come on, I'm missing out on the cinema because of you. Told Colin I was going to see a rom-com so he wouldn't come.'

'So he doesn't know you're here?'

'What do you think?'

Dave sighed. 'Has anyone ever told you you're a master of emotional blackmail?'

'We're all good at different things,' she said, following him into the hall and through to the kitchen despite his insistence that she should take a seat on the sofa, wait for him there. He'd never been totally alone with her for more than a few minutes in her office, and even then there were always dozens of familiar faces and voices a few feet away. It was strange to see her out of context, dressed neither for work nor a party. The make-up was still there, though.

He filled the kettle, flicked it on, stared at it until he felt Crystal beside him. Cue an elbow in his ribs, the tiniest of winks when he looked at her.

'Nice place. You got a cleaner?'

He tutted, shook his head. 'Not all men are animals,' he said, but then when he looked at her she turned away. 'Och, sorry, Crystal. I didn't mean—'

'It's fine. You've every right to.'

'Sorry, anyway. Can I make it up to you with . . .' He opened a high kitchen cupboard, pulled out a packet of chocolate-topped digestive biscuits. 'One of these? Hold it upside down and you can pretend it's healthy.'

Crystal laughed. 'Actually, I'll pass,' she said, rolling her eyes towards her thighs, held tightly under leopard skin leggings. 'Sometimes it's the things we love the most that do us the most damage.'

'One digestive won't kill you.'

'It's never just one, though, that's the problem.'

'Your choice. But go and relax in the sitting room at least, will you? If I'm going to have a guest I might as well make the most of it and act like a good host.'

She smiled, agreed, disappeared.

Thank Christ. Dave stopped all his fussing the second she was gone; stood with his fingertips pressed into his forehead and his eyes closed and his heart whirring even faster than his mind. And that was saying something.

His brain was still processing the now undeniable fact that someone had been in his house when he was out, making repeated phone calls to this stranger called Jonathan Todd. He pulled out his phone and typed the name into a search engine, one eye on the screen and the other on the door in case Crystal reappeared. His phone spat out a few social media profiles and suggested images. But it was a common name. He'd need to refine the search later, gather everything and anything he could about the Jonathan Todd who lived in Edinburgh and who now thought Dave had some kind of campaign against him.

He'd have searched a wee while longer if he hadn't heard Crystal in the hall.

'Enough faffing, Dave. Get your arse over here and talk to me.'

She grabbed her mug off his tray then told him to sit down at the kitchen table. Did she realise she was recreating the layout of her office? One metre and a table between them. Her in control; Dave summoned, forced to confess.

He did what he was told and sat down. Crystal blew on the surface of her steaming tea, took a sip that must have burned her. The silence in the room was so intense that Dave was sure he could hear the hot liquid slide down her throat.

'I've been wanting to talk to you for a while,' she said. 'Away from work.'

'Oh, aye?' Dave wished her gone. No good ever came from conversations that started with that line.

She nodded then pulled her lips tight across her teeth, gave a smile born from sympathy. She probably thought that would help. She'd be wrong. That was what folk did at funerals too; that, and speaking in riddles instead of being honest, calling a spade a spade and a stone a stone and a broken heart a fucking inevitability. He wanted to close his eyes and block out the look of pity on Crystal's face because he didn't deserve it. But he knew what waited in the blackness behind his eyelids: that same scene with Carmen, acted out again and again and that same desperation to change the ending.

He'd killed her and her baby on an otherwise ordinary Tuesday.

His mind often dragged him back to the way that day had started, the two of them walking along the coast from Musselburgh to Portobello as the sun had risen up and out of the sea. A glorious weekly ritual, just for the two of them.

They'd talked about the baby but, as ever, she'd found something to whinge about. She'd been nervous about the twelve-week scan and annoyed at her brother for some snarky comment he'd made about Dave being a dad. Dave, as ever, had taken on the role of resident peacemaker between them. He was a good listener. But it had been hard, sometimes, to make her see sense. And Carmen had never asked how those conversations had felt for Dave, how he'd disposed of the waste she'd dumped on him. Aye, he'd loved that woman; but her love of complaining had been exhausting, irritating, seemingly never-ending. Until Dave had ended it.

Later that same day he'd lost control for one second, maybe two; and the world had lost Carmen and her baby forever.

'Dave? You even listening?'

Crystal's voice dragged him back to the present. Had she asked him a question? Jesus. She looked pissed off, as if she was waiting for an answer.

'You keep disappearing, Dave. And it's not just me who's noticed.'

'Disappearing? Where to?'

Crystal sighed and shook her head lightly, the way dog-owners look at their pet when they refuse to sit despite being told a dozen times. There was affection there, but irritation too.

'You know fine well what I mean, Dave Kellock. You're disappearing into your own head, into thoughts or worries or fantasies or God knows what else, but you're not *here*; not with it. And I'm sure that's what led to the accident today. You're obviously distracted and that's not good for anyone, even less so a bus driver carrying precious cargo across the city.'

'I've already told you I'm fine, OK? You don't need to worry about me.'

'Can't help it,' she said. 'The thing is, Dave, you and I have got much more in common than you think.'

'Is that right?' Dave stared into his tea.

After that, Crystal said his name, too softly; the way folk did when they were going in for a kiss. Dave raised his head and his defences, fired her a look that was easy to read. *Enough*, it said. *Don't go there.*

The shrill beep of a new text message punctured the tension between them. Crystal glanced at her phone, flinched as though a finger had stretched out of the screen and poked her. She stood up and tugged on her jacket. 'Trust bloody Colin. He's on the warpath. I'll need to go. Don't want him turning up at your door.' She smiled, a fake one this time. 'We'll talk more tomorrow maybe? Thanks for the tea.'

'Any time.'

'Think we both know that's a lie.' She laughed, squeezing his arm. 'Take care of your—'

'Wait. How did you know where I live?'

'What?'

'My address. How do you know it? I've never told you.'

'Same reason I know it's your birthday, Dave. I'm your boss. I've got the name and address of every driver in the place.' She rolled her eyes then dropped her phone into her oversized shoulder bag and noisily zipped it shut. 'The world is not against you, Dave Kellock, despite what you seem to think. Get some rest and I'll see you tomorrow, pal. God willing.'

Dave stood and stared at the kitchen door long after she'd shut it behind her. He heard the front door open and close and her final words lingering in the air, taunting him. All around him, the house creaked and groaned, dared him to peer into the darkest corners. His brain did the same. It conjured up an image of the woman on the bus, skin split and eyes stilled.

And he knew one thing for sure: God had nothing to do with it.

CHAPTER 10

Tuesday

Dave stepped out of the taxi, on to a wide street lined with trees that were starting to drop their crisping leaves. He was in the Colinton neighbourhood of Edinburgh, a place made for folk far posher than him. Like, for example, Jonathan Todd; the man targeted by the nuisance calls from Dave's landline.

It had been too late to come here last night after Crystal's unexpected visit so he'd got up early, hoped to get the whole thing done and dusted before the start of his mid-morning shift.

As it was, he'd barely slept; jumping awake a few times, convinced he could sense someone else in the house. He'd got up at around four and walked from room to room, flicking the lights and leaving them on. There was nobody there. Of course there wasn't. He'd kept searching anyway; even went outside in his pyjamas and checked under the big plant pot where his mum used to leave a spare set of keys. But there was nothing there except damp soil and slippery insects, unhappy that he'd wrecked their home.

After that he'd stayed up, spent the next few hours on his laptop, drinking coffee and scouring social media for anything and everything he could find on Jonathan Todd. Dave was a total novice but he'd witnessed it dozens of times in the staff room: a name mentioned in conversation then typed into somebody's phone. Minutes later they'd all be looking at a stranger's home, holidays, dinner, dog.

That was precisely why Dave went nowhere near social media. There was no way he was inviting half the world to turn round and look at him. It terrified him, to think of folk typing his name and seeing his life laid out on a screen to be assessed, picked at.

And anyway, no number of likes or thumbs-ups could shift the shame that had lived in him for so many years. It was always there, festering; hidden under easy smiles and endless activity. Ask Dave what he was doing over Christmas or summer holidays and his answer would always be the same. *Keeping busy,* he'd say, and rare was the day folk would demand more detail or ask the question he dreaded most. *Why?*

They didn't want to know.

He'd googled himself again this morning as well, to be sure the worst of him was hidden. Usually, nothing came up. But now there was the story about the Outstanding Citizen Award, and his big baldy head as a suggested image. He made a note to call the paper, ask when they'd be taking it down. His face printed in a local newspaper was one thing; having it all over the internet was something else entirely. He didn't want the wrong people coming across his face, especially connected with a story like this. But he'd have to tread carefully. The last thing he wanted was a bored journalist wondering what an ordinary man like him was trying to hide.

And what about Jonathan Todd?

From what Dave had found on social media, he had an enormous ego and a wife and a daughter who rarely appeared in photos. The last family picture showed him with his arm around a little girl dressed up as Shrek, face painted bright green. His wife was next to them, but she was bending down, tugging at the seam of her costume so her face was out of view. But that photo was taken almost a decade ago. If that was their daughter she'd be a teenager now, and probably mortified to know that image was available for public viewing.

Instead of snapping his loved ones, Jonathan Todd shared selfies of himself holding up medals and certificates and heavy dumb-bells at the gym, plus photos of golf courses and fast cars and steak dinners. Dave guessed he and Jonathan were more or less the same age, but Jonathan looked as if he'd spent half his life working out. He was immaculate; would have been carved in marble if he'd lived in a different century.

But the key point was this: Dave didn't recognise him.

Did Jonathan Todd know who *he* was? He'd soon find out.

The house was halfway up one of those cul-de-sacs that looked the same everywhere: modern homes with white harled walls built so close to their neighbour you could barely spit between them. Dave took a deep breath then walked up their path and pressed the white plastic button of the doorbell.

Press, wait. Press again, wait. He stepped back to look for any sign of life upstairs.

Nothing. No answer. Game over.

Or was it?

The slatted gate at the side of the house was open. A sign, maybe. Perhaps the Todds were in their back garden and hadn't heard the bell. He might as well check while he was there. Dave glanced over his shoulder then turned and hurried down the side of the house. The path led into the shadows of a tree that hung over from the neighbouring garden. Immediately the light dimmed and the air cooled and the same breeze that made trees whisper tugged gently at the hairs on his arms until they were standing on end. Did this count as trespassing? Probably. But he was here for the good of Jonathan Todd and his family, wanted to help settle their nerves.

So why were *his* on edge?

When he reached the corner of the house he paused and pressed his back against the pink sandstone wall. Heart thundering, lungs tight, thoughts spinning into overdrive. *Breathe, Dave.* He gulped in some air then inched forward, into the garden.

He scanned from path to tree to lawn to shed to fence, and back again. There was nobody there. Beyond the garden a thick woodland loomed, dropping leaves on a damp, dark corner of the lawn. Dave turned to face the house, looking for signs of life. He knocked on the back door then stood on his tiptoes and peered in their kitchen window.

The sill was packed with potted plants that must take half the day to water. Beyond the outstretched branches of basil and geranium flowers Dave could make out a sideboard piled high with letters and magazines and a small table with two chairs. The lights were off, the door to the next room closed.

He gave up on the door and knocked on the window, then pulled out his phone to check how much time he had before his shift started. One hour. He should go. He stuffed his mobile back into his pocket, took a final look inside. And then he heard it.

The creak of wood behind him, the thud of heavy feet on grass, a snort of effort. Then a hand gripped his shoulder. Next came a warm breath in his ear and a voice he didn't recognise. Two words, pushed out through clenched teeth.

'Got you.'

CHAPTER 11

Dave didn't get a proper look at his captor's face until he'd been bundled into the shed and was inside, looking out. It looked like the Jonathan Todd from the photos. He was dressed entirely in beige, with skin to match. The only colour on him was a faded tattoo on his right arm – looked like the symbol of some military battalion – and the flushing in his cheeks. He was breathing too fast, and shaking, looked as if he might keel over and die any second.

'I'm calling the police,' he said, spitting out words between gasping breaths. 'You've got some bloody nerve, I'll give you that, coming here in broad daylight.' He opened his mouth to say something else then changed his mind, closed it. And the door.

The next sound was the metal bolt being tugged into place on the outside.

'There's been a huge misunderstanding,' said Dave, mouth so close to the door he could taste the wood. 'You're Jonathan, right? Let me out and I'll explain. We can talk. Like grown-ups.'

'Don't you talk to me about grown-ups.' The man gave a loud, wet snort. 'You're the one sneaking around in folk's back gardens and peeking in their windows. Not much grown-up about that. And a fiver says you made that hoax call on Sunday. How do you think it felt, coming home and finding police all over the house? Turning the place upside down, searching for blood stains and God knows what else. And then that detective, announcing what they were looking for. A woman and child, killed. Have you any idea of the trauma that's caused? Actually, I doubt you even care.'

A woman and child, killed.

The words were a lightning bolt and Dave was hit, became electric. He stumbled back from the door, chest tight and every other part of him trembling. *A woman and child, killed.* Whoever made the call from his landline reported *that* specific crime? It could not be a coincidence. The blood of Carmen and her baby stained his hands, memory, conscience. For almost twenty years he'd been running from those who knew the truth of who he was and what he'd done. But here, now, somebody knew.

Even worse, that *somebody* had been in his house. But who?

Names and faces swarmed his brain but one stood out more clearly than any other. The woman on the bus. Carmen, back from the dead to do her worst. Even Dave couldn't outrun a ghost.

Or could he?

'You need to let me out.'

'Not a chance.'

'This isn't the fifties, pal. You could be done for this.'

'See you in jail, then.' The man laughed a phlegmy laugh then walked away.

Dave waited a minute then pushed the door and with very little effort it opened far enough for him to wiggle a few fingers into the gap. He grasped around for the bolt on the outside, got a splinter instead. *Fuck's sake*. He pulled his hand back inside and took his phone out of his pocket, eventually found the torch. He tugged at the shard of wood in the palm of his hand. Stigmata, of sorts. But he wasn't any kind of saviour, laying down his life to save others.

The sliver of wood slipped out easily enough, brought blood that he sucked then wiped on his work trousers as he turned on the spot, pointlessly searching for another way out. The shed was bigger than it looked, packed to the gills with transparent plastic boxes and a few made of bashed cardboard. They all had sticky labels on the side, describing the contents. *Dressing Up Clothes. CDs and Tapes. Amy Ski Stuff. Camcorder 1992–6.* This family had a hard time letting things go. A plastic wardrobe in the corner was loaded with gardening tools, smelled of fertiliser and compost and damp earth. But there was no window, no back door, no way out except the bolted door he'd come in through.

This was not good.

He tugged a box down from the shortest stack, used it as a stool. Sat down, head in hands, mind racing. The door would break open if he rammed it but that was the last resort. First, it would mean he'd actually damaged someone else's property and could be charged for it. Secondly, if he fled he'd look guiltier than ever. But would the police even attend something like this? The papers were full of stories about cutbacks and shortages and tales of folk waiting hours for police assistance. The fact that they had been called here two days ago might make a difference, however. There was a history, a suggestion of menace. And, somehow, he was caught in the middle of it.

As far as Dave could see, the nuisance caller had two targets and two missions. The first target was Jonathan Todd and his family.

Mission? Frighten them. Job done.

The second target was Dave. For him, the mission was more complex. By making the calls from his house they wanted to implicate him in the crime, make the police think *he* was the one trying to scare the Todd family. And by specifying what police would find at the house – *a woman and child, killed* – the caller was letting Dave know that They Knew; that, for all his years of running away, the sins of his past were still on his heels. And getting closer.

But why involve the Todd family?

He needed to know more about them and what linked their lives to his. He stood up and turned to face the stacks of labelled boxes that lined the walls of the shed. There was no point sifting through boxes of old dinner plates and bric-a-brac, but if there were papers or photos or letters in here they might help him work out who this family was.

Dust puffed into the torch beam as he hauled down the box marked *Ornaments*. The white plastic lid was cracked and the tape used to seal it had long since gone dry, turned brittle. It was still stuck loosely in place but crumbled when he touched it. He sat it on the floor and went for the next one. Maybe somewhere, inside one of the boxes, he'd find something that would explain all of this; something that would link their life to his, other than the nuisance calls. Phone torch shining, eyes wide, he started the search. But in the very darkest and quietest part of him, in a place he rarely looked, a prayer was forming. Four words, whispered over and over.

Don't find *that* name.

CHAPTER 12

And so I'm here, again.

Today I found newspaper cuttings about the killings; heartbreak, neatly folded and filed away in a box marked Breakables. *That almost made me laugh. Everything can be broken if you try hard enough.*

You'd hidden them under a set of sturdy blue crockery that triggered a memory I could not place. Did you bring that from our home? You'd carefully wrapped each piece inside sheets of bubble wrap that had already been popped. I lifted the pieces out one by one, tried to sense if I recognised the weight and feel of them in my hands. And it was there, beneath those plates and bowls and mugs, that I spotted that red folder, fat with newspaper pages neatly cut out and folded into little rectangles and squares and stored in a place you thought nobody else would find them. There were dozens of them. Did you buy them all, every day?

I think of you in the corner shop, picking up one copy of each paper then inventing some story to tell the man behind the counter so he didn't think you were mad or eccentric. I picture you sitting at our kitchen table with the orange-handled scissors in one hand and with the other you'd be flick-flick-flicking through the newspaper looking for pages that held our story and the why and the what happened next. All of our tragedies and all of our names, packed into one article that was printed in neat columns with a photo above that showed who we were and how we were, before.

How did it feel, to see yourself there? To know how others defined you?

I picture strangers reading about us on trains and in cafés and at kitchen worktops and on sofas, one leg crossed over the other so their leg supports the weight of the paper. They'd turn to the page with our photo and pause, scan the first few lines of our story to see if our lives were anything like theirs. Families robbed of children, hearts broken into shards that stay sharp, always. But somehow the world carried on. There was barely a ripple on the surface of ordinary life. When death came I expected the whole world to scream and sob and dress in black. Instead people in uniform took photos and statements and then they called the clean-up crew to remove the soft bits of humans that were spread on the ground. No trace of her remained, there; but here's the thing: there were parts they didn't know about; pieces of her they couldn't see and scrub clean with a hard-toothed brush and power hose.

And here's my big surprise. Those are the parts I'm bringing home to you.

CHAPTER 13

Dave stretched in the darkness, was poking at the shed's roof joints with his fingertips when he heard the voice of Jonathan Todd, approaching. Probably marching, knees high. His accent was posher now, the soft endings of his words brought to a deliberate point. He'd be spitting with every T and P spoken. Dave saw and heard it all the time on the bus, folk presenting a false version of themselves because they felt like they'd be judged badly if the world saw who they really were. And aye, he could talk.

'Yes, I've got him here. Yes, officer. Certainly. I'll do that.'

Then came a throat, cleared. Fat knuckles, rapped on the shed door. 'The police are on their way,' he said, poshness dropped. 'Might be a while so I hope you're comfortable.'

The morning's excess coffee poked Dave's bladder. 'Could do with a piss.'

Another snort. If Dave ever got out of here he was buying that man a pack of Kleenex. 'As if I'd fall for that old trick. I was in the army, you know. Heard it all before. And worse. You can cross your legs until they get here.'

'Don't say I didn't warn you.' Dave flicked his finger at the door then waved his torch around the shed, looking for something he could pee into. In fact, enough was enough. He'd look for something he could use to force the door. He turned and lit up the final row of boxes with his torch, spotted a big box marked *Kitchen Stuff*. Chances were it held knives and wooden spoons. He could use them as tools. He tugged the box towards him, staggering slightly when it slipped off the stack and on to the floor. Lid off, he then picked out plates and jugs and pots, in search of useful utensils. He peeked into a few packages wrapped in newspaper: white china with a floral design and a gold rim, the kind of dinner set found in the sideboards of grannies the whole world over. On the other side, there was something else solid, not wrapped in newspaper but inside a soft cloth bag. The bag fell away when he lifted it out and he found himself kneeling in the dark in a stranger's shed holding not a milk jug or a teapot, nothing that was part of a matching set.

He was holding an urn.

He held it at arm's length, shoulders hunched, body tensed. Even in the dark of the shed, the rounded metal body gleamed. It didn't weigh much, a few kilograms at most. Certainly not enough for his arms to be trembling this much. His phone was on the floor, screen down, torch facing the ceiling. He moved the urn towards the beam, tilting and turning it in his hands until he could get a good look at it. There was no name inscribed on the side but two swallows in flight were engraved around the base. Somewhere in his brain a memory fluttered, but it was vague; almost out of reach. He turned the urn in his hands, nausea rising in him when he pictured the bone sand inside, slowly shifting. But whose bones were they?

And why did Jonathan Todd keep a loved one's ashes in his shed?

He had to ask him, talk man to man.

For that, he had to get out of here.

Urn, replaced. Box, repacked and returned to the stack. Now he just had to get past that door.

He pushed it hard and held his eye to the gap. Daylight. Grass. Greying sky. The suggestion of a breeze. But there was no sign of Jonathan Todd or his threatened police.

'Hello?'

Nothing.

He stuck his hand through the gap, again, feeling for the bolt on the other side. Tried. Failed. Got another splinter in almost the same place. *Jesus fucking Christ.* His only option was brute force. Deep breath, body braced, and he rammed his right shoulder into the door.

The whole shed wobbled and Dave had images of it collapsing around him the way it would happen in a cartoon. Big baldy Dave surrounded by broken planks of wood, wee clouds of dust puffing up around him, his face coated in filth apart from two blinking eyes.

Instead, it settled. And the door stayed shut.

He tried again, sharpened his elbow and whacked the door directly opposite the bolt. It hurt. But it worked. The door slackened, opened a few more inches. He wasn't a man who could break or even bend metal with his bare hands but he'd loosened the attachments on the door, drawn the screws out of their little wooden beds. He was able to stick his whole hand and forearm through the gap now, right up to his aching elbow. It was enough. His fingers found the bolt and flipped it. He opened the door, let in light and air. Looked, blinking, for Jonathan Todd. There was no sign of him. He headed for the side path, was halfway across the lawn when he heard *that* sound.

A siren, closing in.

Then came the thud of car doors, slammed shut. A latch, lifted. A gate, pushed. Footsteps on gravel. He could hear voices too: Jonathan Todd, and a woman who sounded vaguely Glaswegian. Dave glanced behind him, to the woodland beyond the garden. It was his only escape route. *Jesus Christ.*

He ran to the back fence, wedged his foot into a sliver of dark space between two wooden slats.

A stepping stone, of sorts. Dave groaned as he pulled himself up and over then tugged his leg free. He fell like a sack of old potatoes on the other side. For a few moments he lay where he'd landed, with his eyes closed, wiggling his fingers and toes and gently rocking his neck from side to side. There was no wind left in him but his body was intact. When he rolled over, his cheeks shed browning pine needles, and tree roots dug their knuckles into his ribs. His ears were ringing but he could still hear the voices, mainly Jonathan Todd spitting and spluttering at the sight of an empty shed. He didn't dare look up at the fence, couldn't bear to see disapproving faces pegged along the top. He held himself still and silent until the shed door was shut and the voices had retreated. His body creaked and protested as he eased himself into a sitting position, bones like tent poles clicking back into place. His clothes were damp and spotted with unidentifiable scraps of forest, some with legs and wings. His passengers were in for a right treat today, driven around the city by an old man of the forest. Speaking of which, he was probably late.

He pushed his hand into his pocket, searching for his phone to check the time. It wasn't there. He pulled himself up on to his knees, searched the soggy woodland for any trace of a black screen and smooth silver sides. Nothing. He checked in his backpack; found his work phone but not his own. He groaned, would have kicked himself if he'd had the strength. His phone was either in the shed or had fallen out when he was clambering over the fence. Either way, it was out of reach.

Even if he was strong enough to haul himself back over that fence, there was no way he could risk being seen anywhere near that garden or that shed any time soon. He'd need to wait until nightfall, hope the security light at the back door didn't have a powerful sensor. And hope that nobody else found the phone before him.

CHAPTER 14

Dave was met at the bus stop in Portobello by a massive queue, a chorus of tuts and a few shameless glares from the passengers already on board. The driver he was replacing stood a few metres further down the pavement, eyes on his phone, belly creeping over his belt, mouth sucking on a vape that smelled of rotten fruit. Dave prepared himself for a deserved mouthful of abuse from his colleague. Thank God it wasn't Jimmy Jones he was replacing. He only had to contend with Trevor, a driver from Newcastle who was always cheerful and wearing shorts, despite the fact it was strictly against the dress code.

Trevor looked up, smiled. Good start. Dave decided not to comment on his newly missing front tooth.

'What time do you call this?'

'Sorry, pal. Got my timings wrong.'

'Got ambushed as well by the looks of it.' Trevor nodded to the spattering of brown on Dave's trousers and shirt; the dust of the forest dead. 'Y'aright?'

'Long story.'

'Save it for the staff room, then.'

'Aye.' Behind Dave, sighs and muttering. 'I should get going.'

When he turned, the two grannies at the front of the queue were staring at him, looking for his permission to get on board. 'Ladies first,' he said, arm held out like a suitor as they shuffled forward then ousted a hungover student from the seats at the front that were reserved for the mighty grey-hair brigade.

Dave paused in the aisle for longer than usual, scanning the busy bottom deck before he pulled shut the door to his cabin and checked the view from the cameras. There were four images on his screen, showing the bus from various different angles. The top deck was even more crowded than the bottom one. A group of young folk packed the back few rows. Freshers, likely. Up front there was a man with two toddlers, eating crisps, and behind them a sea of faces; many with their hoods pulled up against the morning chill.

Was *she* among them?

Dave scanned the video images methodically but there was no sign of her. For now. He sighed, then pressed the accelerator and moved slowly forward.

As he followed the familiar route his eyes were on the road but his mind was firmly locked on one single stop: the shelter on Musselburgh High Street where the woman had stepped on to his bus yesterday morning. When it came into view for the first time he slowed; brakes squeezed, heart thundering.

First in line at the bus stop were three spotty boys in grey tracksuit bottoms and football tops. Behind them was a couple dressed in hiking gear and a gaunt girl eating a flaky pastry out of a brown paper bag. No sign of the face he was looking for. He waited as long as he could without pissing off his passengers but she did not come. He'd drive past the same spot four times before his shift was over so there was still time, still a chance he'd see her. But what would he do if he did?

'You blind, driver? The lights are green!'

The voice came from that ginger nurse with the dirty fingernails. She was always running late and blaming other folk for it. Dave turned back to the road, legs shaking as he pushed down on the accelerator and moved slowly through Musselburgh, towards Portobello and up London Road towards the city centre and its omnipresent roadworks. His eyes flitted from churned-up streets to the rear-view mirror to the screen showing images from the top deck. Upstairs, the students were already on their feet. When he pulled into a stop on Princes Street the aisle became a sea of heads as they moved towards the narrow staircase, bumping their way down as the bus shuddered to a halt.

Dave pushed the button to open the doors. This was always one of the most chaotic stops, five square metres of Edinburgh soil rammed with tourists and locals all wishing the council would widen the bloody pavements so they didn't need to step on to the road. He'd seen it hundreds of times: harassed pedestrians leaping on to the road without looking, desperately trying to pass a slow walker blocking their path. Meanwhile, passengers getting on to the bus battled through an endless flow of strangers to reach the door. Dave greeted them with a smile he'd prepared earlier.

First on the bus was a family of five: two crying babies, one whingeing toddler, a sulking teenager and an inexplicably jolly mum. Next was a cheerful backpacker heading to Haymarket to catch the airport tram. He tried and failed to use his bank card then tried and failed to make conversation with Dave while he fished in impossibly deep pockets for change to cover his fare. Behind him, folk tutted and checked their phones and cut through the queue and gazed up at the castle and voiced worries about rain despite the fact that the sky was blue. Dave kept his smile in place and his eyes on the rear-view mirror. There was always a fight to get off. Same thing happened on planes – this desperation for the journey to end and the arriving part to begin. But you're talking ten seconds' difference, twenty at most. Could a life really change in that time?

Aye, it could.

Next up was an elderly man laden with oversized plastic bags from a posh supermarket, bottle of wine sticking out of the top. He was trailed by a pocket-sized wife and the smell of sugar from a bakery. He smiled as he beeped his bus pass, tightened a few of the sagging lines on his face.

'Busy day, son?'

'Every man and his dog,' said Dave, then took the opportunity to twist round in his seat, pretending it was the old man he was interested in. The bottom deck was rammed, new passengers coming in from the front blocking the old ones still pushing down the stairs and down the main aisle from the back. Everybody touching everybody else, the faces of one hiding the face of another. If she was here, he couldn't see her.

Dave turned back to the old man, smiling. 'I'll sort it out for you, pal,' he said, then unbuckled his belt and pushed open the cabin door and squeezed out into the aisle. Better view from here. But still no sign of her. He cleared his throat. 'Can everyone keep moving, please? Be nice. Let folk off before you hunt for a seat.'

The backpacker stepped back to let people off the staircase, blocking Dave's route and view in the process. But he could see movement. Tuts turned to calls of *Thanks, driver!* as folk made it to the double doors and out on to the street.

It was only when the backpacker grabbed the handrail and tugged himself on to the stairway that Dave got a glimpse of the aisle and the doors and the people heading towards them. And there she was, wearing a

yellow jacket instead of the green one he'd been looking for. He hadn't seen her climb on board but the
bus had already been busy when he'd taken over from
Trevor. And it was definitely her, here, now, almost
hidden from sight by three gargantuan rugby twats,
egos as wide as their shoulders.

'Carmen,' he said, but the word came out a whisper. His own voice, rebelling against him. Or maybe it
was his body's way of protecting him from the creep of
madness. He was saying the name of a dead woman;
talking to a ghost, right here on a bus he should have
been driving.

'Carmen?' he said again. Louder this time, but
there was still no response. Not from her anyway, but
the jolly mum turned and started speaking to him,
laughing at her own comment and probably expecting
Dave to do the same. But he stood, staring, willing the
woman to look up and meet his eye and for everyone
else to disappear so they could sit and chat and finally
he'd say out loud the only words that mattered.

Sorry, sorry, sorry.

She was a few steps from the door now, echoing the
footsteps of the people around her but not talking, not
looking, not checking her phone, not being noticed at
all. Could they see her?

'Carmen!'

The world stopped. He'd shouted, surprised himself
with the force of it. Heads turned, tongues tutted, lips

curled, folk whispered the way they do before something bad kicks off. They were like kids, the lot of
them, holding their breaths in the presence of an angry
adult. Dave wished they'd all fuck right off and let him
be, but he was terrified, too, at the thought of being
alone with her. This woman, a ghost.

But the world gets bored quickly, and soon unpaused
itself. The backpacker muttered something and con-
tinued up the stairs and the jolly mum kept chattering
inches from Dave's ear but he heard none of it.

The woman was standing still, blinking; blocking
the flow of passengers heading for the doors. A group
of teenage girls dressed up like rappers pushed past
her, and an elderly lady dressed entirely in purple rested
a vein-streaked hand on her shoulder, and said words
Dave couldn't hear. There were three metres between
them, and a look that was held for long enough to
mean something. Then a skinny lad behind the old
lady leaned forward and gently tugged the woman's
hair. She glanced back, laughing, and just like that, the
connection with Dave was broken. Moments later, she
stepped off the bus then turned left, in the direction of
Waverley Station.

Dave pushed past passengers and stepped down on
to the packed pavement: was pummelled. He could
have been standing in waist-deep Atlantic swells and
he'd have been less battered, less pushed around
by the swirl of life on all sides. If he'd tried this

during the Edinburgh Festival in August, he'd have been scooped up and dragged along by the flow of the crowds, probably ended up two miles down the road, gripping a warm pint in a plastic glass and a dozen glossy flyers, thrust upon him by insistent hands on the way there. But it was September and folk's moods were darkening as quickly as the evenings. He got tuts instead, told to watch where the fuck he was going. But he only cared where Carmen was going, where she'd already gone.

The city's new students were out in force and that, combined with a few rays of sunshine, meant the city centre was mobbed – a place you could easily disappear. Dave put one foot back on the bus to give himself a little more height, scanned every face and head and hood in the thousands of lives bobbing along Princes Street towards the train station and the bridges and the Old Town and the hills behind. *Come back, come back, come back.*

'Driver?'

The voice came from behind, was accompanied by a tapping on his arm that he wished would stop but did not. 'Driver? It's just . . . my boy's got a football game. Are we moving on, or . . .?'

Dave turned, faced the jolly mum; smile now forced. She was making more effort than most of his passengers. A few folk still had their heads buried in their phones but most folk had straightened up, eyes asking the same question the jolly mum had just asked him. *Are we moving on, or . . .?*

Dave stared outside, wordless, then turned back to the driver's cabin.

He'd left the indicator on when he pulled into the bus stop and for a few moments it was all he could hear, the *tick-tock, tick-tock, tick-tock* counting down the seconds to the decision he knew needed to be made. The door was hanging open so he reached across his seat, grabbed his backpack, pushed the red triangle on his dashboard, which set off the hazard lights. Then he turned, nodded to the passengers and stepped off his bus into Princes Street.

Are we moving on, or . . .?

Or.

CHAPTER 15

Dave ran until he came face to face with a group of very round Americans halfway across the North Bridge. They weren't for stopping so Dave pressed himself into the grey paintwork and pushed past, eyes on the bobbing mass of people moving away. He couldn't see her, was losing time. *Come on, come on, come on.* If he didn't catch her soon she'd be lost. The North Bridge connected the New Town with the Old Town; the present with the past. It was one of the most frequently walked streets in the city and the pavement was made even busier by folk posing for selfies and taking panoramic photos with Edinburgh castle on one side and Arthur's Seat on the other. At the top there was a crowded crossroads. Keep going and you'd land on the South Bridge; turn left or right and you'd be walking the cobbled slope of the Royal Mile.

Which way would she go? Dave paused; turning, scanning, hoping, dreading. And then he saw her up ahead, stopped at traffic lights. A woman with a yellow jacket.

He sharpened his elbows and pushed through but she was already on the other side of the road when he got there. The red man came and traffic roared between them. Dave stepped out anyway, ignored honking horns, but the traffic was heavier and faster than he was. Just as he was forced back on to the pavement, the woman glanced over her shoulder. Could she tell she was being followed? Aye, but maybe not by Dave. The skinny lad from the bus had reappeared beside her and they were talking now, faces close. After a brief exchange she hugged him and walked away. For a few moments the lad watched her back; looking earnest. Then he cupped his hands to his mouth, called out to her. 'I'll come, OK? MOB Bar! Tomorrow at eight. I'll be there!'

She looked back and smiled then kept walking.

Dave was still waiting at the traffic lights, cursing every driver on the road as he watched her disappear into the Royal Mile crowds. He'd lost her, but he'd gained *something*.

A time. A place. If he couldn't catch up with her now, then he knew where and when he could find her. *MOB Bar, tomorrow at eight*. For a moment, he felt hope.

Then shame flooded in to take its place. She was obviously a student, maybe even a fresher. And if she was the same age as the lad she'd just hugged then she was far younger than he'd first imagined. She wasn't a *woman*. She was a teenage girl.

What kind of man chased adolescents through the city centre? The same kind of man who followed them to bars, and always found excuses for their own behaviour. What was his? All he wanted was to see her face to face. But why?

To see for himself that, up close, she didn't look like Carmen Martinez at all? To prove she wasn't a ghost? It embarrassed him to even think that thought. And if it *was* Carmen Martinez he was seeing then it was a hallucination.

Death wasn't temporary.

And neither was his job. He had to get back to the bus.

He'd just set off when his work phone started ringing, inside his backpack. He stuck his hand inside, felt for a brick. He knew what name would be on the tiny screen when he pulled it out but winced all the same. This wouldn't be a social call.

'Hi, Crystal, I—'

'Dave? Thank God. I've been trying your personal number but it's switched off. Are you OK? Just had Jimmy on the phone, saying your bus is abandoned on Princes Street? Says your passengers are close to rioting.'

'Och, he's exaggerating as always.' *Bloody Jimmy.* 'I've only been gone five minutes. Ten at most. And I'm on my way back there now.' He switched to a power walk. His legs and lungs protested but he kept going, hoped Crystal couldn't tell he was out of breath.

'But what happened? Why did you leave the bus?'

'There was . . . a lassie. She hadn't paid. I thought I could catch her.'

'Christ on a bike. You abandoned fifty passengers to chase a single ticket? Really?'

'Really,' he said. But it was ghosts he was chasing.

He heard the rattle of Crystal's plastic bracelets then the sound was muffled. A hand had been placed over the mouthpiece. Behind it he heard Crystal sigh, mutter something either to herself or to whoever else was in that office with her. He wished he could hear the words, work out if she was angry or disappointed or worried. All three, maybe. He'd let her down.

And what about his passengers? The majority had given up on him by the time he got back, jumped on a different line instead. As he drove off with empty seats behind him he pictured them, tutting and muttering as they shuffled off his abandoned bus; moaning about missed dates and appointments.

Every action we take spills into the lives of others.

Dave almost cried with relief when he pulled into the depot at the end of his shift. The parking area was empty apart from a few teenagers in the far corner with no jackets and big mouths and lumpy plastic bags at their feet. Even on a Tuesday night they'd probably be stuffed with beer and vodka, bottles to be drained into their bloodstream then smashed on the tarmac. If Crystal saw them she'd be out in a flash, warn them they'd already been caught on CCTV then tell them in no uncertain terms to fuck right off. She had more balls than the men who worked for her, that woman. But so far there was no sign of her tonight.

For once, that pleased him.

He'd give the bus a quick once-over then head home, hopefully see nobody. He collected the worst of the rubbish, the usual selection of greasy newspapers and pizza boxes and crushed drinks cans – then dumped it and headed to the depot.

The door slid shut behind him with a click, robbed him of the comforting sounds of the city. He stepped forward into the darkness, shoes hissing quietly on the lino. He noticed a puddle of yellow light on the floor outside the staff toilet but other than that the place was dark, silent and empty. He patted the wall until he found the big plastic switch then waited for the familiar clunk and buzz and flicker. And then there was light. He dropped off his keys then went to turn off the bathroom light before he left.

The cleaners had wedged open the door and blocked entry with one of those wee yellow sandwich boards that warned about the dangers of walking on wet floors. Dave paused outside, nerves tightening like a drawstring, sharply tugged. 'Anyone there?'

Of course there wasn't. He *knew* that.

And yet he pictured Carmen Martinez, walking out of death and into the darkness of the bus depot, via the women's toilet. *Stop, Dave. It wasn't her on the bus. And there's nobody here now.* Still his mind kept throwing out the same image; that moment when she'd looked right at him, just before that lad tapped her shoulder. Had *she* recognised *him* as well?

He wished there were a way he could have paused the world around him, made the world a party game where everyone and everything holds itself perfectly still until the music restarts. Everyone and everything except him, that is.

He leaned in to the toilets, switched off the lights then headed down the corridor. A CCTV camera blinked accusingly as he approached the main doors. Crystal rarely checked them but he still felt watched. And then, suddenly, an idea slid into his brain.

Maybe there *was* a way to pause the world after all.

He didn't need to chase this woman through the streets or follow her to some student bar like a dirty old man. He could check the CCTV from his bus. The only thing standing between him and the recordings was Crystal's office door.

He turned and headed back down the corridor; stopped by the big radiator opposite her door. Hunching down, he reached in behind it and felt along the wall. When his fingertips hit a lump he used the nail of his index finger to peel back the sticky tape; removed the spare key he'd put in place for Crystal after a day of drama when she'd left both sets at home. Easy.

Just for tonight, her office was his.

CHAPTER 16

Dave's heart fizzed like a mint dropped in cola.

Crystal didn't tend to wear much perfume but when he stepped inside her dark office, the scent of her was there, trapped between stacks of paper files and absorbed by the fabric of those cushions she'd brought in from home to make her chair more comfortable. Dave suspected their real purpose was to give her a few extra inches when she had a lumbering driver glaring at her from across the desk as she picked apart poor behaviour, punished them for it. His cheeks flushed at the thought. He knew fine well she'd be furious and forced to act if she got wind of this. He'd just need to make sure she didn't.

He moved to her side of the desk and fired up the computer. They'd sat here together one day a few months back, watching a CCTV video from his bus after a fight broke out on the top deck. Three drunk neds jumping a rugby fan dressed in an Italy shirt after one of the matches at Murrayfield. Hard to watch but the technology was good so they'd got a decent look at the faces of the lads who did it and the police had caught them, eventually. He'd watched Crystal at work that day, been impressed by how quickly she was able to pull up the right files once she knew the day and time of the incident in question – plus the number plate of the bus involved. He'd watched and learned; and hopefully now he'd find a clear view of that *girl* stepping on or off his bus.

He'd only need to check three files: the footage from his bus on the day of the accident and from the vehicle that collected his passengers after the crash. Thirdly he'd check the recording from the bus he'd driven today.

All he needed was a clear shot of her face and the chance to study it, uninhibited by manners or moving crowds. Chances were he'd quickly realise he was mistaken; that his brain was playing tricks on his eyes. Job done, he could forget about this drama and focus on the ones that were definitely real. The nuisance calls, and the police pointing the finger at him.

First things first, he needed to find the right CCTV files.

He worked on his cover story while the computer warmed up. If someone found out he'd been here he'd tell Crystal he was looking for the customer who'd sneaked on and off without paying. He'd already told her about that, so he'd just need to embellish it a little, claim she'd been riding buses free for months and he wanted to pass her image to the police. That would give him an excuse to be in her private office, on her chair, searching through files.

Dave was rubbish on computers but thankfully Crystal was not. When he opened the CCTV folder he was presented with dozens more, all clearly named. A few were for cameras in the depot and car park, but most were labelled with the licence plate of individual buses. He found the bus he'd just parked and pressed click on the folder marked September. Easy. Except today's footage wasn't yet loaded on to the system.

He tutted. One chance gone.

Now he'd need to find footage from the bus he'd driven yesterday, the day of the accident. He scanned the list of registration plates on screen, hoped one would trigger a memory. Which one was it? There were dozens of buses, and he'd driven most of them. The bus he crashed had been sent to the mechanics for repairs so he couldn't go and check. But no number plate meant no CCTV, unless he opened and checked every single file. He didn't have time for that. Second chance, gone.

He was down to his third and final attempt: the replacement bus that had come to pick up his passengers after the accident. It had been driven by Iris. She'd been there for decades, always got what she asked for and, thankfully for Dave, she always drove the same bus. He located the footage easily, fast-forwarded to the moment his passengers climbed on board her bus at the scene of the accident. Problem: they were all running late and all clambered on at once. He saw a flash of a green coat and nothing more. *Patience, Dave.* He pressed play and leaned forward, waiting; watching, finger resting on the mouse. He'd stop the footage the moment he saw her. If he couldn't see the girl getting *on to* the bus, hopefully he'd catch sight of her getting off.

Ten minutes later, he spotted her getting off in the city centre along with most other passengers. Hood up, head down. Waste of time.

Dave sighed and closed the file.

What now? The best opportunity would definitely be the footage from his own bus yesterday, just before the accident. She'd been the only passenger to get on at that stop so he'd have a clear view of her face. But how else could he find the right number plate?

He went back to the home page on Crystal's computer and scanned the files for one marked *Incidents* or *Accidents* or something similar. Nope. He leaned back in her chair then spun round. Rows of filing boxes lined the high shelves behind her desk. Each was labelled with letters of the alphabet but gave no details of what was kept inside. Was there a chance she'd print off and keep incident forms?

Worth a shot.

He stood up, tugged down the K box, just in case. If there were any printed records with the name *Kellock* on them, they'd be here.

The box barely weighed anything. He opened the lid, expecting papers, letters, files. Instead he found a copy of his contract and a single envelope, bulging but closed with a green elastic band. Dave peeled it off carefully so it wouldn't snap. Inside, photos.

He tipped the envelope and eased them into his hands; felt his heart slide to his stomach when he saw whose face was staring back at him from the top of the pile. His own. The picture had been taken years back on the Isle of Harris, a few months before the killings. Back then he'd still had hair and a smile that hid nothing and the person who took it loved him and was loved in equal measure. It was one of his favourite photos – or used to be.

But why did Crystal have it? And how?

The only copy he knew of was at his house, and yesterday was the first time she'd been there. Even if she'd had some reason to swipe one of his old holiday snaps, it was impossible. She hadn't been on her own apart from those few minutes in the sitting room when he was making the tea. He let his eyes linger on the details of that image then tucked it to the back of the pile, exposing the picture that lay beneath. His own face, again. Another old photo she couldn't possibly have had access to. The ones that followed showed

Dave at work, snapped when he wasn't looking. In one he was leaning over a bucket in the garage, sponge in hand. In another he was in the staff room, back turned to the camera as he poured boiling water into Crystal's mug. But some photos were definitely old, and his: Dave living in a world that Crystal should have known nothing about.

If his nerves had been tugged to their limits before, now they were on the rack, and the wheel was turning, turning, turning. He cleared a space on the desk and laid out the prints side by side, didn't care that he was leaving thumb marks on the surfaces. He turned them over one by one, but there was nothing written on the back. He always wrote the year and place on his printed photos, so at least he'd established one solid fact: they were copies.

And the negatives? They'd be stored somewhere in his attic.

Had *Crystal* been up there?

Dave's eyes fell again to her desk, and the cupboard where all the duplicate locker keys were kept. She knew he kept a spare set of house keys at work. She knew his timetable better than anyone. And now, somehow, she had photos from his attic in her office. Was *she* the one who'd slipped into his house when he was out?

Dave stuffed the photos back into the envelope, replaced the box and closed down the computer. He left Crystal's office exactly as he'd found it. But there was a change in him he couldn't ignore.

He'd found few things of use on the CCTV.

But he'd lost something much more important in there: trust.

CHAPTER 17

Wednesday

Wednesday started with a doorbell rung, far too loud. It ripped Dave out of sleep, woke him up with a thumping heart. He cursed whoever had denied him those brief moments of stillness that the morning usually brought; a few seconds lodged between the waking world and the sleeping one when memories escaped him and he was just here, just breathing. He glanced at his alarm clock. Nine-thirty. One hour after his shift should have started. *Shit.* There were few worse ways to start the day than this: the inescapable fact that you've already let somebody down.

Crystal would kill him. But maybe, just maybe, she'd let him down too.

He hauled his legs out of bed, half-expected to look outside and see Crystal waiting in a rage on his doorstep, having called both his mobiles without success. His work phone was switched to silent mode and his own was still lost, in or around Jonathan Todd's garden shed. He'd intended to go looking for it last night but he was worn out by the time he'd left the depot.

His heart sank at the memory of those photos, hidden in Crystal's office. The only place they should be hidden was right here, inside the supposed privacy of his own home. He glanced at the ceiling, pictured the attic that lay beyond it.

Had Crystal really taken the spare keys from his locker and let herself in?

No matter how hard he tried, he could not imagine her climbing up that wee metal ladder, bangles jangling, pushing cobwebs out of her hair as she crawled from one end of his attic to the other, unseen.

He'd go up there again later, check again for signs of disturbance.

But the fact was this: he had no idea why she had his photos or how she'd got her hands on them. And if she'd seen all those pictures of his past, did that mean she knew what he'd done? Was it *her* who'd made the nuisance calls from his landline? She hadn't been at the depot when he'd finished his shift on Sunday evening, so for all he knew she might have been here, in his house. She could have made the calls and hunted for photos in his attic and taken a snooze in his bed and he'd be none the wiser. He felt sick at the thought of it: him at work while the walls of his home flickered with the shadows of strangers moving through it. And Crystal behind the scenes, pulling the strings.

But why would she?

The doorbell rang again, disturbed his thoughts.

He reached for the curtains, tugged them back. A dark-haired woman wearing jeans and a leather jacket stood halfway up his garden path, one hand cupped over her eyes as she studied his upstairs windows – including the one that framed him, standing in his navy-blue pyjamas. She nodded to him, said something he couldn't hear through the glass.

He opened the window against his better judgement, leaned out. 'I'm in a rush. Late for work. But . . . can I help you with something?'

'Hope so.'

The woman reached into her pocket, pulled out some kind of ID badge. She was probably a volunteer for a charity, doing the rounds. But whatever she was asking for, he'd be strong and politely refuse. No time for that today. He usually had a good chat with them on the doorstep and they'd leave with his bank details and yet another monthly donation. His account was linked to more charities than the National Lottery.

The woman took a step back when she held up her badge.

'I'm Detective Inspector Farida McPherson,' she said, then sniffed long and fully, the way folk did at wine tastings. 'And I'd appreciate a word.'

For a few seconds Dave stayed perfectly still, as if frozen. But he was blazing on the inside.

'I'll be right down,' he said. He shut the window, let the curtain fall, switched his pyjamas for yesterday's work shirt and trousers then went downstairs before his mind persuaded him to flee.

He paused to compose himself in the hall. Took a few deep breaths, snipped his wandering thoughts at the root. Then he opened the door.

There were two of them now. Farida McPherson's sidekick had spiky blonde hair that reminded Dave of some pop singer from the eighties. She introduced herself as Detective Sergeant Effie Garcia. Dave wondered what name Effie was short for and if she'd been a bully at school. Had that look.

'Come on in,' he said, and when Farida walked past he caught the scent of chlorine. So she was a swimmer. Big shoulders, right enough. And a fiver said she'd thrash him in an arm-wrestle, leave the imprint of his knuckles on the wood. 'Sitting room's first on your right.'

'Lead the way,' she said. Not one to take instructions.

Sun streamed in the wide bay window, drawing golden lines on the varnished floorboards and giving halos to the tiny particles that swirled slowly in the air. Not that there was much dust in the place. Dave kept a very clean house, had a deep need for surfaces that held no stains. He went through bottles of bleach quicker than most folk went through wine.

He directed both officers to his sofa, offered tea then escaped to the kitchen.

He filled the kettle and flipped it on, was still debating which mugs to use when the water rose to the boil. He chose three pale blue ones he'd bought at the supermarket, hoped they said nothing about him. His hand went automatically to the biscuit tin after he'd filled the pot. Would that be appropriate? He didn't want them to think he was stingy but it seemed odd to talk with police while munching on a custard cream.

He'd take the tin, let them choose.

His offerings rattled against each other on the loaded tray as he walked through the hall, warned them of his approach. When he pushed open the door with his foot Effie was studying his bookcase and Farida was sitting stiffly on his big grey couch, her leather jacket folded neatly on her knee, her face turned towards the window and the park that lay beyond it, an old industrial site turned to parkland, the ugly made beautiful. When the leaves started falling you could see the summit of Arthur's Seat through the branches and he'd often sit exactly where she was, promising himself he'd climb it again one of these days.

It calmed him, that view.

'Here you go,' he said, setting the tray down. 'I brought something sweet as well,' he said, nodding to the biscuit tin. It was shaped like a bus, an unexpected gift from a customer.

'Just tea's fine.'

For a few moments Dave busied himself with pouring and sipping and offering more milk, filled the space between them with the clink of a spoon on china, the comfortingly familiar sound of liquid poured from a spout. It was better than questions or accusations. But soon all that was left was the drinking. Dave repeatedly blew on his tea as his mind conjured up images of the detectives drinking theirs and leaving without a word.

Farida took a sip then returned her mug to the tray. 'The officers in charge of the hoax call investigation told me you were due to contact them last night. They called your landline but got no answer. Then they tried your mobile too, left a message on your voicemail.' Dave flushed at the mention of his mobile. Farida paused, took another sip. 'Despite *your* promises and *their* efforts, they've heard nothing from you.'

Dave stared into his tea. If there wasn't an actual question, he wasn't answering. But he could sense where this was going.

'If I understand correctly . . . you claim the nuisance calls were made by . . . an *intruder* in your home. Is that correct?'

'It's the only logical explanation.'

She answered with a sniff that Dave suspected was a polite replacement for an expletive. 'And *logically*, if there's been an intruder, there will be evidence of forced entry. My colleagues were hoping you'd provide some. Hence the voicemail.'

Dave shook his head. 'I've checked the house and there's no damage. Whoever's been here got in with a key. I said the same thing to your colleagues yesterday.'

'I see.'

Which clearly meant she didn't.

'May I ask why you've not responded to the message they left on your mobile?'

Think, Dave. And fast. 'I . . . lost it. Think someone swiped it from the bus.'

'How . . . inconvenient. Did you report it to the police?'

'Not yet. Was on my To Do list for this morning.'

She held his gaze for a few seconds longer than was comfortable, then reached into the inside pocket of her leather jacket and pulled out his mobile phone. 'Yours, I believe?'

Dave almost toppled off the arm of the chair where he'd perched, body on high alert. He steadied himself, wished his nerves would do the same. 'Can I have a closer look?'

She handed it over and for a few moments Dave inspected it, killing time, trying to work out what the best course of action would be here. If he denied it was his, he'd be directly lying to the police and, to make bad matters worse, he wouldn't have a mobile phone. If he admitted it was his then he'd basically be making a confession: yes, he'd been creeping around a stranger's garden. And not any old stranger, but the same one who'd been targeted by nuisance calls from his landline.

'It was out of battery when it was found,' said Farida, nodding to the phone. 'But my colleagues took the liberty of charging it.'

The screen lit up when Dave flipped it over, illuminated a photo of his bus in the garage and a slice of Portobello Beach behind. His face flushed. Game over.

'It's mine right enough. Whereabouts was it found?'

He made sure he looked right at Farida when he asked the question, kept his face bright, as if he really was surprised and waiting for an unexpected answer.

Her eyes were something else, like a painting you could stare at forever and still not understand.

'I think you already know, Mr Kellock.' She reached for her tea, every move slow and controlled and gentle, somehow. She was a living yoga pose. Tea blown, sipped, swallowed, replaced as if she had nowhere else to be, nothing else to do. 'But I'll humour you. The phone was found at a property in the Colinton neighbourhood. Officers recovered it while responding to reports of an intruder. A witness spotted a man he described as . . .' She reached for her notepad and glanced at the first page; an act. 'Middle-aged, bald, clean-shaven, grey trousers, white shirt . . .' She paused, fired out a look that almost killed him. 'The witness then proceeded to restrain the intruder by means of locking him in the shed. Does this—'

'Is that not against the law?'

She held a palm out, like one of those oversized Buddha statues staring out of the window at the pound store. 'I think you'll find I'm the one asking the questions here.' A hint of a smile. She was enjoying this more than he was. 'Does this . . . encounter ring any bells with you?'

'Like I said, I thought it'd been swiped from the bus.'

'And you stand by that claim?'

'It's what happened.'

A pause; silence, charged. 'Tell me, are all your buses fitted with CCTV these days?'

'Should be, aye.' *Shit*.

'Then hopefully we can easily find the person who took your phone.' With that she closed the notebook, tucked it into the pocket from where she'd produced his phone. 'I do like it when crimes are easily resolved; and when the culprits have sufficient . . . moral standing . . . to confess.'

She stood up, glanced out of the window to his front garden. He kept his pots there, each one planted with several different flowers that would bloom at different times. At first he used to put four or five identical ones in the same pot, but he'd learned that soil in a confined space supported a finite amount of life. It was a very fine line between a joyful riot of colour and a pot full of sunken, shrunken heads that would wither away to nothing.

'Nice flowers.'

'They're not bad.'

'Got more space at the back?'

Dave nodded. 'Room for a wee veggie garden as well. Lawn. The usual.'

'Lovely. You're lucky to have it.'

'I am.'

'Got a shed?'

The question was a pebble, thrown. It struck Dave right between the eyes, stunned him into momentary silence. He nodded. 'For my tools.'

'Keep it locked?'

'I do, aye.'

'Sensible. Never know who's prowling around – and in my experience it's often not the people you expect.'

A smile, then she nodded to Effie and they headed for the front door. Dave followed, wishing them away. Farida turned to him, one hand on the lock. 'I'll be seeing you, Mr Kellock.'

She left the door open, didn't look back as she walked down his path and climbed into an unmarked car. Dave returned to the sitting room, picked up his phone and swiped open a world of notifications. He had a few missed calls, a dozen texts and three voice-mails. All from Crystal. She'd be furious, wanting to know why he was so late for his shift. Either that or she somehow knew he'd raided her office and discovered the secret stash of photos.

He had to call her back, but what should he say?

His phone rang again before he could decide. Crystal, again. He sighed, swallowed hard, then answered.

'A call, answered? Blessed be thy God.'

He'd heard her use that line with other folk as well, putting on a silly voice when she said it.

'I'm so sorry I'm late,' said Dave. The apology was automatic and he wished he could tug it back inside, start on a stronger foot. 'Look, there's something I need to ask you, Crystal.'

'Ask away, so long as it's a plea for forgiveness? No? Then you can ask me later. Right now *I* want to ask *you* why your arse isn't wedged into one of my buses. This isn't just late, Dave, this is breaking your contract. This is failing to show up for a shift. This is failing to return phone calls. This is me waking up drivers on their day off and begging them to come in and cover your shift.'

'I *am* sorry, but—'

'It's Jimmy Jones who'll be looking for an apology. The man's a total tube but he's got a mum in care, a wee sister in rehab and after today, he's not had a day off in a fortnight.'

Dave sighed. This wasn't the time to accuse Crystal of anything. She was too fired up. He'd try to catch her later, in person, at the depot. In the meantime, all he could do was play along. 'I'll make it up to you. And Jimmy.'

'Too bloody right you will. I've put you on the late shift tonight, four till midnight. But come in early, so—'

'I can't work late, Crystal. Not tonight.'

'Can't or won't?'

'Both.'

Crystal breathed out a sigh so hard she probably lost weight. 'You mind telling me why?'

Dave thought about the MOB Bar, about seeing *her* face to face. He rummaged in his brain for lies. There were plenty lying around that he could choose from.

'I'm meeting someone tonight. An old friend. We've got a restaurant booked for half-seven.'

'And it can't be rearranged?'

'They're only in Edinburgh tonight.'

'You're pushing it,' she said. 'And you still haven't told me why you're late this morning.'

Dave sighed before he could stop himself. 'The police came. I couldn't get away. And before you ask, it was just a follow-up to my interview on Monday. Nothing to worry about.'

'Nothing to worry about? Nothing *new*, you mean. All I seem to do these days is worry about you.'

Crystal's voice was gentler now. Usually Dave found it a comfort but today it sounded forced and instead of a softening heart he felt suspicion. He was sure of one thing alone: all of this must be connected. But could Crystal be the missing link between his vision of Carmen, the nuisance calls and the discovery of his photos in her office? He hated himself for asking that question; loathed himself even more deeply when his brain fired out its answer: a big fat *yes*.

He should never have let himself get close to her.

'Tell you what, Dave – I'll put you down for a half day, OK? Get your arse in here within the next thirty minutes and I'll let you scuttle off on time for your big date.'

'Thank you – really. You're a star.'

'Or a sucker for a nice face,' she said. 'Either way, you owe me, big time. And if you're late tomorrow I'll break you in half. Is that clear?'

'Got it, boss.'

'Good.' He could tell by her voice that she was smiling now, wondered if she was gazing at that photo of him as they spoke. 'One last thing, Dave. Are they still there?'

'Sorry?'

'The police. Are they still with you?'

'They just left.' Funny how in Dave's mouth even the truth sounded like lies. 'Look, if you don't believe me, I'm sure you can call the station and they'll back me up. I know I should have called anyway to let you know I'd be late. And I'm sorry. But I was—'

'Calm down. I believe you. But I was thinking of calling them myself anyway.'

'Really? Why?'

Dave knew her answer before it came, was glad Crystal couldn't see his reddening face down the phone line.

'I'll fill you in when you get here,' she said. 'But long story short? Someone's been snooping around in my office.'

Ten minutes later, Dave left his house without a shower or a shave. He locked up, glanced apologetically at his unwatered plants then headed towards the bus depot, tensed shoulders hugging his ears. They didn't drop an inch until the house was out of sight. But even then he kept stopping and looking back. If someone had been in his house, were they watching him now? He kept expecting to see Carmen there with blood on her face, her dark eyes slowly stilling when they met his.

But there was nobody there; just the grief of it that stalked him instead. It had never left him, would occasionally rise to the surface like water in a plastic bottle, squeezed. Its entrance was heralded by the ache of that lump in his throat that he tried to swallow down but could not. Old wounds, unpicked.

But the question he needed to answer was this: who was doing the unpicking?

CHAPTER 18

Confession one: I've been watching you for weeks, waiting for the right moment to step back into your world, and stay there.

Confession two: I'm no longer acting alone.

Right now you've stopped at the traffic lights and today the same as every day you press three times then pause and press again; as if you think the buttons will pay heed; that the world will reward your optimism. Or it is impatience that drives you? Two schoolgirls with low-slung backpacks scowl and occasionally spit on to the road as they wait beside you and on your other side there's a woman who's young but doesn't look it, dresses like somebody's tired mother. The schoolgirls step out, ponytails bouncing as they grip each other's hands then race across, squealing. I watch you watching them, wait for the pulsing in your cheek that means you're grinding your teeth – which means you're nervous.

Something is on your mind and I think it might be me. I picture myself reaching out and placing a soft hand on that twitching jaw muscle and rubbing it, gently.

119

You'd relax, close your eyes, smile knowingly. Instead you're watching those girls race across the road to the opposite pavement, laughing to draw attention towards themselves and away from the fact that a car had to brake to let them pass. They're giggling, bent over double on the pavement and I hate them for it, the ease with which they embrace joy.

When the green man appears, the people around you step on to the road and tut when you don't. You're a rock in a river, forcing the flow to pass by on either side.

And so it's just us.

Me and you, again, as the lights turn to red.

I inch forward, so close my coat touches yours. The people in cars might see us as strangers but we know different, don't we? When another bus rumbles past you move back from the edge, bump into me and mutter an apology without looking back. 'Sorry, pal.'

Your voice is exactly as I remember it, matches the one I conjure up in memories and imagined conversations. The lights turn to green again and, this time, you walk. You're one of the few on the street without a mobile phone or headphones to distract them from themselves and I wonder what you think about in those quiet moments of life; what and who you allow yourself to dream of when it's just you and the world and a silence you think is yours.

I smile to myself, knowing I could break it if I chose to; wondering what you'd do if I said that name out loud. What would happen if I stepped out of the shadows and stretched out my arms until our finger-tips touched? I picture sparks, flying, and the world as you know it grinding to a halt. But it's still too soon. Instead I turn and retrace my steps to your house, smiling as I slip the key into the back door and step inside. When you left you turned the lock, twice, then tugged the handle to check it held firm. Just to be safe. Just to be sure.

But just so you know: it doesn't make any difference.

CHAPTER 19

Dave's shift passed without event or drama but he'd rarely been so relieved to get home. He grabbed a quick dinner and a brief shower while he waited for a taxi, was still buttoning his one and only party shirt when the driver called to say he was outside. Quick glance in the mirror and he was out and on his way to crash a party for the first time in decades.

On a Wednesday, no less.

The MOB Bar occupied the ground floor of a tenement block near The Meadows. It was one of those scruffy bars that had been built by old men for old men but had somehow become a place of eighties music and rainbow flags. It was years since he'd been in a gay bar. The world had moved on a bit, but all the old clichés were still there and part of him hoped they always would be. The single men stood alone with their backs to the bar, looking towards a makeshift dance floor and the disco ball that spun obligingly above it. A women's football team screeched in one of the old wooden booths and the one next to them was occupied by two older men supping Guinness, seemingly oblivious to the fact that they were ten times straighter than most other customers. One had white hair and a tweed suit. The other was younger, dark hair, looked as though he'd been born worrying. The table between them was cluttered with newspapers and notepads and chewed pens. Looked like journalists. Dave turned his back on them, just in case they recognised him from the awards story – or from the reports of the killings. He did not want to be recognised, especially not tonight.

He did a quick scan of the remaining corners of the bar then headed back outside. The girl from the bus was definitely not in there.

Now it was time to wait and watch.

There were no benches near the bar but there was a church across the road with a low wall to perch on. Perfect. He stationed himself there, crossing and uncrossing legs, leaning and unleaning on elbows, rehearsing and rewriting what he'd say to the girl when she arrived. He jumped when loudspeakers wired to the steeple above him blared out a recording of bells. It was eight o'clock.

Freshers always moved in packs: drunken shoals of new students following each other through streets they didn't yet know, big weans still wanting their mum but being too shy to say it out loud. He heard them before he saw them: the predictable shrieks and whoops of those who drank too much and laughed too loud and tried far too hard to be noticed, liked.

Take away the drinking part and Dave knew how they felt. Nobody grows up, really.

He pulled out his phone when the group got closer, held it to his ear as if he were on a call. Folk on mobiles could look where they wanted and not be accused of staring. They'd be dismissed or forgiven, always had the excuse that their mind was elsewhere; distracted.

He scanned the shifting mass of dyed hair and new tattoos and cheeks reddened by booze. He couldn't see the girl from the bus but his chest sparked when he noticed the skinny lad; the one she'd hugged on the Royal Mile. He had piercings in both ears and thick black mascara around his eyes. In Dave's day, he'd have been punched if he'd left the house looking like that.

A bouncer appeared at the door, blocked it until they'd all waved student cards in his face. They were in. But she was not.

Dave scanned the street in the direction they'd come from. There would always be stragglers, and anyway, the streets were mobbed. It would be easy enough to get caught up in the wrong group of students. Or she might have forgotten her phone or gone for a last-minute pee and missed the bus into town from the university. It might be better this way, anyway. If she turned up late he could get her on her own.

He waited, watching, trying to look relaxed. The church clock struck eight-fifteen. Then eight-thirty. By the time it hit quarter to nine a lassie had puked up chips an inch from his feet, four folk had asked him for a light, and every inch of his backside was frozen solid on that wall. Plus the bouncers from the MOB Bar had started giving him evils. Stuff this for a laugh.

He slipped his phone into his pocket and tucked his nerves behind a gentle smile and a confident walk. The bar was packed, felt smaller. Nothing was still. He pushed past two sturdy women drinking from long glasses near the door, made his way to the toilets up the back so he could get a look at all the tables. The skinny lad and his pals had taken over the booth where the newspaper men had been sitting. The girl definitely wasn't with them.

He went into the loos, took a few deep breaths, then pushed open the swing door and headed for their table, a place of spilled drinks and crisp crumbs and overlapping conversations.

'You guys enjoying Freshers' Week?' Dave had chosen the word *guys* deliberately but it didn't sit right in his mouth. He sounded like someone's embarrassing uncle.

One of the girls glanced at him, top lip curled like Elvis. Translation: you're not wanted.

Dave caught the eye of the skinny lad from the bus. 'I'm hoping you can help me, son. I'm needing to talk with one of your pals. Olive skin, wavy black hair. Sometimes wears a bright yellow jacket.'

The boy pulled a face like he was doing mental arithmetic. 'You mean . . . Amy?'

Dave flushed as a memory started forming in his mind. This was the second time he'd encountered that name in two days. But where and when was the first time?

In Jonathan Todd's shed, handwritten on the side of a storage box.

Was the girl from the bus Jonathan Todd's daughter? If she *was* then that meant Amy and her mother had been the target of the nuisance calls from his landline.

A mother and child, killed.

Amy, who looked exactly like Carmen Martinez, the pregnant woman he'd killed.

Dave swallowed his panic and flipped into bus driver mode, forcing out the kind of smile people usually trusted. 'Aye. That's her. Amy.'

The skinny lad shrugged. 'She's not here yet. She just texted me. Said her mum turned up out of the blue, wanted to surprise her for the big one-eight.'

'The what?'

The boy rolled his eyes. 'Her eighteenth birthday?'

'Of course,' said Dave, blood like hot oil in his veins. He'd killed Carmen almost two years before this girl was even born, but still his brain scrambled to find a connection between them.

126

Maybe Carmen had a much younger sister he didn't know about. Maybe she'd given birth to a daughter before she met Dave – and that child had later been adopted by Jonathan Todd and his wife. An alternative version was this: Carmen had been in some kind of relationship with Jonathan Todd years earlier and they'd had the baby together. That was why Amy Todd looked just like Carmen. Logical. Easy to understand. But impossible. Again, it came back to basic calculations. Carmen and her unborn child had been dead for almost twenty years – and Amy had just turned eighteen. The maths simply didn't work for any of his theories.

He *had* to see her for himself – and her mother.

Why? To quell his fears, or stoke them. Either he was going mad, or not.

'You couldn't give me her number, could you? So I can say happy birthday.'

The boy pulled a face as though Dave had spat in his pint. 'Eh . . . not sure. Who are you exactly?'

'Her mum's . . . an old friend,' he said.

'So why can't you phone *her* and ask for Amy's contact, then?'

'I . . . lost her number.'

'Really?'

'Aye, really.' Dave maintained eye contact, made sure his hands were firmly clasped in front of him so he didn't touch his face. Everybody knew it was the classic tic of liars but he'd long since eliminated the habit, conditioned it out of his system. His lies were too enormous and long-lasting to expose with something as banal as a nose-scratch.

The lad glanced at his pals. Their eyes egged him on. 'No offence, but I—'

'It's really important that I speak to her.'

'Sorry, but . . . I don't think I can help.' He looked around the table for reassurance, realised he had an audience. 'Hang on a minute. Before you go, how did you even know she'd be here?'

Ears pricked. They were all watching now, the wee bastards.

'I *saw* you with her, on the Royal Mile, just after you got off my bus.'

'*Your* bus? Are you a *driver* or something?'

Rarely had the word been said with such disdain. If Dave could have booted himself up the arse, he'd have done it in that moment. He should have said he was a passenger, or not mentioned the bus at all. He was still searching for a decent response when the skinny lad threw out another accusation. He was clearly enjoying himself.

'I don't know about you guys . . .' The lad glanced at his friends. 'But I really don't think a bus driver should be *eavesdropping* on private conversations.'

'You shouted to her, son, and I overheard. It's not a crime.'

'But me and Amy didn't speak until we were *off* the bus. So unless you *followed us* I don't see how you could have heard.' He pulled a stupid shocked face after he said it, blinked far more than was necessary. He could win an Oscar for less. One of his pals muttered something at the other end of the table and a few of them laughed, eyes on Dave. He wasn't close enough to hear but he could guess what they were saying, would probably have come to the same conclusion if it had been him sitting at the table.

'This isn't what it looks like, OK? Can you just give me her number, please?'

'Tell you what . . .' The lad paused, clearly for effect. 'Why don't you give me *your* number. I'll tell Amy what you've told me and if she wants to call you she will. That fair?'

Dave swallowed a sigh, tightened his fists, grunted a yes. When he recited his number the lad uttered a comment under his breath that made all of them laugh. Dave hated them and wished he were them, envied living in a world not yet blackened by the blood of others. They probably dreaded turning out like him and Dave didn't blame them. He felt sick and exposed. He was on the rack and this lot were hoping his nerves would snap.

The skinny lad made a show of typing Dave's number into his phone then read it back to him so loud half the pub would have heard. 'And what's the name?'

Dave hesitated for a second, maybe two, before he answered. Too long. Any trust he'd won was lost. The skinny lad raised his eyebrows then put away his phone.

'Bye, then, *David*.'

More sniggers. Dave turned away, was swallowed up by crowds on his way to the door. He kept his head down, ignoring the piss-take wolf-whistles from behind. The floor was sticky as upturned Sellotape and the bright lights at the bar had been switched to flickers of pale blue and green and red. Faces were softer but full of shadows. A DJ shouted through a microphone then turned up the music so loud Dave could feel it rattle his bones, his breath. The air was thick with sweat and expectation and the hope of love, found. Dave pushed past a crying girl with a crew cut, was almost at the door when a warm cheek touched his and a single word tickled his ear. An old lover's call, with a question mark pegged on the end. '*Chiquito*?'

CHAPTER 20

Him. Here. Now. The disco lights above the bar danced on Dave's face but in any other room you'd have seen his face flip from red to white as all the blood in him bolted straight for his heart. His chest was too full and too hot. He stepped back, trapped some lassie's trainer under his own. She told him to fucking watch himself, shoved him back towards the bar.

And Rafa. Here. Now.

'You come here often?' Rafa leaned in as he said it, added a laugh where a question mark should be. The lights above the bar made his crooked teeth glow bright blue.

Dave blinked a few times, wishing his eyes were a kaleidoscope; that he could twist and change the view. But only the colours changed. He opened his eyes as the DJ switched on the strobe light. A few folk cheered. The crap dancers, probably. Now everyone's movements were jerking, stalling, jumping. Dave felt dizzy. Those eyes were still on him. His mouth moved like a robot. Dave couldn't hear the words over the music but the spit that came with them was lit up with pure white light; saliva like shooting stars.

Rafa leaned in, closer. 'I said, I think you need a drink.' He was already turning towards the bar. He'd have tipped a member of staff at the start of the night to make sure he always got served quickly, wouldn't need to stand waving tenners between strangers' shoulders. Sure enough, a tall lassie with a mohawk and too many piercings nodded at him from behind the bar. He pointed to one of the beers on tap then turned back to Dave, smiling as he waited for a momentary pause in the bassline.

Boom. 'Still on the gin?' Boom.

'I've stopped.'

Boom. 'You kidding?' Boom. 'How about a line, then? For old times' sake?' Boom.

Rafa winked then tugged a tiny plastic bag from his jeans pocket. Cocaine, of course. In the old days he would reserve it for those long, electric nights spent in extravagant hotels that neither of them could really afford. Drugs added to the glamour of it, somehow. For a moment Dave pictured Rafa stretched out in bed, cinnamon skin on soft white sheets. He'd roll a fifty-pound note then breathe in the powder that both united and divided them. They'd both be awake all night and aye, that was the whole point. The hotels were always Rafa's idea, as were the drugs. But it thrilled Dave to be with someone who so readily took chances.

Back then he'd have done anything with him; for him.

Rafa shrugged and slipped the little bag back into his pocket then leaned in, both hands cupped around his mouth. 'Not interested?'

Did he mean him, or the drugs? Either way, Dave's answer was the same. No, no, no. Repeat it enough times and it'd start sounding like the truth. But right now he could barely hear the warning alarms blaring in every part of his brain and body. The music was getting louder. The lights brighter. Dave's heart, fuller. He had to leave, was turning away when Rafa leaned in so close that his finger brushed Dave's cheek. The last time those hands had touched him they'd been curled into fists.

Inside of him a switch flicked to *on*. Dave caught the scent of his shower gel. Same as before. Same one his twin sister used to use as well. One sniff dragged him back twenty years, laughing as the pair of them tutted their way down the bathroom aisle of the big Tesco then ordered Spanish soap in bulk online.

'Last chance. Can I tempt you with water?'

Dave turned away. *Deliver me from temptation.* Elbows sharpened, eyes on the door. He needed out, now. There was only about four metres between him and the exit but there must have been fifty folk crammed into that space. He entered the crowd side-on, one hand held out in front of him like the prow of a ship. Or maybe a dinghy, in his case. Small steps on a sticky floor, every part of him pressed against the damp warmth of strangers' backs and limbs. The world smelled of beer burps and dry mouths and salt from slippery peanuts.

Boom.

A hand gripped his shoulder, tried to pull him back to that voice, that face, that smile, that love. Here. Now. No. It was too much. Too dangerous. Dave pushed forward, squeezed between two overdone blondes and around the far side of a squat man so wide he'd need two seats on a plane. The doorman saw him coming, pushed open the door then shouted at the smokers' colony polluting that stretch of pavement. 'Puker coming through!'

Cue laughs and whoops. They rippled away from Dave all the same as he stood, bent over with his hands on his thighs, breathing too hard. The cold air smelled of hot fat. That was Scotland, home, life as it should be. He spat, then glanced at the empty doorway as he straightened up. He had to get away before he was seen, followed.

He did his best impression of running, gave in to the pleading of his legs once he'd turned a few corners. He stopped and stood in the dark space between two street lamps, back against the wall of a shop long since closed, the window display all sun-faded posters and dead flies. His mind shifted to home, those wasps on the carpet; someone else's hand reaching for the hatch of his attic; and his phone. But who?

He glanced back to where he'd come from, saw a lone figure heading in his direction. Was it Rafa? He couldn't tell, but quickened his pace anyway. He was out of breath by the time he reached the rough bustle of the Grassmarket. It smelled of spilled beer and cold piss. He slowed his step, hoped he blended in with the crowds of tourists and locals and students hanging about on the old cobbles, slurring, squawking, puking, singing, drinking, eating greasy food to soak up the alcohol sloshing through their veins. One of those night-time ghost tours was gathered outside the Last Drop pub, blocking the pavement and pissing off the drinkers as their guide swung his homemade black cloak and put on his radio voice as he told an embellished tale of the last hanging in Edinburgh. An awful way to go; with the weight of that rope on your shoulders and one tiny step between you and the end of everything.

But that was all it took, wasn't it?

He kept walking, his thundering heart and tired legs forcing him to slow as he climbed the sweeping curve of Victoria Street. Must be the most photographed street in the city, Royal Mile aside: the stone walls of every shop painted a different colour; the old window frames stacked up with little panes of glass. It'd catch your eye and keep it, any time of day or year. All around him folk stopped to take photos on their phone while others stood staring at their screens, sharing images already captured. Dave kept his phone in his pocket and his eyes on the ground then ducked through a stone archway between two closed shops. Beyond it lay a filthy stairway known mainly by locals and the homeless. He climbed to a walkway overlooking Victoria Street. From there Dave scanned the faces of folk walking uphill, was relieved to see only strangers. He'd lost Rafa, for now.

He slumped down on a cold stone step, closed his eyes and let his head fall into his hands. His heartbeat pulsed in every part of his body. He willed it to slow down but it didn't listen. His brain ignored him as well when he pleaded, over and over, for the swirl of images to stop. Her face, on his bus. His face, in that bar. First Carmen, then Rafa. Two faces that merged perfectly into one. Carmen and Rafa were non-identical twins, since they weren't the same sex, but looked more alike than any siblings he knew. If Dave and Rafa had married she'd have been his sister-in-law but that was a formality, paperwork. The bond they'd had was worth much more. Carmen had *felt* like a sister. If you could choose your family, he'd have chosen her. She'd said the same about him.

And then? From there, it had all gone wrong.

CHAPTER 21

Dave grabbed a taxi back home from the city centre then sat in the back hunched over his phone. First of all he typed the name *Amy Todd* into the search box, and into all the social media platforms he could think of. But none of the faces that appeared were the girl from the bus. For the rest of the journey he stared at the Messages icon, refreshing his phone over and over. *If* the skinny lad at the MOB Bar had passed his number to Amy and *if* she actually decided to send him a message, he wanted to be sure he got it right away.

But she'd hardly rush to contact him, would she? To them he was an old man in a young people's pub, a nosy bus driver, a weirdo, a loser; a threat. And they didn't know the half of it.

At Dave's request the taxi driver eased into the turning area at the end of King's Road, right in front of Portobello Beach. He'd walk the rest of the way home. Dave paid, tipping too much, then got out and stood with his back to the street; his face to the sea.

There was something magical about shorelines under dark skies. It kept on shifting, whispering, luring him in. Rafa was a useless swimmer but on calm nights he'd often coax Dave into the sea, against his better judgement. They'd dump their clothes and safety concerns at the far end of the beach and run into the black water. Rafa loved to throw himself into turning waves then open his eyes under the surface and stare into a darkness that seemed completely endless.

They'd always end up floating on their backs, fingers entwined as the water rose and fell in time with their breath. It was cold as hell, but warming up afterwards was half the fun of it.

Sometimes the girls came with them too. Carmen was happy floating and splashing with Dave and Rafa – just like the old days – but Suzanne would bring goggles and a rubber hat and a waterproof light that she'd tie to her ankle. Years of swim club had made her shoulders wide and her kicks powerful enough to rock a small boat. Carmen would swoon when she zipped past them like a torpedo. Rafa would roll his eyes then Carmen would tut, tell him not to be so bloody jealous. He hated that and she knew it. But she was his twin sister: always forgiven and never forgotten.

Ahead of Dave, the sea rolled in, almost as fast as the memories.

Then behind him, from the silence, came a sudden screech.

Dave jumped; turned to see a group of thickly painted women staggering towards him. Skirts like belts, hands gripping plastic bags that were stretched by clunking wine bottles. Time to go. Eyes to the ground, key in hand, Dave headed for home.

His street was empty apart from a lad tucked inside a hooded top who swayed as he pissed into a neighbour's hedge. Dave looked away and kept on walking. Almost there. Three, two, one and he'd made it. The garden gate clicked shut behind him. His key was in the brass lock, turning. And then it came. The sound of his name, whispered.

Dave paused and tilted his head. It'd be the sea breeze, playing with his mind. But he didn't dare turn round. He pushed open the front door and breathed in. There was no trace of the unfamiliar smell he'd noticed on Monday. There would be no dead wasps on the carpet. There was nobody in here and nobody out there. He was alone, now, and safe. He was—

A hand grabbed his shoulder and spun him round. Him. Here. Now.

'If I'd known you were frightened I'd have walked you home, Dave. There was no need to pay for a cab.' Rafa laughed, but the sound didn't match his expression.

Dave backed away from him, into the porch, heart thundering. In the very same moment, Rafa moved closer. He smiled, gently, and Dave knew why; could read his mind because his own threw out exactly the same observation: that even after all these years their bodies were still dancing in sync, reading the other in ways that eyes could not. Rafa's body was firmer where his own had grown soft. Dave was suddenly aware of his leather belt digging into his loosening abdominals, of the unflattering cut of his chinos, of shoes bought only for their price. They deserved one of Rafa's exaggerated eye-rolls. He would never have let Dave leave the house wearing clothes that said nothing about him. But these days that was kind of the point.

'How do you know where I live?'

Another laugh. 'It's your mum's house, is it not? I've been here a hundred times.' Rafa inched even closer. Dave could smell him, see the tiny streaks of sweat on his temples. 'I'm sorry if I frightened you, OK? I just wanted to see you. To talk. And to say happy birthday. I know I'm two days late but it's the thought that counts. Right?'

His voice was lower and softer than Dave remembered but the accent hadn't changed. It was one of the things he'd most missed, at first. But he'd destroyed all their videos the day he left, along with that ancient camcorder. He'd gone out to the bins and stamped on them with the heel of his boot so he wouldn't be tempted to retrieve them later.

'But why are you here? I thought you'd have moved away after—'

'I came back,' he said. 'For you.'

Another step forward and Rafa stepped into the beam of the security light. The glare of it exposed his pale, crumpled skin and stripped him of all the soft edges he'd had in the bar. Here his pockmarks held shadows and stains clung to his crooked teeth. Here he was just an old man in a young man's T-shirt and hoodie, beer embittering his breath.

But he was beautiful, still.

'I missed you, Dave.'

Dave shook his head; part disbelief, part warning to the wee spark in his chest that was darting all over the place, trying to find a way out.

'Can we go inside?'

'There's no point.'

'Of course there is.'

'*Was.*'

Rafa's smile loosened, then fell. 'Then at least tell me why you disappeared.'

'I had no choice.'

'Nonsense. You were running away. Still are, by the looks of it.'

It was amazing how love could switch to loathing in the space of a single conversation. But the best thing Dave had ever learned was this: to pause. He blinked and held it, willed the momentary blackness to calm him. Don't fight fire with flames. And anyway, here was something else he'd learned: the comments that stung the most were the ones that held a speck of truth. He needed to find the part that hurt and ask himself if, maybe, it was true.

Was he running? Of course he was.

But somehow, now, the ones he left behind were catching up.

'You don't know anything about my life now.'

'Then tell me.' Rafa leaned against the door frame, crossed his legs at the ankles, thumbs hooked into the pockets of his jeans.

'You need to go.'

'Just tell me where you went for all these years. I looked everywhere, Dave. Asked everyone. In the end I thought you must have . . .' He pulled his hands from his pockets, crossed his arms. 'All this time I've thought you were dead as well.'

'I didn't want to be found.'

'And yet . . .' Rafa smiled. 'Here I am.'

'Aye, but you're just leaving.'

'Don't be like that.'

'I'll *be* any way I want to, thanks.'

'Except honest.'

Another bullseye. Dave stopped, one foot in his hall, the other in the porch. 'What do you want from me, Rafa? It's been almost twenty years.'

'Eighteen and a half, to be precise.'

'So why now?'

'Why *not* now? And by the way, I saw you in the paper.'

'You're kidding.'

'I'm not. Brightened up a fairly shitty September morning. My Dave, back from the dead and getting some big award. The ceremony sounds *very* elaborate and I know how much you love getting all glammed up.' He eyed Dave after he said it, gave the tiniest of winks. 'Seems you'll get your fairytale ending at last. Congratulations.'

Dave started to speak then stopped himself, swallowed the truth that had risen. He'd wanted to tell Rafa he was no longer *his* but left it there, untouched. *My Dave*: a possibility that lingered in the air between them. When was the last time anyone wanted to claim him as theirs?

'How does it make you feel, Mr Kellock? You're officially good, officially loved, officially an upstanding member of the community. Dream come true, no?'

'Fuck off,' said Dave. 'It just means I'm good with grannies.'

'And an expert at putting yourself down. Some things never change.'

'Others do.' He needed to go inside, get away from Rafa and all that he meant. But a question held him back. 'Just tell me one thing: are you here because you've seen *her*?'

'Who?'

The word was a pin that burst him. 'That's a *no*, then.'

Rafa reached for him then; placed a hand on each of his shoulders and tightened his grip. Dave could feel his pulse, smell his sticky breath, see that little scar under his eye shaped like a sliver of moon. There was a new scar as well, near his ear. Looked like a slashing. 'Who did you see, Dave?'

'It's irrelevant.'

'*Entonces porque preguntar*?' Then why ask? he said, but in Spanish. He smiled as he said it but Dave knew Rafa well enough to sense what lay beneath. He always swapped English for Spanish when he was anxious. Dave knew where this could lead. Stretch Rafa's nerves too far and he'd snap.

As if on cue he squeezed Dave's shoulders a little tighter. It didn't hurt, yet. 'You can tell me anything, *chiquito*. You know that.'

Chiquito. Little one. Rafa had called him that since the very first day they'd met in a queue at Almería airport. Dave had been on his way back from a hiking trip in Andalucía, waiting to board a flight, when the crowd behind him had split to make way for a man and woman, running. Rafa and Carmen, dressed for a nightclub but smelling like the sea. Rafa was sweating and out of breath when he raced past the end of the queue and came to a stop right next to Dave.

Neither of them had ever really understood the why of it. Intuition. Chance. Whatever the reason, that was the beginning of them. Dave and Rafa, together; and Carmen by their side.

Rafa and Carmen looked almost identical; and their life paths matched as well. First, they'd burst out of the closet. Then they'd relocated to Scotland to build a new life there, far from the parents who couldn't stand the shame of producing one gay child, never mind two. United, they fled. United, they fell in love. Two became three, then four. And united they remained until that fleeting loss of control that ended ordinary life.

United, until the day that Dave killed Carmen.

There was no way Dave could wake up every day beside a man who looked just like her, and who refused to believe what he'd done. Rafa had insisted the police had got it wrong. Blame belonged elsewhere. The grief of losing his sister was fierce enough without losing Dave as well. But, when the court let Dave walk free, he had packed up his fragile mind and left anyway.

This was the first time they'd spoken since that day. And until yesterday on the bus Dave had avoided saying out loud the name of the woman he'd killed, as if silence made the shame of it any lighter.

What would happen if he said it again, now?

'I thought I saw . . . *Carmen*,' said Dave.

Guilt tried to drag his eyes away from Rafa but he stood his ground, held his gaze. He needed to see

Rafa's face when that name filled the space between them. Right now, it was still. Dave searched for a twitching in his jaw, a tightening of the tendons in his neck. But Rafa didn't even blink. He was calm but Dave's nerves were not. The storm could still be on its way.

'A woman stepped on to my bus and . . . she was Carmen's double. Absolute spitting image.' *You and your mental fragility, Dave.* 'And I don't believe in ghosts, but . . .' *You're pathetic; an embarrassment.* 'That's why I was at the pub tonight. I . . . heard she'd be there . . . and I just wanted another look at her, face to face. Just to check. Just to be sure. I *knew* it couldn't be her but . . .' *But what? Your stupidity knows no bounds.* 'Part of me still hopes the past twenty years have been a massive misunderstanding. That I'll wake up one day and Carmen will still be with us. And her child too. So when I saw that girl on the bus, I thought maybe . . .' He sighed, shook his head at himself. 'Och, it sounds so stupid to say it out loud.'

'Not to me.'

'Really?'

'Really.'

It was both a relief and an embarrassment to confess. Rafa had always had that effect on him. One lingering gaze and Dave would rip open his own heart and expose the contents: good or bad, hopeful or hopeless, inspired, or black and rotten to the core.

Nobody else got a look-in. Dave was staring at the floor but he could tell Rafa's eyes were still on him. Blood rushed to the surface of his skin like a magnet drawn to its opposite force. He was all sweaty palms and belly butterflies and thumping hearts, a middle-aged man with teenage angst. *Pathetic.*

Rafa stepped back, releasing his grip on Dave's shoulders. The heat wafting off him had probably burned his fingers. 'You OK, *chiquito*?'

'Honestly? I'm not sure. Feel like I'm going a bit mad.' He sighed, looked away. 'Just need to get my arse back to reality.'

'You know *I'm* real, don't you?'

'Definitely.' The places Rafa had touched were still tingling. 'But it was a shock to go there, looking for Carmen and then . . . find you instead. What are the chances?'

Rafa tilted his head, looked at Dave the way compassionate teachers look at stupid children. 'I don't think *chance* has got anything to do with it. And I don't think there's anything wrong with you, *chiquito*. Except for the fact that you find that impossible to believe.'

Rafa reached for him again but this time his fingertips touched Dave's jaw and lifted it. They were sharing the same air now; the exhale of one becoming the inhale of the other. Dave closed his eyes, thought of the day he'd ended it. A kiss goodbye and then came punches; fists pummelling Dave's head, back, heart. Then came police.

Almost twenty years later, it still hurt.

'You need to go,' he said, backing into his house without putting the light on. He didn't want Rafa to see it, judge it, see who he'd become without him.

'I will, *chiquito*. But let's talk first. Please. Me, you and a cup of tea. For old times' sake?'

'I can't. I'm working early tomorrow and—'

'Can I give you my number?'

'I *don't want* it,' said Dave. His heart was on high alert, started shutting down and locking up. 'And I *don't want* to see you, OK?'

He pushed the door but Rafa stepped forward, held it open. 'I lost everything, Dave. First my sister, then you. Surely you can spare me five minutes of your time.'

And there it was, right there in front of him: a grief that kept on growing; would not leave.

Dave's throat swelled, a warning sign: tears were on their way. 'I'm sorry, Rafa,' he said, then closed the door.

Finally, a barrier between them. As if that had ever made a difference. He slid down the door so he couldn't be seen through the frosted glass window. The letterbox popped open an inch from his right eye and in slipped Rafa's voice, a love letter from the past.

'Are you back in the closet? Is that it?'

'Neither in nor out.'

'What does that even mean?'

'It mean it's the least of my worries. I've got far more to be ashamed of than who I . . .' He hesitated, didn't want the word *love* to slip out in the wrong tense. Past or present? He was astounded to realise he wasn't sure.

He resisted the temptation to glance back as he stood up and walked up the hall, doing his best to look casual, relaxed, unperturbed. But his guts tightened and curled when he pictured Rafa's familiar mouth, framed inside the polished brass surround of the letterbox. He heard it snap shut once he turned into the kitchen and that was it – as far as his legs would take him. It was impossible, all of it. Seeing Carmen's double on the bus and now Rafa, outside his house. His past, right here in the present.

Dave pulled out a chair and sat down. For the first time in years he wished he smoked, wished he drank, wished there were something he could do to justify delaying what came next.

Tea. He could make tea.

Pot made, drunk. And repeat. He was watching the kettle boil for the second time when his phone beeped. A new message, from an unknown number.

Hi, David, the text said. *It's Amy's pal. From MOB Bar.*

His chest fizzed with adrenaline. Lo and behold, the sniggering skinny lad had come good. Dave had underestimated him, assumed the worst. He was good at that.

A second message arrived. *So you're friends with Amy's mum?*

Dave typed a reply with his thumbs. He might as well strike while he had the lad's attention.

Used to be. Not seen her in years. Are you with Amy now? Can I speak to her?

The reply was almost instant but contained no answers.

She wants to know what you're wanting.

The billion-dollar question. Dave started writing a reply, didn't stop until the massive truth of it filled that tiny screen. He wanted to see her to confirm who she was – and who she wasn't. He wanted to meet her face to face to ease his mind, to reassure himself he wasn't going mad – or to confirm, at last, that he was. He wanted to ask about her family in the hope that he'd find absolutely no connection to his own life. He could have typed all night but everything he said boiled down to the same simple point. He needed to know Amy *wasn't* the ghost or the daughter of Carmen Martinez, the woman he killed all those years ago – and the one person he'd never fully let go.

Type. Read. Send.

The screen blinked, and it was gone.

Dave slammed his phone face-down on the table. He stared at it, heart pounding, then flicked it away like a biting insect. What was he thinking? This was not Carmen or Carmen's daughter, because he'd killed them both. This was a teenage girl, and he was an old man with a criminal record and blood on his hands. This couldn't end well. This would not fix things. Nothing could undo what he'd done. And now he'd made it much, much worse.

He needed to walk away, leave Amy and the Todd family alone. For their sake, and his.

Easier said than done.

Their lives were already linked by those nuisance calls, made from his home to theirs, then to the police. *A woman and child, killed.* The connection was made stronger by his foolishness, sneaking around in their garden and losing his phone when he fled. That detective was watching him, waiting for a chance to pounce.

Walk away, Dave. Delete the skinny lad's number. Leave Amy and her family in peace. She's got nothing to do with you and your sins. She is not the cure because there is none.

She wants to know what you're wanting, the text had said.

And suddenly, a different answer came to him. He wanted to leave.

He'd only come back to Portobello to help look after his mum. But he should never have stayed. It wasn't worth the risk. When she'd died he should have sold her house and fled with a fat bank account, gone somewhere nobody would ever find him. It had worked before and it would work again. He could pack up and leave, right now. End all of this, tonight.

He scraped back his chair and headed upstairs, heart thundering.

Suitcase down, wardrobe open, passport tucked inside.

What else? He looked around the room, found himself staring at the letter tucked into the frame of his mum's old mirror. A single page emblazoned with the Outstanding Citizen logo; proof of his goodness. What a joke. If he left now he'd miss tomorrow's ceremony but it was for the best. His guilt weighed more than any award ever would.

He turned back to his wardrobe, tugged shirts and trousers from hangers then stuffed them into the case. He'd take a taxi to the airport, book flights when he got there.

His fingers fumbled on the zip of his suitcase. Was it the thrill of moving on or the fear of leaving that shook him? He wasn't sure, and wasn't sure it mattered either way. He'd leave and worry about it later. The fact was this: he could go anywhere, do anything, be anyone.

He closed the case and dragged it downstairs.

Back in the kitchen, he emptied the bins and left his mobile phone on the counter to die. Plugs out, curtains shut, lights off.

He was pulling the front door shut when the sound came. It cut through the dark, whispered a sad truth in his ear. *Wherever you go, you have to take yourself with you.* The sound came again, a siren's call coaxing him back inside. He had another text message. The skinny lad had replied.

CHAPTER 22

Thursday

Beneath Dave's feet, five bright white swan arses. There had been six cygnets at the start of the season but three had disappeared after one of the bank holiday weekends, rumoured to have been swiped by an exotic pets gang from Birmingham. The three offspring that remained were keenly watched and fiercely protected by their parents and the community; were now all grown up. God knows how, eating filth. As if to prove the point, the largest one pulled its head out of the water, beak snapping at green slime.

The park was surrounded by roads and houses, and at the far end a railway bridge passed overhead, leading to a train depot and maintenance centre. It was a much-loved *green space* and always busy with dog walkers and runners and parents with pushchairs. Right now Dave's eyes flitted between the swans and the path that circled the pond, willing the skinny lad to appear.

The beep of his mobile phone had lured him back inside last night. He'd vowed to read it then turn around and leave. He'd expected abuse, a virtual slap in the face, a big fat no. Instead, the skinny lad had suggested he and Dave meet first, somewhere public. He'd rather have met with Amy directly, but it was something. Progress, of sorts.

They'd agreed to meet here an hour before Dave started work. But the lad was late. Dave had re-read the text messages far more times than was necessary, hoping to realise he'd made a mistake over the time or the location. But no. He'd got there twenty minutes early and the lad was now ten minutes behind schedule. Should he send another text? Probably. But he'd give it another five minutes.

He popped a piece of chewing gum in his mouth. Helped his nerves. Then he turned his back on the water, stared at the tangled branches of plants and the birds that crept through them. This was the end of the park that was least loved, most overgrown. The railway ran overhead, leading to the depot. Trains that passed here were always empty, row after row of lit-up windows with no faces against the glass. Dave's eyes flitted between the trees and the railway bridge and the metal gates at the park entrance.

Then, in the undergrowth, something moved more clumsily than any animal ever would. Dave straightened up, body tense. Was somebody there?

He narrowed his eyes, stared through a soft mosaic of leaves and branches and shadows and shifting light. Blackbirds and squirrels hopped in the branches, starting their day the same way they always did. Hunting. He held his breath, didn't move, eyes flitting from tree to tree to tree. The trunks were thick enough to hide a human who did not want to be seen.

From where he stood Dave could see the whole park. But he could also be seen; a sitting duck, of sorts.

Had the lad from the pub set him up for a joke? He was probably watching from the trees, sniggering with his pals. Dave wasn't having it.

The wooden walkway over the pond shook when Dave started to run and birds resting on the handrail opened their wings and lifted off to escape him. Then he pushed on to solid ground. When he reached the woodland area he stepped off the hard path and on to the long grass, ran from tree to tree until he ended up where he'd started; out of breath, hope, patience.

He looked back at the walkway, still empty; then checked his phone. The skinny lad hadn't tried to contact him again. He stuffed the phone into his pocket then took it back out, an idea forming. He pulled up the skinny lad's texts then pressed the call button and turned back to the woodland, listening.

There were singing birds and crying babies; a puff of music leaked from a passing car. Barking dogs, owners calling their pets, the clunk of wellies on the hard path. But no phone.

'Your dog off chasing a rabbit?'

Dave turned, met the eyes of a man with a lead slung around his neck like a scarf. 'This one does it all the time,' he said, nodding to a ginger spaniel that was sniffing Dave's trousers. He nudged it away from him then turned back to the woods, searching.

'It's not a dog I'm looking for,' said Dave. 'It's a . . . pal. Skinny lad, about eighteen years old. I'm *sure* he was here a minute ago. You seen him?'

'Nope, but . . . I just got here.' The man grabbed his dog when it went for Dave again, noisily sniffing the smudges of blood on his trousers. It was a stain from yesterday, when he'd cut his hand on the shed door. Dave went to explain but the man interrupted him. 'You OK, pal? I mean, it's none of my business. But you look a bit . . . out of sorts.'

The man kept talking but Dave stopped listening, heard only the thud of his heart and the sound, somewhere nearby, of a mobile phone ringing but getting fainter by the second. Where was it coming from? Dave looked upwards then pushed past the dog walker, ran up the narrow path that led to the railway bridge. It carried tracks and trains over the road and the park, into the depot. But could humans cross it too?

The only people who regularly used this path were workers from the train depot and curious tourists who didn't know the area. If the skinny lad was up there, he'd have very limited escape options. Dave's tired legs slowed as he neared the top. He tried and failed to do the same with his breathing. He needed to calm down, man up.

The first thing he saw when he reached the train depot was Angry Brian from the bus, one hand gripping a roll-up cigarette, the other tugging at the zip of his dirty jeans, or whatever horror lay behind it. He screwed up his face when he clocked the sweaty, panting version of Dave.

'If you're looking for a heart attack you're going the right way.' Brian laughed at his own joke 'Just don't ask me to join you.'

Dave squeezed out a fake laugh as he approached him. 'All right, Brian? Didn't realise you worked here.'

'You've never asked, have you?'

'True, that.' Sweat tickled Dave's temples. He glanced over Brian's shoulder then over his own, towards the viaduct. 'You've not seen a skinny lad run past, have you?'

'When?'

'Now.'

Brain shook his head. 'Just this minute came out here to smoke.'

'And you didn't hear anyone, or . . .?'

'Not a squeak.'

'Is there another way out of here?'

'There is, aye.' Brian cupped his hands around his roll-up, starting flick-flick-flicking a red plastic lighter. He spoke again once the flame took and he'd sucked in a lungful of poison. 'Some folk walk over the bridge, towards those buildings,' he said, nodding to houses and flats that overlooked the park from the other side of the road. 'I wouldn't risk it myself but . . .'

Brian kept talking but Dave stopped listening. He turned to the railway bridge and peered across it, eyes following the route of the metal tracks. In this direction it crossed over the park and a busy road, then sliced through a residential area. Steep embankments ran from the tracks down to the back gardens of homes that lined the track. There was nothing unusual about the scene, except for the one thing in it that was getting smaller by the second. Running down the middle of the railway bridge, following the tracks, was a man dressed in sports gear. Hood up, back turned; exactly in the place a train should be.

Was it that skinny lad, legging it? Dave strained his eyes but couldn't tell from this distance.

He sprinted for the bridge, backpack slapping his back as his feet pounded the ground. He paused when he reached the place where solid ground ended and the bridge began. Both outer edges were lined by a low wall but there were no safety barriers; no nets that would catch him if he tripped. He set off, half-running, half-hopping to make sure his feet didn't catch on the sleepers that rose like squat hurdles between the metal tracks. He cursed his clumpy brogues. God speed, God willing, God knew where this bridge would lead him. Beneath him passed cars and lorries and lives he'd never knowingly be a part of. His heart and feet pounded. His legs and hands trembled; but too much. Far too much. He was halfway across the bridge when he realised why. It had started with a sound he could not place. A hum, then a crackle, then a rumble he could feel as well as hear.

He heard his name being called then too.

Behind him, Angry Brian screamed out a warning. Dave only heard one word of it but that was enough. *Train.*

CHAPTER 23

Dave made it off the bridge before the train, thank Christ. He'd turned on his heels and fled back to where he'd started. He then collapsed in a heap, heart thundering in his chest.

'That runner . . .' Dave looked at Angry Brian, spat out words between heavy breaths. 'Did he make it across to the other side? Before the train came?'

Angry Brian was frozen to the spot, face so white it looked iced over. He was staring at the other side of the bridge, eyes screwed to pinholes. 'I think I saw him jump,' he said, raising his voice as the train slowed and trundled past them and into the depot building. 'Just hope to Christ he landed in someone's back garden.'

Dave hauled himself to his feet, followed Brian's gaze. There was nobody on the bridge or hanging off it. The traffic beneath it was still moving smoothly. Dave forced his legs into another run, heading back downhill towards the park and the road and the homes that lay beyond it. Whoever the runner was, Dave had to find them and make sure they were OK. And if, as he suspected, it was the skinny lad, then he wanted to give him a piece of his mind as well.

The lad had no idea what he was dealing with here; who.

When he reached the park Dave charged past two young mums, knocking one of the prams. They shrieked, and he tossed an apology their way, then raced on to the road in front of a delivery truck that had slowed down as it moved under the railway bridge. It honked its horn but Dave kept going, didn't look back. A squat block of flats cast a shadow on the pavement at this side of the road. Dave paused to catch his breath and make a plan. From where he stood he could see the embankment leading down from the railway tracks towards a shared garden at the back of the flats. But, so far, there was no sign of the runner.

He had to get into that garden, but couldn't see a side path. Plan B, go through the building. He tried the front door, just in case, then rang all the buzzers. Nobody answered.

He paced down the pavement, looking for an alternative way in. The flats shared a side wall with a yoga studio built from red brick. Could he access the shared garden from there? He pushed open the main door and was smacked in the face by the smell of burning incense. Dozens of pairs of shoes were lined up along one side of the reception area and a handwritten sign pinned to the desk read *Class in Progress. Take a deep breath and come back later.* No time for that.

He went back to the front door of the flats, was trying all the buzzers for a second time when he heard approaching sirens, coming from the direction of the beach. Had someone found the runner – and were they hurt? Dave turned, searching the street for answers.

He found Angry Brian, glaring at him from the park entrance. 'I hope to Christ he's no' deid, Dave. Not on my shift anyway. I'm no' meant to let folk anywhere near that bridge.'

Dave was debating whether or not to slap Brian when he heard the front door of the building open behind him. One of the flats must have heard the buzzer after all. He turned, ready to charm his way into a stranger's garden. But the man on the doorstep spoke before he did.

'Have I died and gone to heaven, *chiquito*? What are *you* doing here?'

Rafa beamed at Dave from the doorstep of the building, front door still open behind him. He was dusting himself down, precisely picking scraps of leaves from his running jacket. A lit cigarette was clamped between his teeth. It moved when he talked and somehow he was able to carry it off. Where others would look ridiculous, Rafa was a cowboy, a gangster, the kind of man who made smoking look like a worthwhile habit.

'What . . .?' Dave's head was a blur of questions, flying around so fast they were impossible to grip and hold on to. '*You?*'

'Me,' said Rafa, smiling. He leaned forward and planted a dry kiss on each of Dave's cheeks the way he did with friends and family back home in Spain. His mouth hadn't been this close to Dave's skin in almost two decades.

Dave stepped back and turned, aware of an audience. Angry Brian had crossed the road and stood inches away now with the two new mums and their babies, both of which were screaming their heads off. All three adults were gripping phones and pretending not to enjoy the drama of approaching sirens and spinning blue lights and the grand spectacle of two grown men sharing some kind of kiss, in public.

'How are you here, Rafa?'

'I was going to ask you the same thing.'

'It *can't* be a coincidence.'

'Must be God's will.'

'I'm being serious.'

'So am I.' Rafa stepped back after he said it, just a little. Their faces were almost touching but not quite, not quite. He smiled. Dave tried not to. Failed. Just for a moment, the world felt a little lighter. Then the sparkle turned to stone.

'I need to go,' said Rafa.

'What? You can't just *go*. I need an explanation. I want to know why—'

'Then come with me.' Rafa's eyes flitted over Dave's shoulders as an ambulance and police car turned into the street. 'I'll tell you anything but we need to go, now.'

'But the ambulance is here for *you*. They'll need to check you over.'

'And the police?'

'They'll be here as a precaution, Rafa. They'd hardly arrest you for running over a bridge.'

'Stranger things have happened,' he said, tugging up his hood. 'You coming or not?'

'Where to?'

'Your place?'

'No chance.'

'Then we'll improvise.' Rafa held out his hand as Dave heard the engine slow behind him. Brian crossed the road to greet the ambulance, phone held out so they'd know he was the one who did a good deed and called for help. Doors opened and were slammed shut. Rafa's fingers touched Dave's hand, tugged it. Dave wanted to let go but could not; did not.

And together, they ran.

CHAPTER 24

When they reached the shore Dave draped himself over a metal bench outside the old toilet block. Rafa sat down beside him, laughing. He'd barely broken a sweat.

'Can't believe you're not knackered,' said Dave, words squeezed out between gasps for air.

'I've been working out.'

'I can tell.'

'Is that a compliment, Mr Kellock?' Rafa laughed and Dave looked away, flushing an even deeper shade of red. He inched himself along the bench so their legs were no longer touching; but, at the same time, he hoped Rafa didn't notice.

Beyond the metal barrier a rainbow curled up and over the slate rooftops of the homes that lined Portobello Promenade. It landed in the sea, but if there was gold out there it would be lost; was too far out for even the bravest of cold-water swimmers.

Rafa nudged him back to the present. 'The years have been kind to you as well, you know.'

'You kidding?' Dave laughed, tapping his big bald head. It was warm and sticky, would no doubt be shining. He wished he didn't care. 'In fact, don't answer that. Answer *this* instead. Was it *you* who sent those messages?'

'What messages?'

'The ones I got last night, arranging to meet in the park this morning. It was you, wasn't it? Pretending to be that skinny lad from the pub.'

'I don't know what you're talking about.' Rafa held his gaze while he said it but his eyes flitted over his shoulder when a siren sounded nearby. He stood up and nodded towards the oversized steps that led down to the sea. 'Fancy a walk on the rocks?'

'Will you answer my question first?'

'First we walk, then talk,' said Rafa. 'Follow me.'

They clambered down the steps then turned right, on to rocks only exposed at low tide. This was the point where Portobello ended and Joppa began; where golden sand became black, slippery rocks. They each picked a path over boulders and stones and around little pools of water, movement, life. Rafa stopped when they reached an overhang with a few smooth rocks beneath. 'Your table, sir.' He ushered Dave towards the space, only just big enough for two.

The rock here was cold but dry. Dave sat down, leaned back and stared at Rafa's hands as they deftly rolled a cigarette. When Rafa caught him looking Dave made some banal comment about the sea and the sky-line, as if his eyes had been on the horizon the whole time. Rafa lit up, offered Dave a drag. He wanted one but refused, didn't want a single trace of those lips anywhere near his own.

'So will you tell me why you were there today? And why you ran?'

Rafa sucked on his cigarette then puffed the smoke out of the side of his mouth, away from Dave. 'As I said, I was going to ask you the same thing, *chiquito*.'

'Don't call me that.' Dave's voice wobbled a bit. He cleared his throat, trying to disguise it. 'And please just answer the question. How did you know I'd be there? If it wasn't you who sent those messages arranging to meet, does that mean you were *following* me?'

Rafa laughed, snorted out smoke. 'I think you'll find *you* were the one following *me*. Almost got yourself killed in the process.'

'Nonsense. I was following the sound of a phone, actually. I called . . . that number and heard the ring-tone and ran towards it . . .' He tutted, worried he was saying too much. 'I just didn't think the phone belonged to *you*.'

'It doesn't. You're mistaken. But tell me this – who did you *think* it belonged to?'

'I'm the one asking the questions here.'

Rafa rolled his eyes. 'Don't get so defensive. I'm just trying to understand.'

'Maybe this'll help.' Dave patted his back pocket, was relieved to find the solid outline of his phone. He tugged it out, pressed redial, waited. In the microseconds before the line connected, a thousand thoughts invaded his brain. He wanted Rafa's phone to ring because it would prove his suspicions were right: that Rafa had got hold of his number and sent those text messages to his phone, pretending to be the skinny lad. He'd been set up and made a fool of and would never learn.

It would mean Rafa was bad news.

It would also mean there was still a vague chance Amy *would* get in touch directly – if the skinny lad had done what Dave had asked of him and passed on his number.

But where did all of this leave him?

Another thought nipped his heel before his brain could find an answer. If Rafa's phone *didn't* ring, maybe that meant life was trying to bring them together again, almost two decades after the split. First, a chance meeting at the pub. Then same again at the park. A more naïve man might take it as a sign that Fate was stepping in and playing her strongest hand. *God's will*, Rafa had said. But could he be trusted?

When the call connected, Dave closed his eyes and waited.

He heard the crackle of fire and paper and burning tobacco and the gentle sigh of Rafa releasing the smoke. He heard seagulls screeching their complaints and the rhythmic splash of tiny waves against rocks. He heard the whoosh of a bus engine above their heads on the main road, the momentary beeping of a pedestrian crossing. He heard a car door close, a siren fade, his own heart thunder. But no phone rang.

When Dave opened his eyes Rafa was holding a mobile in his hand, smiling as he stared at the screen. He turned it towards Dave, laughing. He'd taken a selfie of him and Dave while his eyes were shut. 'A wee memento of our . . . *reunion*. I'll send it to you . . . if you give me your number?'

'Nicely done. But no.'

'Was worth a try.' He laughed then held out his iPhone to Dave. It was one of the newer models. 'Take it. Scroll through. Check my calls list and my contacts. Smash it to pieces if you want. But I promise you this – I didn't send you any text messages last night, or ever. And you've never phoned me. We're not connected. Not with technology, anyway.'

Dave stared at the phone, hands clenched into a fist. This wasn't about a phone. It was about trust, and they both knew it. And if Dave checked Rafa's phone, that would be the end of it; of them, again.

He tutted, pushing Rafa's hand away. 'Och, I believe you,' he said.

'Thousands wouldn't.' Rafa stared at the selfie for a moment before closing the app and opening another one. Emails, by the looks of it. He opened one and again held the screen towards Dave. 'And here's my reason for being at the park.'

Dave leaned in, peering at the screen. 'Parkrun? You serious?'

'I've got my first one this weekend but went to the park today to check out the route. I couldn't believe it when I saw you there. Knew you'd think I was up to no good.'

'I didn't say that.'

'You didn't need to,' he said. 'But the point is, you were standing between me and the main gates, so I tried to leave the park by a different route. Had no idea that path would lead me up to the railway tracks, of all places. Or that a train was scheduled. Just my luck. Thankfully it was easy enough to slip down the embankment before things got . . . messy. Only thing broken was the plant pot I kicked over when I launched myself over the fence into that communal garden. Someone had wedged open the back door so I was able to sneak out the front. Thought I'd escaped without you seeing me, almost died when I saw you waiting outside on the pavement. All those acrobatics for nothing. And . . . here we are.'

'And what about the police?'

'What about them?'

'Seemed to me you were running from them as well.'

Rafa's face fell and this time it was him who looked away. '*Pillado*,' he said. *Caught*. 'Sounds stupid, but I hoped you wouldn't notice,' he said, then took a final drag on his cigarette and stubbed it out. 'You obviously deal with all of that stuff much better than I do.'

'Depends what *stuff* you're talking about.'

'What do you think?'

Dave stared at him, knowing but not saying. Every breath said the same thing anyway. *Carmen, Carmen, Carmen.*

'I don't trust them, Dave. Not after what they did to you.'

'Let's not go there. What's done is done.'

'Is it, though?' Rafa's jaw was tight; the veins in his neck wildly pulsing. 'Because we both know who the real killer is.'

Killer. The word was a weapon. Almost twenty years on and the sound of it still spooked him. Dave's heart slithered to the pit of his belly. All words dissolved.

Rafa had enough for both of them.

'You *know* it was all down to her, don't you? *She* killed Carmen. *She* killed the baby. All of this is *her* fault. Not yours. And I *know* you know that's true.'

'So you're a mind-reader now?'

Rafa sighed. It was long and slow and sad and shuddering, a drum roll for tears. He took out his tobacco and started rolling another cigarette. Dave was relieved that his eyes were off him, and that his hands were occupied. Rafa talked as he rolled. 'It should have been *her* who was hauled up in court. *Her* who was trashed in the papers. *Her* who was forced to leave her home and town and job to escape the hell of it. It should have been *her* who left. Not you, *chiquito*. Not you.'

'I chose to go. We talked about this.'

'Maybe. But you forgot to mention the part about staying away for almost *twenty years*.' Rafa laughed, shook his head. 'I waited, you know. And when you didn't reappear I searched for you online, almost wore away the keys that spelled your name. There was nothing. No trace. On bad days I convinced myself you were dead. But part of me refused to believe it, was sure you'd come back when you got your head sorted.'

'Took longer than I thought.'

'Where did you go?'

'Around.'

'What does that mean?'

'That I never stayed anywhere for long,' said Dave. 'What about you? Still working offshore?'

Rafa shook his head. 'Not for years.'

'Get tired of earning a fortune?'

'It was danger money.'

'That was why you liked it.' And why Dave had hated it. Rafa's two-week shifts on the oil rigs had started and ended with a helicopter ride across the treacherous North Sea. A gamble. And a stress for those he left at home. Dave had missed him, always. He noticed a flash of relief in his chest now but pretended he did not. 'And now?'

'I keep busy,' said Rafa, then smiled. *That* smile. 'But enough about me. There's something I want to know about you. In all the years you were away – did you think about me, ever?'

Dave kept his eyes on the sky. He'd known all along that it would lead to this: some kind of confession, an easing open of the heart he'd kept so tightly shut for so many years.

'Of course I did.'

'And what about now?'

The question hung in the air as Rafa cupped his hand around his roll-up and flicked the lighter until it lit. Quick drag to strengthen the burn and he handed it to Dave, somehow knew he'd take it. There was always that sense of the *somehow* with Rafa; the feeling that he could look at Dave and see exactly what he needed and wanted but would not say out loud. Before he took a drag Dave needed to get rid of the gum he'd been chewing since the park. Rafa saved the day, as ever; handed him a crumpled receipt from his pocket. Dave spat his gum into the paper then tucked it away in his back pocket. Then, he smoked.

The nicotine hit him like a punch in the face. He felt dizzy, closed his eyes.

It was Rafa who had been the real smoker in their relationship, but Dave had learned to love the taste of it on his lips and that momentary lightness when he sucked in the poison. He'd given up alcohol after the killings as well, didn't want to water down his guilt. He deserved to suffer, end of story. And anyway, if he'd tried to block out the bad stuff with drugs there would have been no end to it.

That's what had happened to Rafa after the killings, or so Dave's mum used to tell him. Sometimes when they spoke on the phone she'd casually slip in some bad news about the world he'd left behind; tell him she'd spotted Rafa's name in the local newspaper. 'Another court story,' she'd say, then share second-hand tales of drug offences and pub fights. That was why he'd stopped phoning. The man he'd loved was lost, in more ways than one.

Dave sensed movement beside him. He heard the scratch of a match on the box, the tiny triumph when the flame took. Then came Rafa's voice, so close to his own face that he could feel the words as well as hear them.

'There's nothing to stop us picking up where we left off, Dave. We can get back together, for good this time. We can be a family.'

Dave was shaking his head before Rafa finished speaking. 'You know it's too late for that.'

'Says who? There are no rules except the ones we make for ourselves.'

'It wouldn't be the same.'

'It might be even better.'

'No, Rafa.'

'Why not? Is there someone else? Is that it?'

'There's *never* been anyone else.' And there it was, right there; his heart cracked wide open. Trouble was, it was bleeding. 'But when I look at you I see Carmen. I wish I could *unsee* her, but I can't.'

'Thought about therapy?'

'I've tried everything.'

'Maybe *I'm* the cure.'

Dave smiled but he was shaking his head at the same time. 'It'd be a torture for me, waking up next to you every day. To *that* face.'

'Charming.'

'Och, you know what I mean.'

They sighed at the same time then looked out over endless grey water and big white skies. Dave tried to focus on the sound of the water; to match his breath with the inhale and exhale of the sea. Every broken wave became part of the next one that was coming. The sea never dwelt on the past, that was for sure. Rise, fall, smash, remake. And repeat. But that didn't work for humans. And it definitely wasn't how it had worked for Carmen, thanks to him.

He glanced at Rafa. His eyes were tightly closed and his temples were crumpled into splayed crow's feet. A tear had slipped out anyway, was making gentle progress from his eye to the corner of his mouth. The truth always comes out in the end.

'I should go.' Dave gripped the overhang of rock and eased himself up on to his feet. 'Start work in an hour.'

'Spare me your excuses.'

'I'm sorry, Rafa. What we had—'

'Have.' Eyes open, locked on Dave. 'You used the wrong tense.'

A sigh, a sting in his chest. 'Please, Rafa.'

'One date. Please. Then you make up your mind, for good. I've got a surprise for you, Dave. A good one. Give me the chance to share that with you and then see how you feel.'

'I'm here now. Tell me now.'

Rafa smiled, shook his head. 'Good things come to those who wait.'

'Do they?'

'I promise.'

A pause, a temptation, a punishment. 'I can't.'

'You'll regret it.'

'Maybe. I'll add it to the collection.'

A tut, then the tendons on Rafa's neck tightened. Maybe his fists would be next. Dave stepped away, out of touching distance. 'Take care of yourself, eh?'

Now came the clamped jaw and the pulsing below his ear as Rafa gritted his teeth to dust. 'Run, then. Flee the scene when things get hard. You're good at that.'

So this time he was punching with words.

'It's for the best.'

'I wish people would stop assuming they know what's *best* for me.' Rafa sprang to his feet and started pacing back and forth on the black rocks. Dave thought of a sad animal, caged; knew it'd bite if he got too close. 'I know *exactly* who I need to be happy. You, Dave. It's always been you. And I know you feel the same.'

He stopped suddenly and placed his hands on Dave's shoulders, same as the other night. But now they were dead weights, radiating heat, strength, danger. Everything about Rafa was raw and unpredictable and hard to control. He was like electricity: could light you up and strike you down with the same hand.

'You're frightened, aren't you?'

Rafa's face was so close to Dave's that he could smell him, almost taste him. But there was a bitterness on his tongue that would not shift – and it wasn't just the tobacco.

It *was* fear; but not just of Rafa.

Dave was scared of letting *anyone* get close. It was time to go, now, before temptation led him to places he didn't want to be.

He pulled away and started picking his way up the rocks to the road. His ears were on high alert, turned every sound into footsteps. *Don't look back, Dave.* When he reached the pavement he bowed his head and walked in the direction of Portobello High Street. When he'd passed all the shops he took a shortcut to the bus garage through a scrappy area of uncut grass and ugly bushes that nobody would want in their garden. The under-agers took over that place at the weekends, blotted the green with torn crisp packets and crushed drinks cans and blue plastic bags from the wee off-licence they knew would sell them vodka on the sly.

But today it was quiet, had been recently cleaned. Dave paused for a moment to watch a blackbird hop around on the grass, pecking for something he could not see. Carmen used to say they looked like little priests, heads tilted as they listened to confessions. Dave hunched down, held out one hand, told himself that if it moved any closer it was a sign that he was forgiven.

For a moment it held Dave's gaze, shiny black eyes on his. It blinked, hopped a little closer; then flew off in the same moment Dave heard footsteps behind him.

The first blow landed on the back of his neck; the next one on his kidneys. Then someone gripped his collar from behind and tugged him upwards, zip pressing into his throat. The world slowed down. He had to shake himself free, could not, could not, could not. The pressure on his throat got tighter and then came a laugh he recognised. When they let him go he fell forward, face-first into jagged bushes.

After a few moments the blackbird swooped down and hopped towards his face. Again, their eyes met. Then a ball of spit hit the ground between them and strong hands grabbed Dave and rolled him over. Next came a sneer, and words spat out with venom.

'I know what you did.'

CHAPTER 25

Colin's breath smelled minty. He tugged Dave back on to his feet then held him by the collar, their faces inches apart. Crystal would know this view. But where Dave felt sickened, maybe Crystal's vision was softened by the memories of love, or something that went by that name.

'You kept that one quiet, didn't you? Dave Kellock, the killer in our midst.' Colin spat when he spoke. 'Who'd have thought it? Funny they forgot to mention *that* in the papers. You'd have thought the organisers would check first, see if their Outstanding Citizen had a criminal record. But no. They've gone and chosen a sad wee man who killed a pregnant woman. And her poor wee baby. How did it feel to watch them die?'

Dave pushed him, hard; got a smirk in return. 'Temper, temper.'

'Let me go.'

'Still a touchy subject, is it? Let me give you some advice, *pal*. Unless you want the rest of the world to find out – stay away from Crystal. Understand? She's *my* wife. Hear that? My. Wife. Probably wank your-self silly thinking about her, don't you? What a fuck-ing joke. Well, guess what – she wouldn't go near you. She feels *sorry* for you, pal. Tells me all the time. You're a sad case and everyone knows it. And now, I know why.'

'Who told you?'

'Don't you worry your pretty wee head about that. But I know everything. And I'm more than happy to contact the papers. Imagine the headlines. *Killer Bus Driver Stripped of Award. Outstanding Citizen Exposed As Killer.* The tabloids would lap it up. Especially if they got some images as well. What was the lassie's name again? Something Spanish, wasn't it? Whatever, she was beautiful. Would make a good front page photo. Bet you her baby would have been a stunner too. We'll never know though, will we? Thanks to you.'

'How do you know what she looks like?'

'Contacts,' said Colin, winking.

Dave pushed him again. This time Colin stumbled backwards, almost fell. 'Stronger than you look,' he said, laughing. 'And more dangerous. I can't believe they didn't lock you up, but that's soft justice for you. Poor Dave and his *mental fragility*. I'll admit I laughed when I read that phrase. You can't cope with being a killer? Try telling *that* to the girl's family.'

'You've made your point, Colin. That's enough.'

'I'm just getting started. Quite enjoying myself.'

'I can tell. God knows what Crystal sees in you.'

'I was about to say the same thing.'

'You're barking up the wrong tree with that one. We're colleagues and that's that.'

'Oh, really? So what do you two get up to when she's round at yours? Working on rotas?'

'Look, Crystal's been at mine once. *Once*. OK? And only because it was my birthday on Monday. Drank half a cup of tea and she left, end of story.'

'And what about Sunday?'

'She wasn't at mine on Sunday. I was working late. You can check my shifts.'

'Fat lot of good that would do since it's Crystal who makes the timetables. She could easily doctor it to prove your case. Anyway, she *told* me she was going to yours on Sunday so there's no point in denying it. I don't mind her seeing pals, you know. But not every night. And not if she's lying to me. But that's what happened this week. Monday she lied and said she was going to the cinema with her pal and then I discover she's back at yours for the second day running. So don't give me your bullshit, Dave Kellock. Just get it stopped and stay away from her.'

Colin spat again then let Dave go, shoved him in the back when he turned to leave. He was a bully, by the book.

Dave stopped, turned, fists tightening, spine straightened to make himself feel taller. If he wanted he could end this now, knock the lights so far out of that man that all the days ahead of him would be dulled. But for what? And more to the point, for who? It wouldn't help Crystal, that was for sure.

'You're the one who needs to stay away from her,' he said.

Another laugh, released as a grunt. 'She's my wife, in case you hadn't noticed.'

'Then treat her like one,' said Dave, then turned his back on Colin and walked away. He was expecting a crack to the head, another fist to his kidneys, but all that came was abuse and threats of more, all the way back to the beach. He sat on the cold sand and willed his pulse to slow down.

How did *Colin* know about Carmen?

The most obvious explanation was that he'd read old newspaper reports about the killings – for example, the ones that lived in Dave's attic. Bit by bit, the dots were joining up. Was it Colin who'd been in his house when he was out? Maybe *he'd* made the nuisance calls, hoping to give Dave a fright and warn him that somebody knew about his crimes. He clearly hated Dave and was convinced he was having an affair with Crystal. He wanted to cause him harm – but would he take it that far? It was one thing holding a grudge; quite another to break into somebody's house and make a hoax call to the police. He'd have thought that kind of thing was reserved for bored teenagers in the eighties, back when phone boxes were still considered the height of technology. And anyway, it seemed too subtle an attack for a man like that one. When Colin wanted to cause harm, he did it with fists. End of story.

But if not him, who?

Colin claimed Crystal was at Dave's house on Sunday, the same day the nuisance calls were made. Was she using Dave as an alibi for something else? Perhaps. But once again his mind threw out that awful suggestion: maybe it was *Crystal* he should be worrying about. She had access to his house keys and his time-table. She had the photos from his attic in her office. It added up, kind of. But one question remained: why?

It would hurt to ask her if she was involved; but he was hurting already.

He marched to the bus depot, punched in the code at the security door. Damp grains of sand from his fingers stuck to the numbers on the little metal key-pad and when he pushed it didn't open. He wiped his hands on his trousers, inspected them then tried again. Same result. The door wouldn't open. He tried a third time then pulled out his phone and called Crystal, telling her it was broken and asking to be rescued. Should he tell her what had happened with Colin?

He was debating the answer when the door was opened by one of the new lads, Ollie. As far as Dave could tell, he only ate bacon rolls and spoke mainly in grunts. Today, though, he managed a full sentence.

'You've to go see Crystal.'

He turned away before Dave could ask why or when. He'd go now, once he'd removed all trace of Colin. He popped into the toilets, squirted pink soap from the dispenser into his palm then scrubbed his hands as if he were about to perform surgery. He was rubbing them dry when the door was pushed open from the other side, its sharp edge cracking into his elbow. The thud was followed by a yelp, then an apology.

'Crystal?' Dave stepped out of the way to let her in; and the moment he saw her, all the suspicions fell away. It couldn't be her. Not Crystal. Surely. 'If you'd known it was me, you'd have pushed a wee bit harder, right?'

He expected a laugh, a roll of her eyes, one of her affectionate tuts. What he got instead was a head bowed to hide the bruising on her jaw, visible despite the butter-thick foundation she'd plastered on top. That bastard.

'You going to let me past or what?'

Had she caught him staring at her latest injury? Dave flushed, turned his back to the wall to let her past. An inch between them, close enough that the frizzy parts of her hair tickled his face. She usually tied it back but if her bruises were bad enough she used her hair to hide the damage. Dave wanted to open up his arms and invite her in. Instead he stuffed his hands in his pockets.

'The new lad said you wanted to chat?'

'Aye. You can wait in my office.' She went into the cubicle and closed the door, her actions a full stop. Dave tried his luck anyway.

'Can it wait until after my shift?'

'Afraid not.'

'It's just . . . I'm a bit tight for time,' he said. A lie. He *always* got there early to wash his bus, was famed for it. That's why his late arrival yesterday had caused such a stir.

But all he wanted right now was keys in his hand and his driver's cabin sealing him in for eight hours, passengers passing momentarily through his life, smiling or whingeing but never asking difficult questions. He wanted to be far from Crystal and the things he needed to ask her. However he framed them, they were accusations. Crystal was one of the few people on earth Dave had trusted, and he couldn't bear the thought that she'd broken that trust so blatantly.

When she opened the cubicle door Crystal nudged him out of the way and turned on the tap. A blob of soap caught on her wedding ring and when she rubbed it clean it slipped towards her knuckle.

'Best not wash that down the sink, eh?'

'I can think of worse things,' she said, then pulled out a single paper towel and dried her hands slowly, with precision. 'Come on, let's get this over and done with.'

Dave didn't like the sound of that. 'Should I bring coffee?'

'No thanks,' she said, and a tiny fist squeezed Dave's heart until another crack appeared. Their shared morning coffee was Dave's favourite part of the day, a ritual they'd fallen into during his first week and never climbed out of.

When he reached her office the door was open. Crystal sat down and stared at her smartphone screen, tightly gripping its glittery plastic cover. Another phone sat next to her keyboard, plugged in. It was one of those bricks from the nineties, complete with rubber keyboard and a screen so small a midge could barely read it. Must be one of the old work phones.

'Don't just stand there,' she said, then slid both phones into the top drawer of her desk. Slammed it shut, locked it. Then she turned her attention to her computer screen, narrowed her eyes as she scanned the screen. After a moment she picked up her glasses, but instead of putting them on, she pushed them on top of her head. They sat like a crown on her blonde hair. Or a halo, maybe.

Dave moved inside, squeezed cheer into his voice. 'I swear to God in two years I've never seen you *wear* those specs.'

She glanced him, pulled them on to her face. 'Satisfied?'

'They suit you.'

'Bit late for flattery,' she said, then took them off; as if she didn't want to give Dave any reasons to be nice to her. *You like this? I'll remove it.*

'Hard to believe we've known each other that long, isn't it?'

She nodded to the chair on the opposite side of her desk. This was new. A worry. He stayed on his feet, sensing a change. Every muscle in him twitched then tightened, prepared to run.

'I've got news,' she said, and all Dave noticed was the lack of the word *good* or *bad,* which usually meant the latter was on its way. 'Sit down, but leave the door open. We've got company.' She shifted her gaze over Dave's shoulder. He turned, saw a wee man in a big suit walking down the corridor towards the office. You could fit two of him inside one trouser leg.

'James Cardenas will be joining us for the meeting. From head office.'

The wee man nodded to Dave on his way past. He was carrying two takeaway coffees and a paper bag that was slicked with grease. He handed one cup to Crystal, then the bag. 'As requested,' he said.

So they'd already spoken. Made a plan.

James refused Crystal's offer of a seat, just stood in the corner like a sentry, slurping the cappuccino foam off his plastic lid. 'Whenever you're ready, Crystal?'

She nodded to James, glanced at Dave, cleared her throat. And then the show started.

All eye contact was broken and her voice changed, as though she was reading from someone else's script. She kept her head down, talked of *a meeting with My Superiors* and *company policy* and *orders from above*. She spoke of *standards* and how they'd slipped, *too far*. His *wee accident* was mentioned but a bashed-up bus was only the start of it. There was the lingering police investigation into his *private life* – by which she meant the nuisance calls. There was Dave abandoning his bus on Princes Street. There was turning up late for a shift – forcing Jimmy Jones to come in on his day off.

'And now, the big fat cherry on the cake.'

Crystal spun round in her chair then stood up and ran a finger along the shelves behind her, tapping her painted nails against each of the files and boxes Dave had raided. She stopped when she reached the one marked K for Kellock; the one Dave knew contained those old photographs. So, she knew he'd been sneaking around; that he could not be trusted.

But again that question slithered into his mind: could *he* trust *Crystal*?

For now he kept his suspicions to himself; forced them back down. Easy as swallowing cut glass. He couldn't ask anything like that in front of James – and right now it was Crystal who was needing answers.

'Crystal . . . please . . . I can explain.'

'Don't you worry. There'll be plenty of opportunity for that.' She tugged the box off the shelf then slammed it on to her desk. She held the lid half-open with one hand then pulled out a document he knew was his contract, signed, sealed and completely ignored. Rule one: don't break into the boss's office.

'We've had a complaint,' she said. 'Not long before you got here. Someone phoned in, claimed you've been bothering a young lassie.' She looked up, held his gaze. Invisible hands gripped his gut and twisted. *Defend yourself, Dave.* Instead, he looked away.

Guilty, as charged.

'They said you followed her off the bus, waited for her in a pub, then demanded her pals hand over her phone number. They said you acted . . . aggressively . . . when your request was denied. I defended you. Said they must have got it wrong. Said I knew you.'

'You do.'

'Thought I did.' When she frowned like that, the bruises on her seemed to shine more brightly. 'But an Outstanding Citizen Award means nothing in the face of something like this. The rules are right here in your contract. The bus company's got a reputation to think about. We're not wanting a *Me Too* situation on our hands.'

'This isn't . . . *that.*'

'Really? So you're denying you asked for a female passenger's number, as per the complaint?'

'No, but—'

'But nothing. Did you know she's a teenager?'

'Age is irrelevant. I just need to talk to her, Crystal. I can explain.'

'Go on, then.'

'She . . . looks like . . . someone I . . . used to know. That's all. I just needed to check if it was her.'

'Really?'

'Really.'

'Christ on a bike. I thought you'd come up with something better than that.' Crystal shook her head then leaned back in her seat, widening the space between them. She became suddenly small and sad, looked as if she'd been punctured and was slowly losing air.

She glanced at James and he nodded, made every single one of his double chins wobble.

James raised the blade of the guillotine and Crystal let it fall.

The cut was a clean one, but it hurt all the same.

Dave was out.

CHAPTER 26

The wooden groynes at Portobello Beach stretch from the promenade to the water. From where Dave stood they looked like thick stitches holding together square patches of golden sand. But the beauty of the place was lost on him, for now.

He was gripping his phone in his hand, checking it every few minutes. He'd sent another text to the skinny lad, asking why he hadn't turned up at the park this morning, and if it had been him who called Crystal to report his behaviour at the pub. Why would he arrange to meet Dave then phone the bus garage to complain about him instead? To set him up, probably. The texts were written evidence of Dave's plan; his *intentions*. What kind of middle-aged man arranged to meet teenagers in parks before breakfast? Bad ones and stupid ones. Not surprisingly, skinny lad hadn't yet replied. Part of him also wanted Crystal to call just so he could have the satisfaction of not answering, making her wait and worry. It would serve her right, wouldn't it?

She'd suspended him from work, with immediate effect. He'd have a full disciplinary meeting sometime next week and could bring a union representative if he so desired. It was *orders from above*. Nothing she could do. And no, it was *no longer appropriate* for her to attend his awards ceremony that evening. He'd receive his medal and pats on the back from strangers, but she wouldn't be there to clap extra-loud when he stepped on to the stage. Nobody would. The staff drinks would go ahead as planned but she wouldn't be there for that either. That was the final blow.

Even when he was good, he was not loved.

Dave had walked out before she'd finished talking, felt good about it for approximately five seconds. He'd shown her he was hurt and angry but he'd blown the chance to grill Crystal over her potential involvement. So he still didn't know why she had those old photos of him – or if she'd been sneaking around his house on Sunday, making those calls from his landline.

Dave walked up to the viewpoint at the end where he'd stood with Rafa a few hours earlier. He stared for a moment over the long sandy beach and the colourful two-storey houses that lined it, the paths to front doors lined with kayaks and stand-up paddleboards. A few had little wooden benches under the bay window, their armrests no doubt stained by hot mugs. Above their slate roofs another rainbow stretched to the middle of the sea, curling over the promenade and everybody on it. Usually that was the kind of sight that would lift his spirits. But it was made of nothing real, nothing solid.

A bit like his theories on the identity of Amy Todd.

She looked exactly like Carmen, but could not be her. She was born almost two years after Dave had killed Carmen and her unborn child and nothing could change that cold, hard fact. The *only* thing that connected Carmen and Amy was the nuisance calls made from Dave's house to theirs, and that hoax call to the police. *A woman and child, killed.*

There was a chance, however remote, that all of this was a horrible coincidence. The hoax call *could* have been made by a random intruder, reporting the crime at a random address.

Did Dave believe that? No.

But there *was* a chance that Amy *didn't* look exactly like Carmen after all; that all of this was down to his *mental fragility*. It wouldn't be the first time his brain had conjured up her image out of nowhere, back from the dead and staring right at him. He'd run to the other side of the world and reinvented himself and still he'd seen her in crowds, glancing at him mischievously then moving away too fast for him to ever catch her.

Was that what was happening here? The old ghosts were back to haunt him?

Maybe. But he'd only know for sure when he saw her face to face.

He'd searched for Amy Todd on social media but had drawn a blank. Where else could he look? If she *was* Jonathan Todd's daughter then he knew her address, but definitely couldn't turn up at her house without risking arrest. Where else might she be? The MOB Bar. But he might find Rafa there too. *Think, Dave.* What else did he know about her? Only one thing: the place she'd got on his bus on Monday. Musselburgh High Street. A bus ran the route every ten minutes but right now he didn't want to see any of his colleagues and he didn't want to walk in case Rafa was still sitting where he'd left him at the Joppa rocks. Taxi it was, then.

If Amy wouldn't come to him, he'd go to her.

Dave wandered for a while after the taxi dropped him off, unsure of what to do next. He *drove* through Musselburgh most days with his bus but he hadn't stepped foot in the place since he'd moved back to the area two years earlier. The old part of town was prettier than he remembered, its skyline a jumble of towers and steeples and the slate roofs of traditional tenements. The ground floors he saw from the bus were a little less glorious, a plethora of pound stores and betting shops and the classic Scottish cafés selling chips and ice-cream and coffee the wise would run a mile from.

But this might just be the place he'd find her.

He eventually positioned himself on the wide stone windowsill of a High Street bakery. From here he could see the bus stop and everybody who got on and off. Every time he heard the rumble of a bus engine he trained his eyes on the passengers stepping forward from the shelter. And when it pulled into the stop he scanned those who'd been neatly dispensed on to the pavement. This was where Amy had stepped on to his bus on Monday morning, so it could be part of her usual routine. But two hours later, there was still no sign of her.

His arse was cold, his tummy empty, his hope fading. Three more buses and he'd give up, go home. The first bus came and went. Then a second. He was waiting for a third when the door of the bakery opened and a wiry old woman wearing a white uniform stuck her head out, nodded to the windowsill. 'Do you mind? If it's a bench you're wanting there's plenty by the harbour.'

Dave stood up, glancing back at the bus stop as another bus pulled in and passengers stepped off. Still no sign of her. 'I was just leaving.'

'Just as well.' With that she disappeared inside. A few moments later, Dave followed her.

In Portobello the bakeries felt like bars these days, all soft lighting and electronic music and bakers who looked as though they'd spent half the morning with their hands kneading hair wax rather than dough. All quiffs and beards, sculpted to perfection.

Musselburgh was a different story. Here the baker-ies were lit by tube lights and manned by a small army of shrunken women with white curls poking out from under their hairnets.

Dave pushed open the door, breathed in sugar. At first it looked as though the shop was empty but then he caught movement behind the glass-fronted counter and, sure enough, a hairnet rose up over a pile of cut-price doughnuts. The woman smiled, looked friendlier now.

'What can I get you, son?'

'Got anything veggie?'

'Probably just cakes, but let me check.'

She ducked down and for a few moments Dave watched her peer into the warmed glass shelves from the other side, eyes flitting over metal trays loaded with golden-crusted sausage rolls and wee pies with sticky brown gravy leaking out of the lid. She reappeared just as he noticed a fly in there too, swatted; squashed, a life reduced to liquid.

'Cheese and pickle roll?'

'Perfect.'

She ducked down again and tugged a flour-topped bap from one of the shelves then stuffed it in a white paper bag, twisted the corners and set it on the counter.

'Anything else?'

'Just a question, actually.'

She paused, a look on her face that Dave's whispering mind told him was suspicion. He shifted the weight between his feet and his gaze to the ticking clock on the wall just above the woman's head.

'I'm actually looking for a woman.'

'Afraid I'm the only woman going, sweetheart, and you're not my type.' She laughed a loud, tobacco-scorched laugh that belonged in a dive bar, all dim lights and fag smoke and pints that smelled of clogged pipes. He imagined her out of work, dressed in clothes that weren't coated with flour, vodka zipping through her veins instead of milky tea.

Dave didn't join in but didn't talk over her, either. When her laugh trailed to a fading smile she shook her head, as if dismissing the part of herself that had allowed it to happen; letting go, for a few seconds. Dave remembered moments like those, envied her.

'Is that why you've been spying on the bus stop as well?'

'I wouldn't call it spying.'

'Well, I've been spying on *you*, so I should know. But maybe I can help you out. What does she look like, this woman?'

'Olive skin, wavy black hair. Might be wearing a yellow coat. Or a green one.'

'Age?'

Dave cleared his throat. 'Eighteen or so.'

'Eighteen? So it's a *girl*, not a woman.' Widening eyes and a cocked head underlined the word ten times over. Mrs Hairnet was clearly someone else who thought he was a predator, hunting fresh meat. He was already sick of the assumption, wanted to set them straight. But he knew how it sounded and what the reactions would be. Disbelief.

Dave's eyes trailed over her shoulder to a cork pinboard loaded with a few letters and a neon-dotted rota inside a plastic sleeve and a postcard sent from Lesmahagow and a few photos with curling corners, a dusting of white dulling the glossy paper. He immediately saw the old woman's face in one of the photos, shrieking something at the camera, arms slung around two of her pals. Both were women. One old, one young, and the young one had dark, wavy hair.

Dave edged forward, towards the counter and a slightly better view.

The woman turned to see where he was looking, tutting as she tugged the rota to one side so it covered the photo. 'You know what? I'm growing less fond of you by the second.' She folded her arms, started chewing her bottom lip as if it was gum. 'In fact, I think you should leave.'

'Can I just see that photo? Please? It looks like . . . her. I just need to know if she's . . .' Dave sighed. *If she's real. If she's alive. If she's dead. And if she's not dead, how?* What could he possibly say?

The woman answered the question for him.

'That's my *daughter*, pal. So if it's her you're looking for then be warned, her dad'll send you packing.

And I'll set the dogs on you if you go anywhere near her. Now go.'

Dave nodded, paid, retreated with his sandwich. He hoped to Christ this woman didn't recognise him from the buses. He shouldn't have come, not without a script and a credible back story that wouldn't send the masses running for cover. The woman scowled at Dave, then flipped it on its head when the door behind him was pushed open by a runner looking for a bacon roll. She turned to Dave, strained smile fixed. 'Is that everything, sir?'

'For now,' he said, then dropped his eyes to the ground and left.

CHAPTER 27

Dave sharpened his story and spent the next few hours trailing up and down the High Street, telling shopkeepers and café owners he was looking for *his niece*. Nobody had seen her, or at least that was what they told him. But older man plus teenage girl always equalled suspicion. The only people who said anything remotely useful was a couple from Liverpool who ran one of the betting shops. The man said they'd noticed a *delinquent in a hoodie* at the harbour a few times this week; *lingering* close to one of the benches. The wife said they'd been carrying *petrol station flowers* and the husband rolled his eyes, said they'd probably nicked them.

It was Dave's *only* lead and it led him *there*.

He turned his back on the town and on the vow he'd made to himself all those years ago. When he'd fled he said he'd never return. But today he had no choice.

Dave turned up his collar and walked to the place of the killings.

In Musselburgh Harbour the barnacled bellies of boats were dry and exposed, much bigger than you'd imagine when you saw them floating on the surface. Seagulls strutted back and forth on the walkway, looking for attention and dropped chips. Others stood on the sea wall, still as statues on their bright orange feet, heads turned towards the sea. From there Dave could see the grass-backed beach, littered with the shells of mussels and razor clams, every one of them a life long-since lost. Dave had walked there often when he was younger, knew how their tiny coffins would crunch and shatter under the weight of him, no matter how softly he trod.

Everywhere he looked he saw death.

The bitter sea breeze slithered down his neck as he walked the harbour wall. It came in gusts; tugged the ropes hung on boats, turning metal masts to xylophones all jingling at different times. It brought the smell of seaweed and damp wood from the boats, of chips in hot oil and rusting metal.

A dozen wooden benches lined the harbour wall that led from the street to the sea. Each had a metal dedication plate screwed to the backrest: a few words, carefully chosen to remember the dead.

To Isabel, one said. *Thanks for all the stories.*

Dave kept walking. He read a few more of the dedications as he walked to the end of the harbour but it didn't sit right with him. He didn't like the idea of all those souls hanging out together on the harbour, enjoying the view from the afterlife but watching him as well. *They'd* know what he'd done. You couldn't hide your secrets from the dead.

He stopped when he reached the far end. One more step and he'd be in the sea, up to his neck or maybe over it. The last bench was facing the open sea instead of the harbour but the once-varnished wood was now chipped and rotting, looked close to collapse. Sure enough, someone had left a bunch of cellophane-wrapped flowers on top, leaning against one of the armrests. The betting shop couple claimed they'd seen a *delinquent in a hoodie* carrying a bouquet – maybe the card would give him a name. Dave glanced over his shoulder then picked up the flowers and turned them in his hands, looking for a little white envelope. Sometimes they were taped to the side, or wedged between the stalks. But here, now, there was nothing.

Dave replaced the flowers then hunched down in front of the bench, his back to the sea.

This one had no name plate but the backrest was decorated with delicate carvings. They'd been battered by the weather and the sea but the design was clear as day: the outline of two birds, swooping. Dave bent closer for a better look and as he ran his finger over the damp-swollen wood his heart thundered. He could tell by the shape of their tails that they were swallows and, just like that, a memory finally slid into place.

The birds on the bench matched Carmen's tattoo.

He'd only seen it a handful of times, and that was Carmen's intention. She'd had the birds drawn with great precision on her ankle, just below the sock line so few would see them. There were two birds at first but she'd planned to add more. Thanks to Dave, she'd never had the chance.

And that wasn't all.

Dave had seen the same image somewhere else this week. Where?

In the dark, in a shed, on the side of that urn. At the house of Jonathan Todd.

Dave hadn't been in the harbour pub for twenty years but the tables still stood in exactly the same position. He headed for the window seat that used to be his usual, then changed his mind and went straight to the bar. The lad behind it looked up from his phone, blinking behind his finger-smudged glasses.

'What can I get you, pal?'

'Sparkling water. Loads of ice.'

'Coming up.'

Dave sat on the tall stool, thighs bouncing, feet tapping out a beat on the metal supports. The front door was always open in this pub and, even though the main road ran between here and the harbour, he swore he could still hear the sea, the gulls, the rattles and clinks of the boats. From time to time a waiter would pop through a swing door at the side of the bar, shout a drinks order for diners in the bistro through the back. Before the door swung closed Dave would catch the whiff of posh lunches and snippets of chatter and laughter.

He chugged his water then tipped the ice cubes into his mouth and started crunching. It hurt but he welcomed the distraction, hoped the shock of the cold would help calm him down.

First things first, he hadn't found any definite trace of Amy in Musselburgh but he *had* found a potential link between the town and Jonathan Todd. He pulled out his phone and stared at the photo of the carvings on that bench. He switched to the internet and searched *memorials with swallows*; was relieved when dozens of images appeared on screen.

Fact: starlings and swallows and swifts were common motifs on sympathy cards and graves. So it could be a coincidence.

But if it wasn't? Then there was a direct link between the tattoo of the woman he killed and a neglected memorial bench and a *hooded delinquent* carrying flowers and a family he'd been accused of harassing – the family of a teenage girl who, somehow, looked just like Carmen. *And* she had been wearing a hooded jacket the first day Dave saw her, metres from Musselburgh Harbour.

Jonathan Todd would know if his family was linked to that bench, but if Dave turned up at that house again they'd call the police.

So how could he find out for sure who the bench belonged to?

He signalled to the barman to bring the same again, fired out his questions while the lad was scooping up ice cubes with metal tongs.

'Any idea who looks after the memorial benches at the harbour? It's just . . . one of them's falling to pieces. I'd have thought the family would have wanted to keep the place nice. Or the council, maybe?'

The boy laughed. 'Fat chance. Politicians would let the sea run dry if they thought it would save a few pennies.' He pushed Dave's drink along the bar, nodded as he took the payment. 'The harbour area's not their priority. We've had a homeless guy sleeping down there recently as well and they've done nothing about it. Makes the whole place feel a bit . . . scruffy.'

'But you've no idea who it belongs to?'

'What?'

'The neglected bench.'

'No clue.' He screwed up his face. 'How come you're needing to know?'

Dave hesitated; decided honesty wasn't the best option. 'Just seems a shame to have an eyesore in such a pretty spot.'

'You're not the only one who feels that way. Folk are *always* whingeing about the state of the town; say they're going to call the council or the papers but then they do fuck-all so everything stays the same. They're armchair complainers, the lot of them. Or in this case, bar stool complainers. Speaking of which . . .' The boy nodded towards the door, now filled by a wide woman wearing a filthy white apron and black rubber boots. 'Just the usual, Jessie?'

'Make it a double today, pal.'

'I'll bring it over.'

The boy winked at Dave then turned his back on him, scanning the bottles hanging behind the bar. He picked out a single malt whisky, half-filled a squat glass then walked round the bar to reach the woman's table.

'Got a man here looking for gossip, Jessie.'

The woman looked at Dave, cheeks fat as ripe plums, squeezing her eyes to slits. 'You from here, sweetheart?'

'Not really.'

'Not *really*? So you're a man of mystery? Just how I like 'em.' She laughed, then patted the chair next to hers. Dave slid off his high stool, sat where he was told, repeated his half-truth about wanting to find the family of the neglected bench. As she listened Jessie tugged a strand of fine white hair from her bun, twirled it between her fingers. When Dave finished she

207

picked up her glass, took a tiny sip of whisky, smiled as she swallowed it.

'That bench has been neglected for . . . *years*. Decades, maybe. Can I ask why you're so interested in it? Given you're a stranger in town and all that.'

Dave flushed. 'I just . . . like to do my bit.'

'Now *that's* a likely tale.' Jessie eyed him over her whisky glass as she took another mouthful. 'And here was me thinking I was the only fishwife in the place.'

She chuckled after she said it but Dave flushed and looked away, out of the window; towards the harbour. 'I'm not here to cause any harm,' he said.

'I can tell,' she said, then reached across the table and squeezed Dave's arm with her sausage fingers. 'And I'll tell you something else for free. Whatever it is you're hiding, folk won't care as much as you imagine.'

Jesus Christ. So he'd sat down for drinks with the town psychic. Dave dragged his eyes back to the table then pushed back his chair. 'I should go.'

'To the bar? Then mine's a single this time.' She held out her empty glass, winked as she handed it over. 'But make it one of the expensive ones, eh? And when we're settled again I'll tell you all about that bench of yours.'

Dave almost laughed. The woman was a power-house. Once again, he did what he was told.

Six quid later he was back in front of her with a glass that smelled of burnt wood. Jessie thanked him and sniffed it approvingly.

'Like I said, the bench at the end of the harbour has been neglected for years. Decades, maybe. I run a fishmonger's in town, know every man and his boat down there. Over the years I've got to know the mourners too, the ones who visit the benches. Some folk are down there every day. Others, every week. Some folk only come on birthdays or death days or whatever anniversary they've chosen to remember. But in all the years I've had the shop I've never seen anybody at that one. Sad, really, to think you could just be forgotten. But I console myself with the fact that they must have been loved in life. No love, no bench. That's how it goes.'

Dave sighed. 'So you *don't* know who it belongs to?'

'I'm just getting to that part.' A wink, a sip, a smile. 'You've obviously noticed there's no name plate on that one but I wonder if you noticed the carvings?'

'The swallows? Aye, I did.'

'And what about the other one?'

Dave shook his head, adrenaline sparking in his chest. Jessie knew how to hook her listeners, that's for sure. He just hoped she didn't demand another whisky before the punchline.

'Where is it?'

'On the armrests.'

'Another bird?'

This time Jessie shook her head. 'They're quite faint now, swollen with the damp and salt and such like. But on one side there's a little letter C carved into the wood. And on the other, there's—'

'The letter M?'

Jessie tilted her head to one side, blinking. 'Good guess,' she said, then kept on talking. Dave didn't hear a thing. The only words registering in his brain were the ones that matched those initials.

C and M. *Carmen Martinez*.

He knew how that name felt on his tongue, how it sounded with his accent, how it looked in his own handwriting. And he'd pictured, far too many times, how that name would look when it was carved out on cold, hard stone; written on her grave.

When Jessie paused to take a breath Dave thanked her and the barman then headed back to the harbour to see the carvings for himself. The letters were almost worn away completely. But not quite. Dave rubbed his fingertip over the groove of the C and the M, felt his heart crack open a little wider.

Now, surely, there was no doubt. The bench was dedicated to Rafa's twin sister – and the unborn child she had been carrying when Dave had killed her twenty years ago. But who had put the bench there, and why would they let it fall into ruin? More to the point, who had left those flowers there this week? If Rafa didn't know about this, he should.

But Dave had no phone number or address for Rafa, and couldn't find him on online searches. His best chance was returning to the MOB Bar on the off-chance Rafa went there two days running. And if he wasn't there Dave might find someone who had his number. He needed to speak to him, urgently. And this time he'd be honest: tell him everything he knew about Amy, and her uncanny resemblance to Carmen. Only then would he dare ask the questions that were bubbling up in his brain, regardless of how ludicrous they sounded. Because he knew Amy could not be Carmen's baby. But there *was* another way a child could have been born with her face.

And the only person who would know for sure was the one person on earth who shared the same one: Rafa.

CHAPTER 28

Inside, your kitchen smells of curry and the round table is made from cheap pine that's stained with the rings of cups and glasses that tell stories I want to know and wish I'd been a part of. I sit down in the only seat that's not neatly tucked underneath, push one of my fingernails through the varnish until I feel it give way and crack. A tiny scar, from me to you. Then I glance at your knife block, fingers twitching. Five blades, neatly stored, recently sharpened. What would you do if you came home and found my name scored into the table top? Part of you would be happy, surely, and that's the part I'm trying to reach.

Your daily timetable is stuck to the fridge door and inside you have food stored in the right places and no meat and no crumbs that I can see. I open your cupboards, one by one, run my hands over unfamiliar plates and bowls and mugs as if I can coax them into telling me who you are when you think nobody can see you. In the cupboards above it's all lentils and chickpeas and I wonder if you eat like this for health or fashion; or for the good of your conscience.

I move to the utility room. There's an overflowing wicker basket by the window with filth to be washed, and above me clean clothes are drying on the long wooden slats of a pulley hung from the ceiling. It's all clothes I do not recognise: sports gear and a few smart shirts and tea towels from some of the places you've visited or where others have gone and thought of you and bought a rectangle of cotton to prove it. They're all signs of a life, lived. Or of someone trying to control the few parts of life that allow it. But your dirty laundry can be cleaned and hung up to dry here, inside, where nobody can see it. I reach up and pull the hanging sleeve of a grey hooded top, hold it to my nose and inhale, but I can only smell detergent.

I smile. Very soon, my clothes will smell the same and will hang here, right next to yours.

It's almost time.

Tonight I'll be watching you with someone else beside me; someone who you don't yet know but should, and don't yet love, but will. There are things about you that only I know, and the time has come to share them.

Mark my words: tonight the world will change.

CHAPTER 29

The city centre was jumping, mainly with new students squeezing the last few days out of Freshers' Week. Dave watched the hordes through the window of his taxi, hoped the MOB Bar would be more serene. He asked the driver to stop at the church across the road; stepped out of the taxi and into a puddle of fresh vomit just as the bells struck four o'clock.

Bloody students.

He cursed the lot of them as he wiped his shoe clean on the pavement, then headed for the bar. Inside, the place was empty except for two older women sitting on the same side of a booth, drinking sparkling water and reading dog-eared paperbacks.

There was nobody behind the bar either but Dave went there anyway, stood with his elbows on the polished wood and his eyes on the massive gold-framed mirror that was a relic from the pub's previous owners. The original name – The Old Stable Yard – was painted on the shiny surface, and beneath those golden letters Dave could see himself. Was this really the face of an *outstanding citizen*?

Little did they know. The ceremony started at seven so he'd have to go straight there from the MOB Bar, still wearing his grubby work uniform instead of the expected kilt and smart jacket. It was apt, somehow, that he'd prove to be a disappointment.

He forced a smile into place when he heard movement through the back, got two in return from the bar staff when they pushed through a bead curtain, puffing out the reek of tobacco when they laughed. The older of the two looked as though he'd been brought up in the eighties and decided to stay there. He left his colleague fiddling with the music system, sauntered over.

'Sorry to keep you waiting.'

'Needs must.'

'What you having?'

'I was wanting to speak with your pal, actually.' Dave nodded to the woman behind him. She was now standing on her tiptoes, doing her best to untangle a multitude of cables that led to and from a speaker on the back wall.

The eighties man whistled to get her attention. 'Linda? You're wanted.'

'Two seconds.' She tugged a few more wires then shrugged and let them go. The speaker crackled then made a popping sound as she walked towards them.

She had even more piercings than Dave had noticed the other night but today her mohawk had been flattened and every few seconds she'd flick the curtains of bleached hair out of her eyes.

'If I were you I'd shave it right off,' he said.

'Hair tips from a baldy bastard. Love it,' she replied, laughing. 'What you needing?'

'Gossip, basically.'

'You've come to the right place.'

Dave caught a glimpse of himself in the mirror when he smiled. He looked the opposite of how he felt.

'There was a guy in here last night, at the bar. You seemed quite pally with him. Tall, olive skin, built like a brick shithouse. He was wearing a white T-shirt with a big green arrow on it? Anyway, he gave me his number but I . . . lost it and . . . och, I'd like to see him again. Wondered if he's a regular, if he's likely to be back in?'

She laughed. 'You've just described half my clientele.'

'He probably tipped you at the start of the night, a good chunk.'

A smile creased her eyes. 'Oh, *that* guy. What's his name again?'

'Rafa.'

'That's right. He's not been coming for long to be honest but he's proving to be quite . . . popular. There might be a queue when you find him.'

'I'll wait,' said Dave, trying to kid himself and the world that news like that didn't sting. 'What's the chances of him being here tonight?'

'Your guess is as good as mine. But Thursday tends to be one of our busiest nights so if he's on the pull then he'll have good pickings. Speaking of which . . .' She slouched and leaned across the bar, lowered her voice. 'Don't look now, but the lad who just walked in will know more than I do. I've seen him and Rafa together a few times. Can't guarantee he'll want to share phone numbers with the competition, though.' She winked. 'Best of luck.'

With that she straightened up, smiled over Dave's shoulder as the man approached the counter. Dave pretended he was looking into the mirror, stared at the man as he made easy conversation with the mohawk girl then ordered himself a pint of some artisan beer she recommended. He was Irish, had good chat and eyes that constantly wandered. He smiled when he caught Dave looking at him.

'Cheers, then,' he said, then nodded to the cardboard beer mat sitting in front of Dave. 'You're not thirsty?'

'Just waiting . . . for a pal.'

'Can I buy you a drink in the meantime?'

'Go on, then.'

'What's your poison?'

'Zero beer if they've got them?'

'Coming up.' He winked, turned back to the bar. 'Linda, you got one of those beers for poofs?'

Predictable, but she laughed and he laughed and Dave forced himself to join in. When you're gay you can make all the gay jokes you want. And anyway, if this man could help him find Rafa he'd laugh at every single thing he said. They *needed* to talk.

They'd just clinked glasses when Dave felt the sudden warmth of someone standing on the other side of him. The Irish lad's eyes flitted over his shoulder, a quizzical expression momentarily denting his smile. Dave was about to turn when soft words stopped him in his tracks, spoken in a voice that he'd have recognised underwater.

'Fancy meeting you here.'

CHAPTER 30

DI Farida McPherson nodded towards one of the empty booths at the far side of the bar. 'We need to talk.'

Dave glanced at the Irish lad then back at her. 'I'm kind of busy.'

'Last I checked, our conversation wasn't optional.'

Dave heard the Irish lad – John, his name was – do one of those whirling whistles that folk used to do at school just before someone got a kicking. Farida was already walking away; she tossed her leather jacket into the booth then slid in after it.

Dave shook his head, swallowed a sigh. 'I'll buy you one when I'm done, OK? Don't go anywhere.'

John winked then turned away, was making both the bar staff laugh before Dave had reached the booth.

'Thanks for joining me, Mr Kellock.'

'Didn't have much choice. Mind telling me why you're here?'

'I was about to ask you the same thing,' she said, but didn't wait for an answer. 'I was actually planning to . . . pay you a visit later, at home.'

'For?'

'You've got no idea?'

'Can't say I do.'

Farida nodded, seemingly to herself. 'I heard you were suspended from work.'

'News travels fast. Who told you?'

'I have contacts,' she said, then leaned back in her seat. 'But I'd appreciate it if you'd explain the reasons for your suspension.'

Dave sighed, still couldn't believe it. 'There are numerous. All nonsense, I should add.'

'Could you elaborate?'

'Should I get a lawyer?'

Farida stared at him, her face unshifting. 'As far as I'm concerned you're just helping with enquiries.'

'Enquiries into *what*? Those nuisance calls? Because if that's the case I can't see why you need to document my every move. I've told you before and I'll tell you again: I've done nothing wrong.'

'I'll be the judge of that,' said Farida. 'But please consider this an informal meeting. You're free to leave at any time. Does that seem reasonable?'

'Most reasonable thing I've heard all day,' said Dave. 'Now, if you can please tell me why you're here, I'll decide whether or not I'm staying.'

Farida took a sip of her drink then reached into her shoulder bag and pulled out a bright red folder. For a few minutes she kept it closed, both hands resting on top. Her nails were short and Dave noticed dry skin at the flattened tips of her fingers. Rafa's hands were the same: the scars of a guitar player. He always teased Dave, said he had a woman's hands. Long and thin and soft and hairless. But that didn't mean they couldn't cause any damage.

'Where were you last night?'

The words snapped Dave back to the room. 'Here, for a while. Then home. Look, if this is about me giving my number to that lad then I'll tell you exactly the same thing I told my boss at work. I was just—'

'Why this bar?'

'Why not?' He blushed and hated himself for it.

'Is this a bar you . . . frequent?'

Dave knew what she was really asking. But if she was talking in code then he would as well. 'Last night was the first time,' he said.

'I see.'

'But do you, really?'

She tilted her head. 'I think it's best if you let me ask the questions.' She cut eye contact, looked at the folder instead. She peeled open the edge of it with her thumb, held it for a few seconds then let it go. Long enough for Dave to see the corner of a photo but not the face it captured. 'After speaking to your bosses at the bus depot I understand you spoke with a group of students here last night and subsequently gave your mobile number to one of the men in the group.'

'I did, aye.'

'You were looking for a friend of theirs? A teenage girl?'

'I didn't know she was so young. I thought—'

'Would you like to tell me your motive?'

'There was no *motive*. You're making it sound worse than it is.'

Farida cleared her throat, straightening up. The air in the room shifted with her. She might as well have rolled up her sleeves and asked him to step outside. 'According to my . . . sources . . . this all started when you followed the girl *off* your bus. You then listened in to a private conversation she had with a friend, during which they mentioned the precise time and place they'd be meeting. You came here last night specifically because you thought she'd be here.'

'There was something I needed to ask her.'

'That's irrelevant, in my book. I'd have thought a driver of your experience and . . . standing, would have been aware of client–customer guidelines. And I'm sure you know that teenage girls don't much like a stalker.'

'I wasn't *stalking* her, for Christ's sake.'

Farida reached into her inside pocket and pulled out a notepad. She slowly flicked through, pausing at a page near the back. She read it, then raised her eyes to Dave.

'Let's run through the facts again, shall we? You followed her off your bus. You eavesdropped on her conversations. You gatecrashed her birthday drinks.

222

And then? When it became apparent the girl in question was absent, you asked for her phone number. Her friend refused, at which point you gave him your own number – noted here if you want to check – and asked that she get in touch?'

'That's one version of events.'

'And what's yours?'

Dave stared at Farida, hated her and hoped it showed. 'You want to know my view? This whole thing is ridiculous.'

'I'd appreciate answers rather than opinions,' said Farida. She opened her folder, picked out the photo, held it where only she could see it. Her face was impossible to read. She could have been staring at a selfie or a photo of a sliced-up human and he was quite sure her expression wouldn't change. There would be no flinch, no movement over which she did not have control. Dave was the opposite, felt himself flush when her eyes flitted from the photo to him.

'I'd like you to have a look at this,' she said, then precisely placed the photo on the table before sliding it towards him. Dave leaned forward, looked without touching. He could see the smudge of Farida's fingertips in the corner and he kept his eyes there, studied swirling lines caught on glossy paper, as if that was why she'd brought him here.

'Well?' Farida slid the photo a little closer to him so he lost sight of those smudges and found himself staring instead at *that* face. This was what he'd been searching for all week; what he'd been looking for when he'd searched the CCTV recordings in Crystal's office and when he'd followed her off the bus and through Edinburgh city centre. This was the face he'd hoped to see last night at the MOB Bar.

This was the face; captured on a little rectangle of paper, trapped under gloss. It *was* the face of Amy, the girl from the bus. She looked exactly like Rafa's twin, Carmen.

But that wasn't all.

Dave blinked, over and over, as if the image might change between one flash of black and the next. It did not. Farida's eyes were prodding fingers, wanting to see what he saw. But he could not believe or understand it, and would not say it out loud. Yes, he looked at her and saw the face of the woman he'd killed. But he could see traces of someone else there too.

It was dream and a nightmare rolled into one. The unthinkable, made real. A glaring fact with no logical explanation. It wasn't only Carmen he saw when he looked at Amy's image.

He saw the father's face as well.

CHAPTER 31

Dave sensed movement at the bar and dragged his eyes away from the photo. John was necking the dregs of his pint and pulling on his jacket. Leaving. More than ever, Dave needed Rafa's number. He could not let that man go.

He planted his hands on the table, stood up. 'I need to go.'

'As you wish.' Farida stayed seated as he edged out of the booth. He was half-in, half-out when she spoke again. She reached out an arm, forced him to pause. 'She's gone missing, you know.'

Her words were a lasso; choking him, reeling him in. He sat back down. 'Missing?'

A nod, a sniff, a slow blink; but her eyes didn't leave him.

'Missing *how*?'

'It's very early days, not even twenty-four hours. But given the nature of the hoax call on Sunday and the nuisance calls to the family home, this case is being treated with . . . urgency. Her mother phoned us this morning, in a panic. She saw Amy last night for her birthday dinner. That's when she told her about the nuisance calls and the police turning up at the house. Naturally, Amy was upset. Her mum went to visit her again this morning at university, to check she was OK, but Amy couldn't be found. Bed not slept in. Phone switched off. She doesn't have a boyfriend and none of the neighbouring students have seen her – but a few reported hearing a door being thumped, late last night. Others claim they heard a man's voice, saying her name.'

'You think it's something . . . serious?'

Farida observed him for a few moments before she spoke, blinking slowly as her eyes scanned his face, searching for signs of lies. Dave clenched his fists and stuffed his hands into his pockets. They couldn't do any damage in there.

'Teenage girls love to be rebels,' said Farida. 'They love to take risks. But ultimately, they're highly vulnerable. And easily led.' A pause, a sniff, her eyes on his.

Dave's phone burned an Amy-shaped hole in his pocket. He *should* tell Farida he'd received those texts from the skinny lad last night; that they'd arranged to meet early this morning in the park. That he hadn't turned up; and that Dave had spent the whole afternoon searching for Amy in Musselburgh instead. But she'd already accused him of stalking the girl, and all of that would incriminate him even more. He *should* tell her about the connection he'd found between the urn in Jonathan Todd's garden shed and a neglected bench at the harbour – but that would immediately expose him as a liar: he'd told her he didn't know the Todds and didn't know how his phone had ended up in their shed. Any trust would be blown to bits if he confessed now. Maybe it was better to back off, step away, stick with his original plan for now: find Rafa, tell him about Amy and see if he could shed any light on the truth of it.

'I think I've helped you all I can.' He was glad his voice sounded calm. He was a good citizen, ready and willing to aid the authorities. And aye, he'd remain innocent until charged. 'Whatever has happened to this lassie has nothing to do with me.'

'And I've made no such suggestion,' she said. 'I'm not here because of *you*, Dave. I'm here because her mother told me Amy was due to come here last night with friends. She changed her plans when her mum turned up. They went for dinner. But nobody knows what Amy did *after* that. There's a chance she might have come here later on, so I need to speak to staff and any regulars, see if they remember anything. Who she was with, what time she left, her mood. We're keeping it out of the papers for now, but we've all seen how these stories can end.'

'Aye,' said Dave then looked away, breaking eye contact. But this woman could see right through him anyway, probably smell the guilt from twenty paces. He had to leave, now, before she prodded too deeply and broke down his barriers and saw what lay beneath.

He stood up again, too quickly, knocking the table. Farida's drink sloshed in its glass but her hand was on it in a flash. She stilled it, sipped it; was the cool, calm eye of a shitstorm.

Dave nodded to the glass. 'You always drink on the job?'

'You always flee when something touches a nerve?'

Touché, Farida.

'I'm leaving because I've got a date.'

'And I'm drinking tonic water. I'm in a bar because I have questions, and that's not so different from you. We've got good reason to believe the missing girl is the same person you were looking for last night. So here we are, the pair of us, both looking for the same girl.'

'And hopefully we'll find her,' said Dave, pushing out of the booth just as Irish John pulled open the pub door. A cool breeze crept in as he stepped out. Dave had to leave now, follow, if he wanted to catch him. This man could help him find Rafa.

But what about finding Amy?

He hesitated, turned back to Farida. 'Is there a way I can contact you? If I . . . hear anything?'

'Thought you'd never ask,' she said, shifting her gaze from Dave's eyes to the business card already in her hand, pinched between two strong fingers.

She held it towards him, flashed a momentary smile when he took it. 'I'm sure we'll speak soon.'

Outside, the street smelled of bacon. A woman with a stroller walked past, white flour puffing from a greasy roll as she took a bite. Dave hadn't eaten meat for almost twenty years but still the smell made his stomach rumble. Every body has its urges, regardless of the rules set for them by brain, logic, morals. The bacon woman turned left and Dave was debating which direction to choose when he heard his name, called.

'You legging it to avoid buying me a drink?'

He turned, saw Irish John reappearing from an alley down the side of the church; smiling as he stubbed out a cigarette against the low wall. 'Went to have a fag with the dead,' he said, nodding towards the small graveyard that lay behind the main building. 'They've got better craic than most folk in the MOB Bar, I'll tell you that for free.'

'Sorry, I . . . got held up.'

'I noticed. Thought you'd gone and turned straight for a second there. She's a pretty one, right enough. But a bit . . . serious.'

'That's one word for her.'

'You definitely look like you're needing a drink. Maybe something stronger this time?'

Dave glanced back at the MOB Bar, caught sight of Farida, still in the booth, sipping her tonic water as she talked to somebody on her mobile phone. The file was open on the table and she was studying that photo of Amy; the girl with *that face*. Amy, who'd now gone missing. He felt sick, scared, confused, guiltier than ever. He was some kind of modern-day Medusa, cursing the life of anyone who dared look him in the eye. Was John next? He couldn't risk it. 'I should go,' he said.

'Lucky for us that *should*s don't exist, then.' John nudged him. 'And anyway, Linda told me your secret.'

Dave's heart was lead, but he forced lightness. 'Oh, aye, and what's that?'

'That you've got an ulterior motive,' said John, smiling. 'Only want me for my contacts list. Now come for a drink – just one – or you'll be getting nowhere near it.'

They ended up in an old pub with a big beer garden surrounded by high stone walls. Most of the wooden picnic benches were empty. Suited Dave just fine.

He got them both a drink, wondered how long he should wait until he mentioned Rafa directly. The awards ceremony started in – he looked at his watch – just under two hours, so he had time. Right now it was patience he lacked – and any good bones in his body. Here he was, flirting with a stranger to try to get Rafa's phone number while the police helped the Todd family search for Amy, days after a hoax caller had told them they'd find her and her mum dead in their own home.

He should be out there, helping. But what could he do? He'd been trying to track her down all week without success, so there was no reason to think he could help find her now.

But he *could* have been honest with Farida instead of lying to save himself.

He should go back to the pub, or call her, tell her everything he knew.

'Earth to Dave: you here to daydream or to drink?' John was smiling at him from across the table, pint held aloft. 'Here's to good health and . . . to the real reason you're here.' He clinked his glass against Dave's bottle of zero-alcohol beer then pulled out his phone and held out a selfie of himself and Rafa. 'This is the lad you're looking for, is it not? His name's Rafa.'

'Aye, I know. I . . . know him, from a while back.'

John laughed. 'I think he *knows* half of Edinburgh, this one. He's got some body on him. Small reward, I suppose, for spending all those years behind bars. Personally I'd rather pay the gym membership.'

He laughed after he said that. Dave did not.

John went to take another sip of his pint then paused and put down his glass. He leaned across the table again. A smudge of beer foam was clinging to his top lip. 'Ah, you didn't know that part, did you?'

'Of course I did,' said Dave. 'I just . . .' His cheeks weren't listening to his lies; he could feel that they had flushed so red he'd glow in the dark. Was this the real reason Rafa had suddenly reappeared out of the blue? Had he just been released from prison?

John reached out, touched Dave's arm. 'You OK?'

'Of course.' He forced a smile, mind racing. 'You know what he was in for?'

'Your guess is as good as mine. But from a few things he said, I'm guessing he'd been in for a long stretch. A good few years.'

'You didn't ask specifics?'

'I wasn't really there for the conversation, if you know what I mean?'

'Aye.' Dave flushed, didn't want to picture Rafa reaching out for anybody else. Those hands. Those *fists*. Had Rafa been jailed for attacking Dave the day they broke up? It was unlikely. He'd surely have heard about it – and anyway, it wouldn't have been a long jail term. But what life had Rafa led once Dave was gone for good? He thought again of the stories his mum had told him on the phone, her voice a blend of sadness and disapproval as she'd read articles from the local paper. Rafael Martinez was a man on a downward spiral; his name linked to drugs and brawls and petty crime. His life was branded as *chaotic* by lawmakers and *tragic* by those who defended him. Even then, Dave wished he could help. But he could not; did not. Eventually he told his mum he didn't want to hear about Rafa and so the stories stopped. But did the crimes? If he'd been locked up for *years* he must have done something bigger, darker, more damaging.

'Don't let it put you off, though,' said John. 'We've all made mistakes we don't want to be judged by.'

They both went quiet after that, took a few sips in silence. Then Dave necked the remainder of his drink in one extended gulp, pushed his empty bottle into the space between them. 'I need to use the bathroom,' he said, then pushed back his chair and headed inside without looking back. The cubicle smelled of some-body else's shit and the white walls were adorned with the usual graffiti. Often he'd read them, search for the funnies. But not today. He locked the door then slumped down as best he could between toilet bowl and door. He closed his eyes and let that old memory roll in again.

When Dave had walked free from court that day the press were waiting for him.

But so was Rafa, in a taxi, door wide open. They hadn't seen each other since Carmen's funeral, nineteen months earlier. Dave had reluctantly climbed in before reporters and photographers spotted him and together they'd returned to Musselburgh Harbour. For closure, Rafa had said. He'd whispered a prayer for his dead sister and pleaded for a new beginning with Dave. The distance had made his love even stronger, he'd said.

And just like that, Dave had known his plan had backfired.

He'd only stayed in Scotland because of the court case. He'd been banned from travelling abroad while he was on bail but after Carmen's funeral he'd fled Edinburgh and everyone in it. He'd built a quiet life for himself on the Isle of Harris; six hours from the mainland by ferry. Far enough away that loved ones knew he wasn't hoping for visitors. He'd hoped the time and distance would help Rafa understand that he'd meant what he'd said the day he'd moved out of their flat: their love wasn't enough; would hurt rather than heal him. Why? Because when he looked into Rafa's eyes he saw Carmen there as well.

He'd told him the same thing that day at Musselburgh Harbour. The court case was finally over, for good; and they were too. The family they'd hoped to build with Carmen and Suzanne had been blown to bits by the killings; as had his heart.

There was no going back.

First came tears. Then fury.

The first blow had landed on the back of Dave's head. Even now, so many years later, Dave remembered the shock when his face had hit the wet concrete of the harbour. When he'd rolled over he'd got a kick in the ribs for his efforts. Then Rafa had knelt down and leaned over him, one hand wiping away the tears that streamed from his beautiful eyes.

'*Please* don't leave again,' he'd said, as though he'd really believed a beating would convince Dave to stay.

A passer-by had called the police and Dave had sat on a bench with his back to the sea and his eyes on the ground as Rafa was dragged away by two police officers, screaming declarations of never-ending love. He'd refused to accept Dave had really ended it, for good. But Dave had made his decision.

The *we* that they were was over.

But what was time, or distance, when it came to a love like theirs? He was still looking for the answer when he heard the bathroom door open.

'Dave? You in there, pal?' John's voice was both soft and strong, somehow a comfort.

'With you in a sec.'

'Dodgy tummy, is it?'

'Something like that.'

'I believe you. Thousands wouldn't.' A pause. He stepped closer. 'You want to be left alone?'

'Aye,' said Dave, then realised he didn't. His mouth was on autopilot, automatically firing out the same old responses. He stood up, tugged open the lock, opened the cubicle in the same moment John pushed open the swing door to leave. The Irishman turned his head with the hinges.

'Was it something I said?'

'It's not you. It's . . .'

'Rafa, right?'

'Aye,' said Dave. He looked away as John's face fell. 'There's nothing going on with us, OK? I just need to ask him something. That's it. Me and him ended a long time ago.'

'Something tells me that's not entirely true. But either way, I've got bad news for you. I don't have his number. He didn't offer and I didn't ask. And I think you've missed the boat with that one anyway. Last time I saw him he said he was meeting an old boyfriend this week, seemed pretty sure they'd be getting back together. So maybe it's time you started looking for someone new?'

'Like you, for example?'

'Perhaps.' John smiled. 'Look, can I make a deal with you?'

'You can try.'

'I can't give you Rafa's number, but I'll buy the next round if you give me yours?'

Life whispered, *Say yes*.

Dave said no.

He left alone, walked up through the Old Town to The Meadows. He needed wide-open spaces and big skies, the opposite of tight nerves and the same thoughts on repeat. What had Rafa been jailed for? When would Amy be found? Who had been in his house and made the calls? Who had left those flowers at the memorial bench? And how was it all connected?

One thing at a time, Dave.

He sat on an empty bench beside one of the paths that crossed the playing fields. From there he could see

Arthur's Seat and the Salisbury Crags and the jumbled rooftops of university buildings and the old hospital now made into posh flats. Behind him a group of students played football on the damp grass, whoops and yelps the soundtrack of goals and saves. From time to time runners and dogs panted past, puffing out clouds of warm air. But mostly it was just him and his phone and the thunder of his own pulse in his fingertips as he typed *Rafa Martinez* into Google and pressed Search. If Rafa had been jailed for attacking Dave the day they broke up, almost twenty years ago, then it was unlikely to appear online. But more recent crimes would be all over the internet and social media.

Dave's brain worked faster than the internet, had painted dozens of detailed scenarios in his mind by the time the search results appeared on screen. The only photos and stories featuring that name were linked to a Spanish basketball player. Dave scrolled the images, searching for a match. Nothing.

Any stories featuring *his* Rafa were buried.

How else could he find out why he'd been jailed?

Easiest option was to ask Rafa directly but he still had no phone number, and no guarantee he was even in the city any more. What about DI Farida McPherson? If Rafa had been in jail in Scotland there was a chance she'd know the reason. But given their history she was unlikely to do him any favours. Who else could he turn to?

The only other people with an obvious connection to all of this were Amy's family: Jonathan Todd and his wife. The urn in *their* garden shed had the same bird motif as the neglected memorial bench that *must be* dedicated to Rafa's sister Carmen. It could be a coincidence – or it could mean their family was somehow connected to Carmen and Rafa. Would they know why he'd been jailed? Maybe. But with Amy missing they wouldn't be in the mood for a chat – especially not with Dave. They might even call the police if he turned up at their door again.

But right now he had no other options.

He checked the route on his phone. A bus went right past the end of that street but he couldn't bear the thought of being seen or questioned or pitied by colleagues. News of his suspension would have spread quicker than Covid. He flagged down a taxi just as the rain started. The driver was talkative, filled the twenty-minute ride with a non-stop moan about her last holiday in Gran Canaria. Not the same as it used to be, she said, and Dave wanted to shake her, tell her nothing was, ever.

'You can drop me here,' said Dave, slicing in two a story about cockroaches crawling up the plugholes in a hotel bathroom. He opened the car door, pulled out his wallet, paid his dues. The rain was belting down now so he bowed his head and tugged up the hood of his jacket as he walked. Just outside the Todds' house he stopped mid-step, right foot suspended above the brown shell of a snail that was heading in the same direction he was. He sank down, one hand on the ground to steady himself. When he reached out, the snail sucked its eyes inside its shell for protection. Rafa had read a book about snails once, kept coming out with all these facts about their teeth and how far they travelled in a single night and how, in desperate situations, the females could somehow reproduce without a male mate. But most of all he loved the scars on their shells, jagged lines drawn in a paler colour that meant the shell had been cracked or broken but had then regrown. Rafa had been amazed by that, would often hunch down and check the spirals on snails for signs of previous damage. *They're survivors*, he'd say, and Dave would tell him not to be such a soft bastard. And he was, at times. But on the days when anger blinded him he'd stamp on their shells for the fun of it.

Dave bent down, moved the snail off the pavement then opened Jonathan Todd's front gate. The first thing he noticed was a CCTV camera, mounted on the wall above the front door. It looked brand new, and blinked at him as he stepped forward to press the bell.

Was someone on the inside watching him right now? And if they saw *him* on the doorstep, would they answer?

After a few more nervous breaths he had his answer. Stomping footsteps in the hallway and the rattle of keys. He braced himself for the rage of Jonathan Todd. He'd either be dragged back to the shed or smacked in the face; was debating which he'd prefer when the door was pulled wide open. Dave's heart leapt into his throat, ready to jump out of his mouth and run.

It wasn't Jonathan Todd.

Instead, framed in the doorway of that house, was a woman he'd thought he'd never see again: Suzanne Forsyth. She was Carmen's heartbroken wife, Rafa's furious sister-in-law, the woman whose dreams of a family had been destroyed by the killings.

She greeted him without looking at his face, had one of those tired smiles born from good manners: gently tugged lips ready to catapult polite apologies to unexpected callers. *Not today, thanks.* She was gazing over his shoulder, already thinking of someone, some-where, something else.

Then Dave pulled down his hood and spoke to her for the first time in almost twenty years.

'Suzanne,' he said, and when his voice reached her she stiffened as though he'd plugged her into a wall socket. Now she looked at him. Now she was listening.

The last time they'd stood this close his scalp had still been covered in thick brown hair that he would run his hands through when he was nervous. He'd been wearing a short-sleeved shirt to show off a new tattoo that said more than a wedding ring ever would.

A name inked on to his arm could not be shifted or lost, swapped for another one when he got bored. Today it was faded and hidden; served only to remind him of all the worlds that had been lost between that day and this.

He wished she'd speak, but she was already pushing the door shut. Dave reached out, held it open. Why was Suzanne here, now, in the house of Jonathan Todd? Was *she* Amy's mother? Dave's thoughts raced, became a blur. 'What are *you* doing here, Suzanne? I don't understand how—'

'Have you taken her?'

'What?'

'Amy. She's . . . missing. And I know it's you who made that hoax call, telling the police they'd find our bodies here. You're sick in the head, Dave. And I know you were here the other day, sneaking around in the garden when I was out.' She pushed against the door again, trying to shut it. 'If you've done something to Amy, I'll—'

'I've never even talked to her, Suzanne! I—'

'Only because she wasn't stupid enough to phone you. The police told me all about the pub, Dave – that you told her pals me and you were *old friends* so they'd trust you, give you her phone number. And don't try to tell me that wasn't you.'

'I admit that was me, OK? But—'

'Save your excuses for the police.'

EMMA CHRISTIE

Even from where he stood, Dave could see the trembles that shook her hands. *His doing.* She started punching a number into her phone, but dropped it. Dave reached forward, picked it up, handed it over. But not before he'd seen the screensaver photo. Suzanne and Amy, side by side, arm in arm. The sight of it shook him. Those two faces, together again, twenty years after he'd ripped them apart. What was going on?

'I followed Amy off the bus, OK?' he tried again. 'But only because . . .' He looked away, couldn't bear to see her face when he said it. 'Only because I thought she was *Carmen.*'

Suzanne flinched and drew back, blinking, as if she'd been slapped in the face.

The last time that name had passed between her and Dave, the body of Carmen and her unborn child had been there as well.

CHAPTER 32

Carmen was three months pregnant when Dave killed her, on his twenty-eighth birthday. The date became a death day, his age irrelevant, every passing year a reminder of those he'd stripped from others. He'd only lived his half of the story but he'd heard the rest of it so many times in court that it felt like a memory of his own.

*

It started with Carmen, roaring up to Musselburgh Harbour on her motorbike and thumbing for Suzanne to climb on the back, as usual. Suzanne, her wife. Suzanne, the one person on earth she loved more than her twin brother. Suzanne, angry after yet another disagreement with Rafa. Suzanne, insisting on driving so she could let off steam.

Thought it would *do her good*.

As they switched places on the bike and secured their helmets and prepared to set off, Dave was approaching Musselburgh in his car. He was thinking of birthday drinks on the beach, maybe a barbecue if the weather held. He spotted Rafa as soon as he turned into the harbour. He was standing at the far end, hood up, back turned to the sea, arms tightly crossed. There was no sign of the women. Dave tooted his horn, felt his insides glow when Rafa looked round, found him, smiled. Just like that, everyone else faded away. Dave was in love and felt blessed and sure that was unchangeable. As he glanced at Rafa he pictured them here as old men with whitening hair and withering bodies, still enjoying walks and pints at Musselburgh Harbour; still exchanging lingering looks that held more meaning than any words ever could. He imagined Suzanne and Carmen as well, strolling behind them along the harbour they all loved so dearly. But soon there would be children too, and he wondered again how these new lives might change them. Would there be enough love in him for all of them?

All of this in the time it took for his eyes to meet Rafa's and for love to rise up and fill every part of him. Three seconds, maybe four. A look, a smile, a calm certainty that this was It.

And then, a thud.

The impact was a bubble, burst.

It was a soundless, tiny fraction of time, a pea under a tower of mattresses. He braked hard, saw a flash in the wing mirror, the momentary shifting of light and shadow on glass. He stopped, checked both mirrors and at first saw nothing and nobody. It was just him and the car and the world framed by the windscreen: a rare blue sky over Musselburgh Harbour, punctuated by Rafa's waving hand and the swaying masts of little boats. He often paused his memory there, enjoyed just for a few minutes more the weightless joy of a life without tragedy, grief, regret, guilt.

It never lasted. He climbed out of the driver's seat and into hell.

Both women were sprawled on the road behind his car.

For a few seconds everything stopped except the motorbike's engine, still running. Its heavy metal body lay on top of Carmen. She was still and silent in her leathers, going nowhere. The glass visor of her helmet was slicked with blood on the inside. Beside her, Suzanne was moving, groaning, trying to roll on to her side.

'Don't,' said Dave, because he knew what she'd see.

Suzanne's first scream was muffled, trapped inside her helmet. She tugged it off and pulled herself on to her feet and shouted at Dave to not just stand there, to help her move the damn bike. He did as he was told and then she was on her knees again, leaning over Carmen. She pressed her ear into her chest and then her belly, the places where hearts should be beating. Dave dropped to his knees too, desperately checking and rechecking for a pulse in Carmen's neck, chest, wrist. All he found was blood, oozing. It was warm and sticky on his hands and would leave a permanent stain.

Behind them, chaos.

A fisherman was calling an ambulance and someone else was directing traffic away from the scene, shushing the drivers who were honking their horns. A young lassie sprinted over from the pub across the road, said she was a medical student and would do what she could and then she was on her knees beside them and trying, trying, trying but there was nothing to be done. Behind Dave an old lady was saying the Lord's Prayer, getting half the words wrong. It was only when she finished and placed a hand on Dave's shoulder and crossed herself with the other that he realised she'd been praying for him; for forgiveness, probably. It was already too late for Carmen.

Over Suzanne's shoulder schoolkids stood like weeping statues, holding each other's hands instead of shaking them off. It was like being in a play, a full cast of extras gathering round the tragedy at the centre of the stage.

All eyes were on him and Suzanne and the body between them.

There were no sirens yet but there was another sound, a *tick-tock-tick-tock* that would not shift and never lost its rhythm. A flash of orange drew his eyes back to his car and the indicator that had been seen too late or not at all. Dave hunched down beside Suzanne and placed a hand on what used to be Carmen and wished the sound were coming from deep within that body. A heart, restarting. A life, not over. Their world, cracked but not broken.

Tick-tock-tick-tock-tick-tock.

When Rafa burst through the crowd Dave wished he could freeze the world and everything in it. He was running towards them, calling out the name of the only person who had never let him down. But now, for the first time, she wouldn't answer.

Dave stood up and stepped around the body and blocked Rafa's path, tried to hold him back. 'Don't,' he said, again.

But Rafa did. When he reached the body he roared at life and at death. And then at Suzanne. Rafa's words were almost blocked out by the approaching sirens but Dave heard all he needed to hear.

Your fault, your fault, your fault.

Sirens were silenced and doors were slammed and footsteps came, quickly. Paramedics brought the sound of fat zips and ripped Velcro and words that Dave didn't know the meaning of but understood anyway. When they'd done all they could, a paramedic with long hair approached them. She smelled vaguely of turpentine and said her name was Stef and she was kind and efficient and good at her job but Dave willed her away because he knew she'd bring something he could never escape from.

Those words, said out loud for the very first time. 'She's dead.'

It wasn't so much a declaration of war as the words that ended peacetime. There was nothing fancy about them, nothing overtly emotional. It was just a statement of fact, a simple sentence that a toddler could probably string together if you gave them half a chance. It was a textbook phrase on a foreign languages course. Subject, verb, adjective. She was dead.

And that was it: the end of a chapter.

The next one featured a police station and a courtroom.

When Dave was charged, Rafa called the police and the papers and Suzanne every name under the planet. It was *her* fault. *She'd* been driving the motorbike. *She'd* been angry and driving dangerously as a result. *She* was the killer.

The police disagreed.

When Dave pleaded guilty to causing death by careless driving, Rafa called out to the judge and was removed from the courtroom. Then came doctors and psychologists who spoke of Dave's *mental fragility* since the accident and his *previous good character* and the *significant risk* of self-harm and the debts piling up in his bank account. He'd left his job but refused to claim benefits because he didn't deserve help. His lawyer spoke of heartache and tragedy, claimed that Dave had been punished enough. The judge agreed. He was given a two-year suspended sentence – meaning he wouldn't be jailed. He'd serve his time at home.

The courtroom erupted. He was guilty, but he would walk free. Outside court, Rafa was waiting for him with a broken heart and open arms and a taxi to whisk him away from the reporters who wanted to talk about justice, and Dave evading it. They all tossed out the same predictable question: *How do you feel?*

Dave left without answering, with Rafa; then he left Rafa, for good.

He was still loved, aye, but he did not deserve it.

He'd gone to Suzanne's house that same day, before his sentencing at court. He'd expected to be jailed and wanted to apologise, face to face, while he still had the chance. But she wouldn't let him in. They'd spoken through the letterbox and Dave had said sorry in a dozen different ways, sworn he'd only maintain contact if she asked him directly. *I'll get in touch when I'm ready*, she said. Then never did.

But here, now, almost twenty years after the killing, here he was.

CHAPTER 33

'You need to go.' Suzanne grabbed her phone from Dave's hand and shoved the front door, trying to close it. 'I'm going to call the police, right now. I warn you.'

'Just give me a minute.'

'I'm giving you nothing.'

'Please, Suzanne.' He stepped closer, climbed the first step. From there he could smell the bitter tang of alcohol blended with the thick reek of tobacco on her breath. Her skin was a map of red blotches connected by lines too deep and dark and grey for a woman her age. Guilt tugged his chest a little tighter. 'I'm just trying to understand.'

'There's nothing for *you* to understand. Just tell me where Amy is. And bring her *home*.'

She slammed the door so hard the whole house shook. Dave bent down and pushed open the letterbox, could see Suzanne still standing in the hall, shaking; staring at the door. Last time they'd spoken it was a different house and a different door. But little else had changed. Suzanne, bereft. Dave repenting. Carmen, dead. And somewhere in the shadows was Rafa, alone with a grief that had festered and turned into fury.

'I swear to you I've nothing to do with Amy disappearing.' He spoke softly, slowly, as though he was coaxing her back from a cliff edge. 'And I promise I didn't know *you* lived here or I'd never have come.'

'Then why did you?'

'It's actually Jonathan Todd I'm looking for.'

'My *landlord*?'

'He's your landlord?' Dave's jaw dropped, feelings sliding from stunned to stupid. 'But I thought he . . . lived here? I thought he was . . . your *husband*. I thought Amy was his *daughter*.'

'I'll assume that's a very bad joke?'

'He's listed online as owning this property,' said Dave, holding open the letterbox with one hand. Suzanne glared at him. Even from there, her expression was easy to read. *Disgust*.

'Jonathan owns both houses. He lives next door with his own wife and his own daughter. Not *us*. Me and Amy rent this place from him, have done for years. And by the way, after all the trouble this week Jonathan's fitted security cameras at both properties – so this is being recorded. They're checking footage at the university halls as well, trying to see when Amy last left there, and who she was with.'

'I promise you it wasn't me.'

'Then who was it?'

'Have you thought it might be . . . Rafa?'

'Impossible. He's in *prison*; there's no way—'

'He's out. I saw him when—'

'Out?' The look on Suzanne's face switched from disgust to something far worse. *Fear.* 'Are you *sure* it was him?'

'Positive.'

'Where?'

'The same pub I went to, looking for Amy.'

As soon as the words left his mouth, Suzanne clasped one hand over her open mouth then slumped down on to the bottom step.

'No, no, no, no, no.' She looked up, red eyes leaking all over the place. One hand was cupped over her mouth. With the other she held her belly. 'If you know where Rafa is, you need to tell me. If there's *any* chance he's got her . . .' She squeezed shut her eyes, shuddered. 'If he harms her, I swear to God I'll kill him myself.'

'Come on. I don't think Rafa would—'

'You don't know, do you?'

'Know what?'

'What he . . . *did* to me?'

'I know you and he don't see eye to eye, but—'

'Are you two back together? Is that it?'

'I've seen him but nothing happened. And nothing will happen.'

'And he didn't tell you?'

'Tell me *what*?'

'Got some advice for you, Dave. Next time you see him, *ask*. Ask why he was jailed. Ask him what he did to me. Then maybe you'll understand why I don't want that man anywhere near my daughter.'

She gripped her belly, hands shaking, then turned her back on him and clambered upstairs. Dave called again through the letterbox, trying to keep his voice soft. Nothing.

When his own phone started ringing he pulled it out, sighed when he saw who was phoning. Diane from the National Museum. She was co-ordinating the awards event – and he was late. They'd all been asked to arrive early for a photo shoot with the Lord Provost. All the good people of the city, gathered together to be honoured and thanked. They were told they could bring *loved ones* with them to the event. Dave felt sick at the thought.

He cancelled the call and ducked down to Suzanne's letterbox but his phone started ringing again. Crystal now. He cancelled the call and silenced it, stuffed the phone into his pocket. They could all wait.

When the next call came in, his phone stayed silent but vibrated against his leg. He'd switch it off, had enough on his plate without this. But when he pulled it out there was a new message on his screen instead of a missed call. It was his next-door neighbour, sending a photo of several cigarette butts, bent and twisted and soggy on varnished wooden decking.

They were roll-ups, homemade.

We need to talk about your Airbnb, the message said. *Urgently.*

Dave screwed up his face, quickly texted back to avoid more calls. *Wrong neighbour.*

His phone rang almost immediately. Dave went to cancel the call but answered by mistake, got an earful from his neighbour before he had the chance to hang up.

'I won't keep you. Just to say, I know you're running a holiday let from the flat and I know you probably don't have the right paperwork for it. The council need to give permission, don't they? So in theory I should report you. But I won't, OK? We'll keep it between us. But can you ask them to stop flicking their cigarette butts into my garden? I'm convinced the decking will disappear in a fireball and I'd rather it didn't.'

'Who's *they*?'

'Come on, Dave. The ones who've been staying. A couple, I assume. I heard them on Sunday afternoon when I was out doing my roses. She was upset. He was doing a bad job of comforting her. And they're at it again. Smoking and crying. I was tempted to speak to them myself but I thought I better take it up with you directly. If it was only once I'd let it go but I've found a dozen roll-ups in my rose beds and it's beyond a joke. Obviously they can smoke all they want. It's your garden and it's a free country. I'm just annoyed when I find fags in my garden. No offence.'

'None taken.'

'Anyhoo, I trust you'll take it from here? As I said, they appeared to be having another disagreement just before I left. She sounded really upset, and he sounded like an arsehole, if you'll excuse my French. Didn't seem like the right time to pop my head over the fence, so—'

'Hang on – are you saying they're at my house *right now*?'

'Yup – or at least they were when I left a few minutes ago.'

'Did you *see* them?'

'No, but I could hear them well enough. Unless I climb on a ladder I can't see past that big tree of yours – in fact, that's something else we need to talk about. Another time, perhaps?'

'Aye,' said Dave. Then he hung up, stunned. Now he knew for sure that somebody had been in his house on Sunday when he was out – and they were there *right now*. According to his neighbour it was someone who smoked roll-ups. It *had* to be Rafa. And who was the woman he was with?

The obvious answer was Amy.

Dave ducked down and shouted loud as he could through the letterbox. 'I think Rafa's got her, Suzanne. And for some reason they're . . . at *my place*. Call the police, send them to my mum's house. Tell them I'm on my way there.'

She didn't reply. But before Dave left he heard her voice; raised and in a panic. By the sounds of it, she was already talking to the police. Suzanne told them she had an intruder outside her house, as well as information linked to the disappearance of her daughter. She spoke quickly, stumbling over her own words again and again. But Dave got the message loud and clear. Words tumbled out of her, but two hung in the air; left a stink that would not shift.

The first word was Rafa. The second? *Rapist*.

CHAPTER 34

The stitch in his side was a killer. Dave stopped and bent over, heart thundering, hands on his knees, parched lips sticking to his teeth. Half-past seven on a Thursday evening and there were no bloody taxis anywhere. Or buses, for that matter. But he'd run all the way to Portobello if he had to; even if the effort gave him a heart attack. He had to reach Rafa before the police did.

He knew Rafa better than anyone, knew how to cool the rage in him instead of fanning the flames. If Amy *was* with Rafa and she *was* in danger, Dave was the one man on earth who could probably help. Send in the cavalry and Rafa would be furious – and that was bad news for everyone. Dave had been there, bore the scars to prove it.

And now it seemed Suzanne did too. Rafa, a *rapist*.

Sickened didn't capture it. Had he misheard or misunderstood? There *must* be another explanation. But as he ran, Dave's mind raced; threw out memories of Rafa's tiny revenges. Rafa had always loved telling the story of the time he'd got his own back on a boss who'd called him useless. He'd made him a coffee laced with laxatives – and the scraps of rotting insects he'd peeled off the fly paper in the staff room. He'd crushed their crisping bodies with his fingers then sprinkled the dust of them into the coffee, hidden under a cap of frothy milk. His boss had drunk the lot, then leaked at both ends.

The story always triggered groans and laughs and Rafa always lapped them up. Same thing had happened when he had told friends about the time he caught an ex-boyfriend cheating on him – with a woman, no less. He'd hacked into his ex's email account and sent intimate photos to every one of his contacts – then phoned the woman's husband to let him know his wife preferred sex with gay men. Bomb dropped, he then stood back and admired the damage.

It was easier to react with aggression than to sit down and calmly deal with the hurt; easier to close down than to open up to grief and all that it meant. Everything was easier than forgiving.

The way he presented them, Rafa's tales were about honour and restoration of justice and him standing up for himself. But, looking at them now, Dave could see the source of his actions was something much more childish; and, at the same time, something much darker.

They were revenge attacks, plain and simple.

Hurt me and I'll hurt you back, but worse.

And, if Rafa had already raped Suzanne but still wanted revenge, what was his intention now?

Dave upped his pace, almost wept with relief when a black cab pulled in to the kerb to drop off an older couple with a little white whippet. He signalled to the driver, got a thumbs-up and collapsed, exhausted, on to the back seat. The driver punched Dave's address into the satnav then pulled into the evening traffic jams. The sight of static cars on all sides tugged Dave's nerves so to distract himself he pulled out his phone, and typed Rafa's name into the search box. Same as before, the Spanish basketball player dominated the search results. Then, with disbelief, Dave typed those four awful letters. *Rape*. Surely a story like that would have made the papers

Sure enough, the search engine dragged a few suggested articles out of the archives. The words he'd typed appeared in an academic journal about male prisoners reoffending once they were in jail. *Rapist Rafael Martinez* was one of the men used as an example. The words were written in bold in a sample of the article. Dave didn't click to read on, couldn't stomach it. The taxi pulled into the bus lane and accelerated, whizzing past dozens of static cars, while Dave hoped speed alone could release him from the crawling of his own skin.

The lad who'd picked him up looked too young to be driving and spent the whole journey talking to his girlfriend on hands-free. They were leaving that night for a holiday to Greece, were debating how many euros they'd need and how many bottles of sunscreen to pack and what time they'd need to leave for the airport. Dave wished for such simple worries.

He got dropped off in front of the garden gate.

From here, everything looked normal; exactly as he'd left it.

But what about the back garden? His neighbour said they'd been sitting there when he left. With any luck they'd still be there – whoever *they* were. Dave stepped off the path and on to the narrow gravel lane that led to the back of the house. It was always cold and damp and in shadow. Dave placed each foot as softly as he could, listening for voices. Nothing. He inhaled, a sniffer dog searching for traces of tobacco in the air. Nothing. When he reached the corner he stopped for a moment, then took a deep breath and stepped into his own garden. It was empty.

Dave wasn't sure if he felt relieved or disappointed. Either way, that initial feeling was blown out of the water when he turned towards the house. Something was very wrong.

The back door was wide open, kicked in. Someone was inside, standing with their back to the kitchen window. Dave ducked back on to the side path, heart thumping in every inch of his body. What now? He closed his eyes and listened, was almost sure he could hear a man's voice, talking quietly. Was he on the phone, or was someone in there with him?

And was it Rafa?

He should definitely call the police, right now. Or call Farida directly? Better. He patted the back pocket of his jeans, fished out the card she'd given him at the pub. *Detective Inspector Farida McPherson.* The one and only. He dialled her mobile number and pressed the call button, felt sick when it started ringing. He had to get her here, fast. And quietly.

'DI McPherson speaking.'

She'd answered on the second ring, efficient as ever. Dave crept back towards the front door; spoke in a half-whisper with his hand cupped round the mouthpiece. 'It's Dave Kellock. I'm at home and—'

'Sorry, who is this? I'm struggling to hear.' Behind her voice were the sounds of her job, life, world; all the things he hoped she wouldn't bring here. Sirens, slamming doors, raised voices.

'It's Dave. Dave Kellock.'

'Mr Kellock? You'll have to speak up. There's a lot of background noise.'

At the other end of the line, Dave heard the sound of a woman shouting. Then Farida covered the mouthpiece with her hand, muffled the sounds of the world where she stood. Dave strained to hear, then realised after a few moments that a woman was shouting at his end of the line as well. And, close by, movement.

Heavy steps, moving from his back door down the garden path. From there, if they turned, they'd see him. And from there, if he spoke, they'd hear him.

'I'm at my house, in Portobello. Get here, fast,' he said, loud as he dared, then hung up. He flipped the volume control to silent then quickly typed out the same words in a text to Farida. Job done, he stuffed the phone back into his pocket and held himself tight against the side wall.

The footsteps stopped and instead came the sound of someone shaking the wooden door of his shed. He kept his lawn mower and garden tools in there, sealed with an oversized padlock that was supposedly impossible to pick. It'd keep them busy anyway. Dave took his chance, retraced his steps to the garden and his back door. The woman who'd been shouting wasn't there. He glanced towards the shed then sprinted from the corner of his house to the back door. And he was in.

He stood for a moment in his own kitchen, dazed; staring at two unfamiliar jackets that had been tossed over the back of his chair. He'd grown up here, knew every corner of the place. But today the air was different; no longer his. He could definitely smell tobacco. It caught in his throat, dragged his mind to Rafa.

The next thing he noticed was the spray of blood on the wall.

He raced from the kitchen to the hall, heard the bathroom fan. He ran upstairs, taking them two at a time, the same way he did when he was wee. When he reached the top of the stairs he glanced over his shoulder, crept forward. In the same moment that he reached for the bathroom door the person on the other side turned on a tap. He heard the rush of water, the firing up of the boiler in the landing cupboard, the splashes of someone washing their face. But that wasn't all. With all of that came a sound that he knew well and had heard almost every day for the last two years. But it did not belong here. That sound would usually cheer his heart a little as he clocked on for a shift and headed towards the staff kitchen. Today it sickened him. Beyond his bathroom door he heard the familiar jangle of plastic bangles on a wrist. It wasn't Amy on the other side of the door.

It was Crystal.

CHAPTER 35

Crystal was dressed up fancy, draped from head to toe in leopard-print clothes. Her chest was laden with twisted plastic necklaces. She was holding her hands under the tap and her face in a grimace as she studied a blackening bruise on her upper arm. She didn't look up when Dave pushed open the door, nor when he stepped into the room and slowly moved towards her.

'Believe me now?' she said, dabbing at the swelling with a handful of wet toilet paper. 'He's not here and he's not in the shed and I'm only here because I'm worried about him, OK? And if you were a decent man, you would be too.'

'I'm right here,' said Dave.

Crystal whipped her head round, eyes wide. 'Dave! You *are* here!'

'Last I checked it was my house. Not yours.'

'I can explain.'

'Keep it for the police. I've already called them.'

'You're kidding.'

'Not laughing, am I?'

'What, you think I'm here to nick your shampoo or something? I'm here because I'm *worried* about you. I know I said I wouldn't go to the awards ceremony . . .' She shrugged. 'But that was *work* Crystal. *Boss* Crystal. Once I calmed down I knew I couldn't miss it, in spite of . . . everything. I nipped home, put on my finery and headed over there. First person I saw was Diane, in a total flap. She told me you hadn't turned up and weren't answering her calls. I *knew* you wouldn't miss something as important as that if you were feeling . . . like yourself. When you ignored my calls as well I thought maybe . . .' She bit her lip, cut eye contact. 'I just came here to make sure you were OK. When you didn't answer the door I came round the back, peeked in the window. Almost dropped dead when I saw blood on the wall. I really thought . . .' She sighed, stepped a little closer. 'After everything that's happened I thought maybe you'd . . . *harmed* yourself. There. I've said it.' She reached out, went to squeeze his arm, then hesitated. 'But if it's not your blood, whose is it?'

'I was about to ask you the same thing.'

'Meaning?'

'Have you hurt her?'

'Who? You're not making sense, Dave. The only thing that's hurt is your back door – and your shed, probably. Colin's work. He saw me getting dressed up and assumed I was off for a night of passion somewhere.

Followed me all the way to the National Museum and then here and is convinced you're now hiding to escape his wrath. He's on a rampage. I'm really sorry he kicked in your door – but at least it meant I could come inside and look for you.' She smiled. 'I'm *so* glad you're OK.'

'Who says I am?'

The words were still hanging between them when the bathroom door burst open.

'Hope I'm not interrupting a lovers' tiff?' Colin snorted after he spoke then marched inside, stood between them with his chest puffed out and his hands on his hips, the way a superhero would stand for the closing credits of a film. 'Where were you, then? Hiding in the laundry cupboard? I've kicked down two doors looking for you. Back door and shed door. And all at the request of my beloved wife. She got dressed up for you, Dave. Even got the razor out, so she was clearly hoping for some action. That's more than I get these days. Practically have to beg and, to be honest, it's rarely worth the effort. But then you know that already, don't you?' He grabbed Crystal's arm and pulled her away from the sink. 'Come on. We're leaving.'

'Get your hands off her.'

Colin laughed, turned to Dave. 'Or what? Want some more blood on your hands, do you? I guess you must have a taste for it.'

Colin dropped Crystal's arm and stepped so close to Dave that for a second their noses touched. The minty breath from before was tainted with stale tobacco. 'I'm sure Crystal would love to know all about it as well, so tell us. How did it feel to watch them die? I'm intrigued. Which heartbeat stopped first? The mother's or the baby's?'

Dave didn't answer. Crystal was staring at him, gaze as sharp and unwavering as a laser. Eventually Colin laughed, then stepped triumphantly into the awkward silence.

'While we're all here, I've got a question for my dear wife as well. Crystal, my love, would you like to tell Dave why you were here on Sunday? He told me he doesn't remember you being here.'

She flinched when he said that, glared at Colin. He sneered in return. 'You told *me* you were here though, didn't you? So either you lied to me, or Dave here is playing dumb. Which is it?'

'I was . . .' Her eyes flitted between the two men. 'I think we should talk about this at home.'

'And I think you should learn to tell the truth. You *know* what happens when you don't.' Colin reached for her, far too roughly. 'I'll get our coats.'

This time, she let herself be led. Dave blocked their path. 'You're going nowhere until the police get here.'

'You reckon?' Colin barged past Dave and out of the door, a silenced Crystal trailing behind.

Dave stopped halfway down the stairs, torn. Could he trust her? If what Colin had said was true, she'd been here on Sunday as well – exactly when the nuisance calls were made. He couldn't bear to watch her suffer, and yet maybe, just maybe, she was the source of all of this.

Colin dumped her in the hall then disappeared into the kitchen.

She looked up. Dave looked down. Their eyes locked. His heart cracked a little more. There wasn't room enough for all the rage in him. 'Before you go, will you at least tell *me* the truth?'

'I'm leaving,' she said, just as Colin reappeared with a coat in each arm. He handed a bulky purple coat to Crystal then tugged himself into a tight leather jacket made for younger, thinner men. 'Get a move on, woman.'

He waved a hand in front of Crystal's face, as if to check she was still alive. She stood still as death, staring at a yellow coat that was tucked inside her own. She was like one of those statues in Greece, a sombre face poking out from a mass of rumpled cloth, a hundred folds and creases making soft the stone. Then Colin yanked the yellow one out of her hands. 'It must have been hanging over the chair already,' he said, turning back to the kitchen.

'*Wait!*' Crystal's voice was trembling. 'It's not my coat. But it's . . . hers.'

She bit down on her bottom lip now and turned her head back towards the staircase; to Dave. She took the coat from Colin's hand and held it towards him. But it wasn't an offering.

It was an accusation.

The coat was bright yellow, with two rows of buttons up the front. The first time Dave had seen the girl on the bus she'd been wearing a green coat with the hood pulled up. But the second time he'd seen her she'd been wearing a coat just like this one, hanging loose over blue skinny jeans. She was wearing it in the photo Farida had shown him. Why?

Because that was what she was wearing the last time she was seen.

CHAPTER 36

Crystal held the yellow coat with both hands, studied the front then flipped it round and looked at the back, the sleeves, the cuffs, the buttons, the collar, as if somehow she'd find a logical explanation there, caught between the threads. But all she found was a few discarded hairs, stuck to the soft cloth.

'I saw her photo on the community Facebook group,' she said. 'They said . . . she's missing. Nobody's seen her since last night.'

'I've no idea where that came from,' said Dave, nodding to the coat. 'Or the blood in the kitchen. I'm trying to *protect* the lassie, not do her harm. Someone's trying to set me up. You've got to believe me, Crystal.'

'Actually, I don't.' Crystal slipped her hand into both pockets, started tugging out the contents and handing them to Colin. 'With any luck she carries ID,' she said. 'I want to be sure it's definitely the right person . . . before we call the police.'

There was a scrunched-up paper hankie, a crumpled receipt with the change wrapped inside. A hair bobble that had lost its elasticity. A few loose coins, including a euro. A stub of a chewing gum packet with a few squashed pieces still inside.

A business card for Charlie's Cabs taxi company.

Crystal held it up to the light, flipped it over a few times so she could read both sides. The card had a glossy surface and bashed corners and a logo Dave recognised and the power to change everything. He reached into his back pocket, pulled out the bank card receipt Rafa had given him at the shore. Dave's chewing gum had hardened inside but he unfolded it carefully, without ripping. Most of the writing was obscured by Dave's gum but the name along the top was clear. It was a payment to Charlie's Cabs.

It could be a coincidence. Charlie's Cabs was a fairly large taxi firm, based a few streets away in Portobello. They'd have dozens of cars and hundreds of customers. It looked as if both Rafa and Amy had used them recently – but had they taken a taxi together? And if they'd left from Dave's house – *without Amy's coat* – where had they gone?

'We need to call the taxi firm,' said Dave. 'Maybe they can tell us where she is. And who with.'

Crystal glared at him. 'Let's leave the investigations to the police, shall we?'

Rarely had he seen a look so precisely and deliberately sharpened into a dagger. The gentle camaraderie that had always bound them had hardened into something else; something jagged and brittle and ready to snap.

His last bridge was burning. The fuel? Facts.

A girl was missing and her jacket was in his house.

A girl was missing and there was blood on his kitchen wall.

A girl was missing and Dave was already accused of harassing her and her family.

'I know how this looks, Crystal. But if you just let me explain? I—'

'Leave it, Dave.'

'I think she's in danger. *That's* why I called the police. I wouldn't do that if I had something to hide, would I?'

'We'll be the judge of that.' Colin grabbed Crystal's elbow and led her to the kitchen. Dave stayed where he was, listening to them argue in muffled tones. Then he pulled out his phone, dialled Charlie's Cabs and prayed for them to pick up fast.

They didn't. Moments later Colin reappeared, snatched Dave's phone out of his hand and cancelled the call. 'If you're phoning a friend, you're too late. We've called the police. They're on their way. And with any luck you're on your way to court, *again*.'

Crystal came out of the kitchen, mobile clutched to her chest. Her cheeks were flushed – either from stress or a hard slap. She spoke like she was reading auto-cue, announced they wouldn't leave until the police arrived in case Dave *tampered with the evidence*, or tried to *flee the scene*. Then she looked right at Dave and said she wouldn't forgive herself if *something bad* had happened to that girl.

So that was how she saw him now: both a criminal and a coward. He wondered if part of her was enjoying the drama of it. Everybody gets a wee thrill from blue lights and sirens until the day they stop outside your own front door.

Colin ordered Crystal to stay in the hall, with the jacket, waiting for the police. Meanwhile, he led Dave to the kitchen, pulled out a chair and nodded for him to sit, the way a bad cop would do in a crap TV show. He stationed himself at the broken back door, arms crossed, legs wide, somehow managing to chew gum and sneer at the same time. He was like that bouncer nobody wants to meet outside a club, the one who'd cause problems rather than cure them.

'So Crystal tells me you're a bufty boy.'

Dave hadn't heard that phrase since school. It was almost comical to hear it now, and from a teacher who was touching fifty instead of some scrawny bullies with baggy jeans and a fear of their dad.

'You'll get plenty of action in the jail, then.' Colin sniggered, clearly delighted with his originality. 'Here was me thinking you were up to no good with my Crystal. But you probably wouldn't know how.'

Dave didn't grace him with a response. He was just stunned that Crystal had ever agreed to marry a man like this one. There must've been a large sack of cash involved. Either that or he had something on her. Did Crystal have secrets she didn't want the world to see?

Not much was clear in this situation but one thing was definitely true. She'd lied to them both. Crystal had told Colin she was at Dave's house on Sunday. But Dave knew nothing about it. If Crystal *had* been there on Sunday and the nuisance calls were made on the same day, it was logical to think it was her who'd made them. It was either that or he'd had two intruders in one day: first Crystal, then the nuisance caller. But that seemed unlikely. She'd admitted breaking into his house today, for reasons she claimed were virtuous. But could he believe her? If she'd broken in today then it was possible she'd sneaked inside previously, most likely using the spare keys from his locker at work. That would explain how she got her hands on his old photos. But for what purpose? And was it really a coincidence that Amy's jacket and the blood splatters appeared at his house at the same time as Crystal and Colin?

Dave's gut kept telling him the same thing: he was being set up. Someone out there wanted to ruin his reputation, and ensure he was finally punished.

His mind was dragged back to the present by the sound of his doorbell, quickly followed by Crystal's voice in his hall, ushering police through to the kitchen like unwelcome dinner guests. The officers stopped in the doorway and introduced themselves. Detective Constables Deborah Halliday and Greg Martin. Colin switched back into teacher mode, offered his hand for shaking and his clichéd wisdom to anyone who'd listen. 'It's always the quiet ones, eh?' He tilted his head to Dave after he said it, face like one of those weeping virgins at the church.

Except Dave would slap it silly, given the chance.

'We'll take it from here, pal.' Constable Halliday waited until Colin left the room then knelt down and studied the blood spatter on the wall. She glanced at her colleague, eyebrows high. 'Best call the boss?'

Her partner nodded and went back to the hall, radio crackling. Halliday was now examining the splintered wood that used to be Dave's back door.

'Want to tell us what happened here?'

'That arsehole happened.' Dave nodded towards the hall. He could hear Crystal talking with the other officer but she was speaking too quietly for him to hear any details. He could imagine well enough. 'They've got the wrong end of the wrong stick. I've got nothing to do with that girl going missing, OK? But I *think* I know who she's with. We need to call Charlie's Cabs, right now. If Amy took a taxi with them they'll tell you where she went, won't they? Then you can focus on getting her back home instead of wasting your time here with me.'

'Always give advice to the police, do you?'

'No, but—'

'But nothing. We'll do things as we—'

'Rafa Martinez.'

'Sorry?'

'You need to find Rafa Martinez, urgently. He's not long out of jail, will be on your records. I'm *sure* he's with Amy, the girl who's missing. And he's . . .' Dave paused. What words could possibly fit? Dangerous? Desperate? The love of my life? Or that other, awful definition and all that it meant. A convicted rapist. It could not be right, surely.

But why would Suzanne lie?

'He's unpredictable,' said Dave. That much was true.

Halliday finished her inspection of the door then sat on the seat opposite Dave, studied him instead. What she couldn't see was this: he was just as splintered as that bloody door.

'And what is he to you?' she asked.

Rafa had been everything, once. And now? Would the love he felt finally dry up and peel off like old skin? Did rape and murder make old love disappear?

'Me and Rafa Martinez . . .' Those words had thrilled him in the beginning. He loved loving someone with a name that felt so foreign on his tongue. 'We were . . .'

'Together. Correct?'

The voice came from behind him, was followed by a sharp sniff. Dave whipped his head round. Farida McPherson was standing in the doorway with her sidekick from the other day; DS Effie Garcia. 'We'll take over from here,' said Farida.

A nod, a scurry, and the uniformed officers left.

Farida took Halliday's place at the table but occupied the whole room.

'This is quite the drama you're cooking up, Mr Kellock. We've had numerous calls to the emergency line, urging us to come to your property. Plus *your* call and text to *me*. Can I assume you've *remembered* something of use in relation to the missing person case?'

'I called because I thought she was here. Amy, I mean. But I arrived and found those two inside my house.' He nodded towards the hall. 'And they'd kicked in my back door.'

'I see that.' Farida scanned the room, processing every detail. Her eyes twitched when she saw the blood on the wall, then returned to Dave. 'Let's return to what you were telling my colleague. About Rafael Martinez.'

It was years since Dave had heard anyone use Rafa's full name; his Sunday name, the one they'd have read out in court. The one they'd use in prison. Farida did everything by the book.

'You know him?'

'I'm asking the questions. You're a couple, correct?'

'We were, a long time ago. But we're not now. And won't be.'

'Save your breath. We've got footage.'

'Of?'

'You and Mr Martinez. Together. This week.' She pulled out her phone, started scrolling. 'I've got it here somewhere. Perhaps that'll help to jog your memory?'

'My memory's just fine, thanks.'

She put down her phone, screen against the table top. Then she leaned forward.

'I'm going to ask you some very simple questions. I highly recommend you answer truthfully. Did you see Mr Martinez this week?'

'Yes, I did. By chance.'

'Just the once?'

Dave winced. He knew how this would sound. 'Twice. But it wasn't planned.'

'A happy coincidence, was it? Serendipity at play?'

'Something like that. But—'

'And what about the missing girl? We both know you tried and *apparently* failed to find her at the MOB Bar. But how many times *did* you see her this week?'

'Twice. On my bus.'

'Never here?'

'Never.'

'And yet it appears her jacket found its way into your kitchen.' Farida's face was carved in stone. Not a twitch. Not a single hair would dare move without

278

written permission. She stared at him until he looked away then pushed back her chair. 'We need to continue this conversation at the station,' she said, standing up and signalling for Dave to do the same.

He stayed put. 'Are you *arresting* me?'

'Not yet.'

'Then I won't go. We're wasting time. I think Amy's with Rafa. And I think . . .' Dave bowed his head, studied the table top. He'd had this thought in his head for hours but hadn't allowed it to fully form, never mind saying it out loud. But here it was, the inexplicable truth: the reason Amy looked exactly like Carmen and Rafa. 'I think he's her dad,' he said.

CHAPTER 37

The word *dad* was still hanging in the air between them when Halliday knocked on the kitchen door then stepped inside. Her face was red and sweating and one arm of her uniform was smudged with white dust. 'Boss? You got a minute?' She widened her eyes after she said it; she'd be crap at poker. What had she seen?

Farida nodded. 'Mr Kellock was about to accompany me to the van. Perhaps you can escort him? It's parked directly outside.'

'I've already said I'm not going.' Dave stood up, headed for the back door. Farida blocked his path. 'I'm telling you,' he said, 'it's *Rafa* we need to be looking for here. And if you lot won't look for him, I will.'

'Rest assured it's under control.'

'Meaning?'

'We're very well aware of the . . . connection . . . between him and . . . the missing teenager. I can discuss this case with you only because the details are in the public domain. But I do wonder if you know the full circumstances of the . . . incident?'

'I know enough.'

'Based on what you just told me, I doubt that. Let's continue this conversation later,' she said, then she and Effie left. The stairs creaked as they climbed them. Dave tried to work out which room they were heading for. His bedroom, probably. But then he heard it: the metallic groan of the attic ladder. What had they found up there? He hadn't gone up there since Monday – but had somebody else?

'Come on, you.' Halliday talked to him as if he were a misbehaving dog. She thumbed towards the front door, expected him to obediently follow. He did. Until she stepped into the porch. Then he slammed the inner door behind her, flipped the lock and sprinted up his stairs two at a time. The landing was empty but the attic ladder was down. He grabbed both sides and hauled himself up. Farida and Effie were crouched at the far end. Their heads turned when Dave pulled himself inside but they were too far away to stop him; and too late to shield his eyes from the chaos that lay beyond them.

The stacks of neatly labelled boxes had been moved, opened, tipped out. The floor of the attic was a sea of old crockery and vinyl records and some of his mum's old tablecloths. But that was nothing compared to the walls. Someone had pinned photos to every inch of every surface in the attic. The pictures were all his, peeled from the old albums that he'd packed into boxes and sealed with thick tape and not looked at for years. Now the albums were lying open on the floor with broken spines and sticky yellowing pages. He'd left them here when he'd fled Edinburgh all those years ago; found them again when he was clearing out the house after his mum died. Part of him had wanted to bin them or burn them, deliver himself from the temptation of ever opening, looking, remembering. It would do him no good to see once again the worlds he'd destroyed. But in the end he'd felt guilty at the thought of dumping them. It would have been a final insult to the dead. Instead he'd shoved them to the back of the attic and his mind, done his best to forget about them.

'Please leave,' said Farida.

Dave heard, but did not move or look at her. His eyes scanned the walls, the scraps of his old life, on show. Every photo showed the same thing. Dave, back in the days when he had hair and hope for the future. Rafa, when all he was was loved. Carmen, full of life that would be stripped from her before age could wrinkle her cinnamon skin. The photos screamed love.

But the absence in them screamed even louder.

Suzanne was missing from every photo; not because she'd been behind the camera or was somewhere else when they were taken. Time and again, her face had been carefully cut out with scissors.

Dave looked again at the floor and he saw her there, rough circles with Suzanne's snipped-out face on one side. She'd been beheaded, over and over. The four of them, reduced to three not by death but by a sharp metal edge. In every photo, Dave, Rafa and Carmen were together, without Suzanne; just like the old days Rafa so clearly idealised. And if you didn't know about Carmen you might think it was somebody else standing with them. Amy.

'Who would do this?'

'I was about to ask you the same thing, Mr Kellock.'

Nothing felt impossible now. Rafa had been jailed for raping Suzanne, but was that brutal act enough to quell his loathing for her? From what he'd said to Dave it was clear he still blamed Suzanne for the death of his sister; which in turn had led to the end of him and Dave. Did Rafa feel as if he'd punished her enough, or was there worse to come? Dave could see the answer now, staring at him from the attic walls. Suzanne would be removed, discarded.

Maybe it wasn't Amy who was in danger after all.

'You need to get someone round to Suzanne's house, right now,' he said. 'When I left there she—'

'You've been to her home?'

'By accident. I thought it was Jonathan Todd who lived there.'

'The last time we spoke, you told me Jonathan Todd meant nothing to you. Now you tell me you were trying to visit him? Which one is it?' Farida's look could have killed from forty paces and aye, Dave felt halfway to dead.

'It's not what you think.'

'Heard that one before. Now tell me – when and where did you see Suzanne Forsyth?'

'I was at her house half an hour ago. She told me what Rafa did. That he . . .' Dave paused, plugged his stinging eyes with his fingertips. If he let the grief start running it would not stop. 'I honestly didn't know she lived there, OK? And I didn't know Rafa had . . . raped her, until today.'

'Ignorance is bliss.' She edged along the attic floor towards him, swallowed his shadow with her own. 'But be sure of this. Ignorance of the law does not remove one's responsibility to act in accordance with it.'

Farida turned to Effie, spoke too quickly and quietly for Dave to hear. She nodded, then tugged her radio and sent an incomprehensible coded message to someone in a room far different from this one. When Farida turned back to Dave her message was loud and clear.

'Given the fact that you *forgot* you knew Jonathan Todd, there's something else I want to double-check. One question, and I want the truth this time. Where is Amy?'

'I've no idea.'

'Shall I phrase it in a different way?'

'The answer will be the same. *I don't know*. I'm racking my brains here, trying to think where Rafa might have taken her.'

'Try harder. You'll have plenty of time on the drive to the station. Let's go.'

Effie moved past Farida, forcing Dave back towards the metal steps. She went down first, probably to stop Dave fleeing. He followed, took a final glimpse at the attic before he lowered his head. All the scraps of his life, scattered. He vowed to bin the lot of it if he ever made it back home. Nostalgia was a waste of time; never did anything for anybody except hold them back.

'Get a move on, pal.' Effie was standing with her hands on her hips on Dave's landing, staring up. Dave moved one foot off the top rung, was lowering himself downwards when he heard a crunch and muttered curses from Farida. Composure, lost, when she thought nobody was watching. Dave knew only too well the weight of an armour like that one.

He paused, lifted his head above floor-level again as Farida reached out and gathered pieces of broken glass and wood in her palm. A photo frame, crushed. Even from there Dave could tell which one it was and what it meant. It held a photo of him and Rafa with Carmen and Suzanne, lounging on a boat they'd rented one weekend from a fisherman in Musselburgh Harbour. The day Rafa had asked him to marry him.

The day Dave had said yes.

Rafa had made a framed copy for all of them to mark the occasion but Dave had left it behind when he'd fled the city after the end of his court case. He'd packed it into that box, hidden under old crockery alongside the newspaper cuttings about the killings. His little tortures, packaged up and hidden out of sight.

But now the photo was here, on the floor of his attic.

There was only one person who'd know to look for it, or care if Dave had kept it. He thought of Rafa at the Joppa rocks, refusing to accept Dave's rejection. Why? Maybe because he'd been here, found the framed photo and come to his own conclusion about what that meant. Why would Dave keep it all these years? Because he still loved him.

In Rafa's mind it would prove that they weren't yet broken.

But if it *was* Rafa who'd been prowling around his house, was he also the nuisance caller? A penny dropped, hard. Maybe the calls had been made *not* to incriminate Dave but to frighten Suzanne, to let her know one terrifying fact: she was not yet forgiven.

Farida turned then, still holding the broken pieces in her hand. 'Should have watched where I was going,' she said, and Dave remembered how those same words had felt in his mouth, back in the place where all of this had started. Musselburgh Harbour had always been Carmen's favourite place, but after the accident Suzanne had vowed never to return.

Dave stared at the broken pieces and thought about punishment, about all the ways humans made each other suffer. Rafa blamed Suzanne for killing Carmen and her unborn child, then losing Dave. But what twisted logic had driven him to *rape* Suzanne?

Surely it wasn't about sex, but control and power and settling scores. Surely it was inspired not by lust, but by loathing. It was a textbook act of revenge; violence triggered by the misguided belief that it would make him feel better.

You ruin my life; I'll ruin yours. But revenge never heals a wound. It keeps it open.

Meanwhile, Suzanne had kept going, had the child, grown a flower in the mud. Amy, who looked just like Carmen – and just like Rafa. How did it feel for Suzanne, to look into that face every day? And had Rafa known about Amy before his release? When he saw *that face*, he'd be in no doubt that she was his. It made sense, kind of, that he'd want to be part of her life.

But if Rafa had Amy, where would he take her?

Dave searched the faces in that photo and, just like that, found the answer. He knew Rafa's mind and how it worked. If he wanted Suzanne to suffer even more he'd take Amy to the place Suzanne feared most. She would be desperate to find Amy; would do anything and go anywhere to get her back. And if Rafa wanted to add to Suzanne's suffering, he'd lead her back to *that place*.

Musselburgh Harbour, the place Carmen was killed.

Effie tapped Dave's foot, impatient. Dave glanced at Farida above him, thought of the van that waited for him outside. If he ended up in some interview room at the police station he'd be there for hours. Anything could happen in that time.

Anything.

Decision made. If they wouldn't do what he asked, he'd have to do it himself.

Dave reached into the attic, grabbed the broken wooden photo frame. With one hand he tossed it into Effie's upturned face. It was enough to take her by surprise, make her step back, blinking, cursing. Enough time for Dave to zip down the stairs and flee. First came shouts, then footsteps followed behind him, along with a few warning words from the voice in the attic, and in his head.

'You'll regret this, Dave Kellock.'

He ran through the kitchen and out into his garden through the smashed-up back door. Nobody was watching the side path and Farida's van was parked to the right of his front gate, flanked by Halliday and Martin. Dave turned left and legged it.

A few minutes later he arrived, out of breath, at the office of Charlie's Cabs.

The door was open and inside there were three desks, two of which were occupied by balding men and all of which were messy: stacks of paper folders, takeaway cups and open bags of boiled sweets. The walls were decorated with fading maps and photos of Edinburgh's most famous landmarks, snapped in the sunshine then trapped forever inside a clip frame with silver edges. Every phone in the place was ringing but nobody was answering any of them, apart from a young lassie in a white tracksuit who was doing her best to slouch on one of those rigid armchairs that usually only exist in old folks' homes. Pink plastic, cushions hard as a kick up the arse.

Dave cleared his throat, got a nod in reply from one of the men. 'With you in a second, pal.'

Two or three excruciating minutes later, he turned to face Dave, eyes sagging like a washing line hung with wet towels.

'Where you heading?'

'It's not a taxi I'm needing,' said Dave.

'We're not hiring, if that's what you're after.'

'It's just some info I want.' He put on his best Cheerful Bus Driver voice. Light, jovial, trustworthy. He'd rehearsed what to say during the run there, repeated the story. He was needing to know all the days and times he'd taken a taxi in the past week. 'A request from my boss,' he said, remembering to roll his eyes when he said it. 'I use the taxis for work. The boss is wanting details.'

'You could just have phoned and asked us, pal.'

'Och, I was passing anyway.'

The man wrote down Dave's address on a scrap of used printing paper then headed back to his computer, humming a tune Dave vaguely recognised but couldn't place. He typed with one finger, eyes plodding between the paper and the screen to make sure he was spelling it right. Dave could have typed quicker with his big toe. After a dramatic poke of the return button he leaned back in his chair, looking as though he'd just defused a bomb.

'Got you. Last taxi left your address about an hour ago. There was another yesterday. And the day before . . .' The man started clicking his tongue. 'There's been one a day, pal. All of them heading to Musselburgh Harbour. All booked by someone called . . . Rafa Martinez.' He squinted doubtfully at Dave's pale, Scottish face. 'That sound right?'

'Aye,' said Dave, as all the blood in him rushed to his cheeks. It sounded right.

But it meant something was very, very wrong.

CHAPTER 38

Dave called Farida on his way to the harbour. When she answered he spoke quickly, told her everything he knew before she had the chance to read him his rights. 'Rafa's got Amy,' he said. 'I'm sure of it. He took a taxi from my house to Musselburgh Harbour, less than an hour ago, and I think Amy was with him – without her coat. I'm arriving there now but you should come, quickly. And tell Suzanne, please.'

He hung up before she could respond then pushed open his door before the taxi was fully at a halt. He dropped twenty pounds on the passenger seat and ran in the direction of the sea. The streetlights painted orange circles on the pavement but the harbour area was poorly lit. Few were the folk who wanted to come and stand at the water's edge once the sky was black.

He paused next to a ramshackle building at the entrance to the harbour, peered into the darkness. When the tide was in, as it was now, the water would be well over the head of any man. And cold. Humans could die within minutes in a sea like this one.

He ran down the harbour wall, towards the neglected bench.

He was sure that he'd find Rafa here, with Amy; that he could ask questions and be answered.

But no. There was no sign of any human here except for the names on the memorial benches – the ones who were already dead. Dave turned, shivering as he peered into the darkness.

The only movement came from the fishing boats bobbing in the blackened harbour, flag ropes tinkling against the metal poles. None was illuminated, but a few of the larger ones would have a lower deck, sealed off from searching eyes.

He could probably climb on board a few of the boats from the harbour steps, see if he found them there. But the hard reality was this: even if the taxi had dropped them here they could be long gone; could be in a flat or a car or in a boat that had already lifted its anchor and sailed off.

And aye, he'd missed it.

Then from behind him, a fizz and a gurgle. A bottle being emptied, water being sloshed on to a hard surface. He turned back to the black water and the boats it held.

'Is that you, Rafa?'

Dave's voice boomed in the still night air. He called out again, as loud as his dry mouth would allow. Nobody replied. He was about to try a third time when he heard a clatter and a clunk. Then, from the darkness, came a voice that used to light up every part of him.

'You come here often, *chiquito*?'

Dave froze, eyeing the endless dark. 'Rafa?'

'The one and only. How did you know I'd be here?'

'Let's call it fate.'

'I knew you'd see sense in the end.'

Dave followed Rafa's voice to a narrow stone staircase at the end of the harbour, leading downwards. The black sea lapped the bottom steps. Two or three fishing boats were moored there, painted hulls squeaking as they bounced gently off buffers made of used car tyres. The smallest was old and white with a fat green stripe and the name *Freedom* painted on the side. It was the same boat they'd rented all those years ago. At one end was a cabin big enough for two men. The other end was open to the elements. A narrow bench ran along one side. And on it sat Rafa.

He tapped the bench and smiled, signalling for Dave to join him.

'Knew you'd come running back to me in the end.'

'I'm not here for you, Rafa. I'm looking for Amy.'

'Aren't we all?'

'Where is she?'

'Come here and I'll tell you.'

'This isn't a game.'

'Of course it is. You're just choosing not to play.' Rafa shrugged then looked away, turned his attention to a roll-up cigarette that he was flipping between his fingers. 'Fag?'

He laughed after he said it and something like rage sparked in Dave's chest. Nerves tightening, jaw clamped, fists following suit. He slipped the moment his feet touched the top step, swallowed a yelp, flattened his hands against the damp walls to steady himself. After that he pulled out his phone, used the torch to illuminate the slippery black seaweed that coated some of the steps. One false move and he'd be in the water.

When he reached the bottom step Rafa stood up, reached out a hand. 'Welcome aboard,' he said, and Dave wished he had the balance to refuse Rafa's outstretched fingers but it was that or the freezing sea so he took it.

Rafa's hand was sticky to the touch. Dave felt the boat lower in the water as he stepped on to the tiny area of deck. He wobbled again and Rafa gripped tighter. His saviour, as always. But when he regained his balance Dave tugged his hands free and rubbed them on his trousers. They stayed sticky. He peered at them in the dark, then looked at Rafa. He'd sat down again but his eyes were on Dave, watching his shifting reactions; enjoying them.

Dave turned his torch beam on himself, then Rafa. Rafa held up his hands in protest, palms out. 'You trying to blind me now?'

Dave didn't answer, couldn't take his eyes off the smudges of blood dotting Rafa's soaking-wet T-shirt. Every part of him was drenched, dripping wet with something else that was thicker than water. It took Dave a few seconds to register what could be so greasy, so sticky to the touch, so pungent on the air. Petrol.

Rafa clamped the roll-up cigarette between his lips, spoke out of the side of his mouth. 'You got a light?'

Dave backed towards the cabin, gripped it for balance. The paint was rough against his fingers, flaked off when he tried to get a firmer hold. The water in the harbour was calm and still but the boat lurched from side to side when they moved, controlled by the weight of them. 'Don't do anything stupid, Rafa. Please.'

'Too late for that.'

'Where is she?'

'Who?'

'Amy. Your . . . daughter.'

Rafa laughed. '*Daughter*? Says who?'

'I worked it out.'

'I'd love to see your evidence.'

'I know you . . . *attacked* Suzanne. I know you were jailed for it.'

Rafa laughed again, but it wasn't the sound Dave remembered. This laugh came from an empty place rather than a full one. 'I can assure you I'm not Amy's dad.'

'But you did . . . *rape* Suzanne?'

For a moment silence divided them. Dave prayed for an angry denial. He'd choose a fist in the face over a confession like this one.

'I thought hurting her would help,' said Rafa, and something in Dave's chest slammed shut. Maybe that was it; the moment love ended.

If Rafa felt the change it didn't show. He kept talking, blaming.

'But I've done my time, and then some. I got ten years, then eight more for protecting my cellmate when the junkies jumped him. Bastards came at me with a knife, slashed my face, and somehow I was the one who ended up with extra jail time.'

'Why, Rafa?'

'Ask the prison wardens.'

'No – I mean why hurt Suzanne like that? Why would it even occur to you?'

'I wanted her to suffer as much as I had, to leave a scar on her.'

'And you didn't think she'd been punished enough, losing her wife and baby?'

'What about me? I lost my sister thanks to her. And I lost *you*.'

'She didn't force me to leave.'

Rafa sighed. 'There you go, defending her as usual.' There was anger in his voice now, rising.

Dave glanced at the harbour steps, his escape route. Now, the steps were further away than before.

'Surprise!' Rafa held up the mooring rope, untied. The boat was drifting away from the harbour.

Dave sidestepped, leaned over the edge, reached for one of the old car tyres hanging on the wall. The boat lurched to one side and Dave with it. He gasped, sucked in the smell of petrol. They hadn't drifted far, but still dry land was out of reach.

'Maybe *now* we can have a proper conversation?' said Rafa, tucking his cigarette behind his ear. He budged along the bench to make room for Dave then tapped the space with the fingers of his right hand. And in his left? He now held a lighter.

CHAPTER 39

Dave sat down, as far away from Rafa as possible. Still, there was only an inch between them.

'I'll give you five minutes, Rafa, then I'm calling the police.'

'Good luck getting signal out here.'

'Then I'll shout. Or swim. Whatever's needed. But please: tell me where Amy is; what you've done to her.'

'You've got that question the wrong way round.'

'Meaning?'

'You should be asking what *she's* done to *me*. And the answer is? *This*.' He tugged his petrol-soaked top. 'It's *this* or I go back to prison, and I just won't. All I wanted was for us to be a family, Dave. Me, you and her, together forever and all that. That's why I wanted her to see your house: to know she had another home, with us. I didn't think you'd mind once—'

'Wait. It was *you and Amy* who broke in?'

'We didn't *break in*. I used a key.'

'What key?'

'Your mum's spare one, from the plant pot.'

'You're kidding.'

'Nope. Poor show, Dave, not checking. I wonder if your mum left it out there for you, hoping you'd come home when she was still well enough in the head to recognise you.'

That hurt. Dave clamped his jaw, tried to pretend it didn't. He didn't want to fan the flames. Hoped there would be no flames in the first place.

'How did you know you'd find me there?'

'I didn't. Went there as soon as I was released from prison a couple of weeks ago, expecting to find your mum. I was going to ask her for your phone number, or an address. Nobody answered the door, so I waited. And then I saw *you*, walking up the street with a key in your hand. The bald head confused me a little but I'd recognise you anywhere. The way you hold yourself, the way you walk.'

'And you didn't think of saying hello, rather than stealing a key and sneaking inside?'

'I was worried you wouldn't want to see me.'

If only. 'How many times have you been in, since then?'

'Only a few. But listen. None of this was planned.'

'Does that make it any better?'

Another shrug. 'I wanted to see who you'd become, if you'd found someone else, if you still . . . thought about me. I went back early the next morning and when I saw you leave for work I sneaked round the back and checked that old plant pot. When I found the key I took it as a sign. Promised myself I'd have a quick look inside and go. But I felt happy there, among your things. The prison set me up in a hostel but I wanted a *home*.'

'So you hijacked mine?'

'I didn't *hijack* it. I want to share it with you. And with Amy. As a *family*. When I found that framed photo of us in the attic – on *this* boat – I knew that deep down you wanted the same thing. If you *really* didn't want to marry me, you'd have dumped that photo a long time ago.'

'A man's allowed to change his mind.'

'True. Not so easy with the heart, though, is it?'

'And what about *Amy's* heart? Did she *want* any of this before you barged in and blew her world to pieces? How did you track her down in the first place?'

'Easy. I found Suzanne on social media and searched her contacts list. Sent Amy a private message, explaining who I was and asking if she'd consider meeting me. She replied the same day, told me she'd spent her whole life looking for a face that matched hers. She was still too young to apply for information about her blood family but had been planning to start researching as soon as she turned eighteen. I saved her the hassle. We met on Sunday afternoon, almost twenty years to the day since the accident. But it was perfect timing. She'd just moved out of home to start university, so we could meet without Suzanne knowing anything about it.'

'And you took her to *my* house?'

'I couldn't take her to the homeless hostel, could I? She wanted to meet in public the first time so I brought her here, to Musselburgh Harbour. Sat her down on the bench I put in place for Carmen twenty years ago and told her the truth about Suzanne. Explained that she wasn't really her biological mum. That she'd killed Carmen – and the baby that would have been her sister. I told her about you as well, you know. About *us*. I showed her that article in the paper. I'm proud of you, Dave. And Amy will be too.'

He looked at Dave, smiling. But the venom soon flipped it.

'But you know what *Suzanne* had told her? That she'd got pregnant with an anonymous donor from abroad, that she'd never find out who her dad was. Amy had been lied to her whole life. And then she met me.'

Rafa paused to silently congratulate himself. Dave eyed the lighter but he'd passed it to his other hand. Dave would have to stretch across Rafa to reach it.

'I'm the only person who's ever told her the truth. About who her dad is. About who her mum killed. Amy had never even *heard* of Carmen. Can you believe that? She was very upset, obviously. I suggested she could come back to *mine* to calm down and talk some more; told her we could even phone her mum and demand the truth.'

'And that's when you took her to *my* house?'

Rafa nodded. 'I knew you wouldn't be there until much later on – thanks to the work timetable on your fridge. Might sound silly but I thought Amy would trust me more if she saw I had a nice home. Once we got there she called Suzanne a few times to get her side of the story but she was too nervous, kept hanging up the moment Suzanne answered.'

'And you called from *my* landline, right?'

'How did you guess?'

Dave sighed. 'The police told me *someone* had been making nuisance calls to that number, from my house. And that *someone* had then called the police from my phone to report a serious crime, claiming they'd find the body of a woman and child at Suzanne's address.'

Rafa smiled for a second, but then it hardened. 'And they would, if they looked hard enough. Before she left Amy told me that years ago she'd found an urn in the garden shed, decorated with swallows. Her mum told her it belonged to some distant relative. But it *must* be Carmen – the swallows would match her tattoo. Can you believe that? Carmen and her baby, packed away in a garden shed to rot. I was furious, called the police to give her a fright, and to let her know I was on to her.'

'I think you've caused Suzanne enough damage already,' said Dave. 'Did you tell Amy *that* part of the story? About why you were jailed?'

Rafa's smile dissolved. 'She knows, OK? And I'd have told you the truth as well, when the time was right. And then . . . it would have been like the old days, wouldn't it? Us and Carmen. Before Suzanne came along and fucked everything up for all of us.'

'You're . . . deluded. Amy's not Carmen.'

'I *know* that. But she's got the same blood. We're family. Me, you and her.'

'I'm not part of that family any more.'

'What are you talking about?' Rafa screwed up his face and then, suddenly, he pulled his eyes as wide as Dave had ever seen them. Just for a moment, his face softened and Dave caught a glimpse of the man he'd loved, once.

This was his chance.

He leaned in, slowly, as if for a kiss. The smell of petrol caught in his throat when he drew in a breath and pushed down with his feet then launched himself forward, snatching at the lighter in Rafa's hand.

He missed. The soles of his shoes were wet from the steps, made him slip and tumble off the bench instead. He was pathetic; fell clumsily into the puddles that dotted the deck. They were cold and sticky but not made of seawater. An empty petrol can lay on its side by his feet.

And, above him, Rafa still held the lighter.

The boat was a bomb, ready to blow.

Dave closed his eyes, waiting for the flick of a lighter. There was a certain inevitability to it, a comfort even. The wait was over. For twenty years he'd known he'd get the punishment he was due: that he'd burn, one way or another. He had just never imagined it would happen right here, in the same place as the killings. He'd never use a word like *karma* in public but maybe that was what this was. All he could smell was salt and petrol and the blood that was leaking from his lips. All he could hear was the gentle gulp of the sea against the bottom of the boat and Rafa breathing; too fast, too heavy. It'd stop soon enough.

'You really don't know, do you?'

Dave opened his eyes, saw endless black skies and stars that shine long after the flame in them is dead. And Rafa, waiting for an answer; smiling as if he loved him.

Dave felt sick, sad, defeated. 'Don't know what?'

'That she's *yours*.'

'Who is?'

Rafa opened his mouth to speak but then sounds from beyond the boat came between them. A car door, slamming shut. Footsteps, getting louder, closer. Then Suzanne's voice, screaming the same word over and over. 'Amy!'

CHAPTER 40

All of Dave ached. He tried to sit up but could not. Rafa's feet pressed down hard on his chest. He struggled to talk. Any harder and he'd struggle to breathe too. Maybe that was the point. And maybe that would be better than burning.

Back on the harbour Suzanne was still shouting into the darkness. 'Where are you, sweetheart?' The sounds of the sea almost swallowed her. 'Please, Amy. Please.'

'There's no need to get hysterical, Suzanne. You *know* what happens when you're angry. People get hurt.'

'Rafa?'

'The one and only.'

'Where is she? If you've *hurt* Amy I'll—'

'She's not here.'

'But the police called me, said they thought you *had* her. Dave said the same. When they mentioned the harbour, I just knew . . .' Sobs shredded her voice. 'They said they were sending officers here, told me not to come, warned me you were dangerous. As if I didn't know that already.'

Dave felt sick, needed out. He forced his chest upwards, tried to wriggle free. Rafa pushed down harder. 'Nice try, *chiquito*. But you're staying here with me.'

'Who are you speaking to?' Suzanne's voice was closer now. She must be right at the edge of the harbour, by the bench. Standing in Carmen's favourite spot. 'Amy, are you there?'

Dave went to shout but Rafa covered his mouth with a petrol-sticky hand; answered for the pair of them.

'It's just me and Dave.'

'I *knew* it. *Knew* I couldn't trust the pair of you.'

'You're a fine one to talk.'

'Meaning?'

'Meaning you can't be trusted either. Dave still doesn't *know*, Suzanne.' Rafa laughed that empty laugh. 'So should you tell him or will I?'

'Just tell me where Amy is.'

'Only if you tell Dave what he needs to know.'

'Please, Rafa.'

'Begging won't help. I thought you'd have remembered that.'

'What have you done to her?'

'All I've done is tell her the truth.' Rafa smiled as he spoke; he was enjoying this. 'You should try it some time.'

'Don't you dare tell me how to be a mother.'

306

'And what about Dave? Should we tell him how to be a father?' Rafa leaned forward after he said that and whispered warm words in his ear. 'She's made of you, *chiquito*.' Then he touched Dave's face and softly turned it towards his own. He smiled, and it reached his eyes. There was love in there somewhere. 'We can be a family. You, me and Amy. I'm her uncle. And you . . . you're her *father*.'

A bomb could have dropped in Musselburgh Harbour and Dave would barely have noticed. '*I. Can't. Be.*' Every word hurt, for a hundred different reasons. 'Carmen's baby . . . died . . . with her.'

'There was one embryo left. One of Carmen's.' Rafa paused, let the enormity of that fact sink in. It was too much, too much, too much; a whole world shifting.

Dave had been a key part of Suzanne and Carmen's beautiful plan.

Once the embryos were created, Carmen would carry Suzanne's child and Suzanne would carry Carmen's. Their two children would be born of both of them, and Dave.

The pregnancies would come from bank loans instead of biology; trips to foreign IVF clinics instead of early nights at home. The family would be theirs but Dave and Rafa would have been part of it; related by blood to the new lives Dave had helped create. But it was Dave who'd travelled abroad for appointments with Suzanne and Carmen, gasped when they'd told him how much it cost. But it was the only way the two women could create new life together, to know that the humans they made belonged to both. Each child would be born with the face of the other.

They'd all agreed from the start that Dave would be present in their lives as a friend but not as a father. He didn't want the title or the responsibilities it would bring. This was their dream and their children, not his. They'd got pregnant at the same time but Suzanne's had failed and the grief of it had surprised them all. Doctors used words like *high-risk*, suggested she *think twice* before trying again. Meanwhile, Carmen bloomed. Pregnancy suited her, and the growing excitement eased the pain of Suzanne's loss.

Then the accident smashed their beautiful plan to pieces.

Suzanne's biological daughter had died with Carmen and as she'd sobbed with Dave on the bloody tarmac she'd said the same thing over and over: that was the end of their family. Nobody had ever spoken of the embryos that remained, and after the court case, Dave had fled; never imagined that one day he'd come face to face with one of them on his bus.

But now he knew.

The girl on the bus was not the ghost of Carmen, Rafa's twin sister and the woman he'd killed. Nor was she a baby created with hate instead of love, when Rafa raped Suzanne. Amy was Carmen's child, made twenty years ago in a laboratory test tube, with Dave's help.

Amy had been carried by Suzanne. But she was Dave and Carmen's biological daughter.

'You know the worst part?' Rafa raised his head now, spoke loud enough for Suzanne to hear. 'There was only one tiny part of my twin sister left on this earth and *Suzanne* took it. Told nobody. Not even me. Not even *you*. Why do you think she didn't show up at court? She was *already* pregnant with Carmen's embryo and didn't want anybody to know. Lucky for her you pleaded guilty and she didn't need to stand as a witness.

'She must have been worried she'd be found out, when you turned up at her door after court. You told me yourself you thought it was odd when you went there and she wouldn't even open the door. Made you speak through the letterbox. That's why, Dave. She didn't want to be seen. Didn't want you to know she was carrying a child that wasn't rightfully hers.'

'And when did *you* find out?'

'The day you left.' Rafa looked away, towards the horizon. 'After our . . . *argument*, at the harbour.'

'The only person arguing was you, Rafa. All I was trying to do was help you understand why I had to leave. Didn't expect a fist in my face for the effort.'

'I was heartbroken. And angry.'

'That's no excuse. You should have respected my decision.'

'But it *wasn't* really your decision, was it? You came to meet me after you'd talked to Suzanne and suddenly you wanted to leave me again? What poison did she plant in your mind? When you walked free from court I thought that was the start of a new chapter, not the end of us.'

'And you thought punching me would make me stay? And getting arrested?'

'I wasn't *arrested*, Dave. The police gave me a warning then let me go. They warned me to stay away from you and I agreed. But they didn't mention Suzanne so I went straight to her house from the police station. I just wanted to *talk* to her, Dave. To get an explanation. To find out how she'd persuaded you to leave. But she wouldn't open the door and when I pleaded she laughed and said you were better off without me. Said Carmen would have been *ashamed* of me. That was the final straw. I was sick of playing the game by her rules when she was to blame for all of it. So I went round the back, kicked in her kitchen door, found her cowering in the kitchen like some kind of pathetic animal. I noticed the bump right away, asked her straight out who the baby belonged to. When she told me . . .' Rafa's head and hands were shaking with the fury of it. 'She betrayed us all, Dave. Said there was no reason for her to tell us that she was carrying Carmen's child. *No reason?* That child is my *only* blood relative. My *only* family. But you didn't care about that, did you, Suzanne?'

Rafa turned his eyes and attention back to Dave. His voice relaxed but his words were loaded. 'I was so angry, Dave. I'd have killed her there and then if it wasn't for the fact she was carrying part of Carmen with her. And part of you. That baby was made of you and her and I loved her even then. Our Amy. I'd *never* have caused her any harm.'

'But you thought it was OK to *rape* her mother?'

Even if Rafa had replied, no words were enough.

Then into the space between them slipped a sound Dave had spent twenty years dreading. A police siren, getting closer. Dave turned his head, saw blue flickers in the black sky. He heard footsteps, thundering along the harbour, getting further away. Suzanne must be running towards the police cars. She'd bring them here and he'd be saved; safe. They both would.

For a moment, hope surged in him.

But then he felt Rafa tense, tighten his grip on the lighter. What would happen if the police tried to take him by force? Dave knew Rafa well enough to know he'd never back down. He'd flick-flick-flick until the flame caught, and took them with it.

Dave had to get off this boat.

'I want to see Amy,' he said.

'Join the club.'

'Can you take me to her?'

Rafa shook his head. 'I wish.'

'She's reported as missing, you know. Not been seen in almost twenty-four hours; since last night.'

'And what – you think I've *harmed* her? You've all lost your minds.'

'So you've not seen her?'

'That's not what I said.' Rafa rolled the lighter between his twitching fingers. 'I only went to the MOB Bar last night to meet her and her pals. *That's* why I was there. We'd arranged it.'

'But at mine, you said—'

'That I hadn't seen her there. And it's the truth. She didn't show up. So after I left yours I went to her university halls. I'd collected her there on Sunday, the first time we met. That's how I knew where her room was, and why I didn't think she'd mind me showing up. But things were different last night. It was late when I got there and she was with that stupid friend of hers. I wanted to chat but she turned me away, talked to me through the closed door, said if I wanted to speak I should phone her.

'When I asked what was wrong she told me she was just back from dinner with her mum. First time they'd seen each other all week. Said Suzanne broke down in tears the moment she saw her, then reeled off her sob story: how she'd got home from work on Sunday night to find the police inside, expecting to find the pair of them murdered. Suzanne had asked her if she had any clue who might have made the hoax call and

Amy had lied, said she had no idea. She knew it was me, of course, but didn't want her mum to know she'd met me behind her back. She didn't want trouble with her mum – or with the police. Told me she wanted to lie low for a few days and didn't want to see anyone. Not me, not her mum. Nobody apart from that friend of hers. Said she was going to stay with him. I warned him not to contact you, by the way.'

'What? Why? And how did you know—?'

'I overheard you chatting with them, just after I arrived at the MOB Bar. I was right behind you, Dave, heard everything you said – including your phone number. When I went to Amy's flat later I asked if he'd texted you yet. When he said no I warned him off, told him you were bad news anyway. Then I texted you myself.'

'*Pretending* to be him?'

'That was *your* assumption. Nothing I said in those texts was a lie. I said I was the man from the bar, and I was. I said I wanted to know what you wanted with Amy. Also true.'

'You manipulated me.'

Rafa shrugged. 'I was surprised you fell for it.'

'But I rang your phone later, at the beach. And it didn't ring.'

'Never heard of flight mode?'

Dave sighed deeply. 'Why would you do that, Rafa?'

'Because I knew you wouldn't agree to meet *me* but you were clearly keen to see that boy. I know how your mind works, Dave; knew that if we *accidentally* crossed paths again you'd think it was fate. And it was, kind of. But fate with a little help from me. Didn't expect us to end up on a railway line but . . . that's life.'

'It's not *life*, Rafa. It's lies.'

'For the greater good. And even if that lad *had* passed Amy your phone number, she wouldn't have got in touch anyway. Her mobile's been switched off since last night, probably to avoid my calls. I went back to her room early this morning but she didn't even answer the door. And she's blocked me online. Have you any idea how hurtful that was? So she's not *missing*, Dave. She's been hiding, *from me*.'

'Why would she put her mum through that?'

'Because I told her the truth and she's furious with her. She wanted her to suffer and I don't blame her. Suzanne had fed her lies from the day she was born.'

'Doesn't mean she doesn't love her.'

'And it doesn't mean she *does*.' Rafa gritted his teeth. 'It was *me* knocking on her door. *Me* who was calling her to make sure she was OK. *Me* who was sending messages online, letting her know she had a new house and a new family waiting for her whenever she felt ready. All I ever wanted was to bring the three of us together. That's why I was *so* pleased to read your text message confessions and see how desperate you were to meet Amy. It should have happened today, you know.' He glanced at his watch, smiling. 'Right now, in fact. I was going to bring her to the awards event and when you walked off the stage we'd have been there, waiting. Me and her. You and your *loved ones*, just like it said in the papers.'

Once again Dave had no words, and Rafa, enough for both of them.

'But that stupid friend of hers fucked it up for all of us. He texted me back this afternoon, said Amy needed to ask me something, face to face. I thought you'd be at work so I persuaded them to come to yours, so we could chat in private. She eventually agreed, but I could tell from the second they walked in the door that something was wrong. Amy didn't look at me the way she did the first time. She didn't look at me at all, in fact. Then the boy piped up, said they'd been shocked to find out I'd made that hoax call to the police and decided to do some research on me. Found out I'd been in prison. Knew I'd been done for rape. But the papers don't name the women, do they? And that's what Amy wanted to know. She said she'd never trust me again unless I told her everything. So I confessed, told her what had happened with Suzanne. And that was my first mistake.' When Rafa spoke again his voice cracked. 'She told me she never wanted to see me again. Then she said . . .' He was sobbing now. 'She said she wished I'd burn in hell.'

Tears dropped from his face to his elbow to the pools of petrol on the deck.

'I didn't mean to hurt anybody. But that boy . . . he wouldn't shut up. I just pushed him, not hard. But he fell, bumped his head on your table on the way down. Started bleeding. I tried to help but Amy pushed me away, got him to his feet. Then she screamed at me, said she was going straight to the police. Then they ran. Everybody runs from me in the end.'

Dave heard slamming doors and footsteps, someone comforting Suzanne. He couldn't hear what was being said but he'd recognise that voice from a mile off. A Glasgow accent, lightly rubbed down at the edges. Farida McPherson was here. And she wasn't alone. A third voice sounded on the harbour. Another soft voice, talking to Suzanne, through sobs. *I'm sorry,* she said, over and over. Dave didn't recognise the voice, but Rafa did. He sprang up, shifted his feet from Dave's chest to the wet deck.

'Amy? Is that you? I'm sorry, OK? Can we talk? Please. I didn't mean to hurt him.'

Dave eased himself up off the floor, into a sitting position. His body was cold and stiff and creaked with every move. He twisted round so he was facing the harbour. The boat had drifted even further from the steps, bobbed gently between the two stone arms of the harbour. On one side, Musselburgh; on the other, open sea.

He blinked when a beam of bright yellow light flashed over his face. Someone on the harbour had

316

a powerful spotlight, and they were in it. Farida McPherson's voice carried over the water. 'David Kellock? Rafael Martinez? Return to shore, right now.' Dave heard Suzanne's voice too, saying three words over and over.

I knew it.

Dave needed her to know this wasn't his doing. He tried shouting to her but his voice came out as a croak. He was desperate for a drink, and dry land. He tried again but only Rafa could hear. His grip on Dave tightened.

'Please don't tell me you're taking *her* side now, after everything?' Rafa reached for Dave, gently tugged his chin upwards so they were looking at each other, inches apart. For years Dave had woken up beside that face and felt only love. Now he saw the face of the woman he'd killed and a man destroyed by the grief of it.

'She ruined everything,' said Rafa. 'After Carmen died you were all I had and then . . . you left me too. I'll never understand why you did that to me.'

'Isn't is obvious? I had to escape the shame of it.'

'Of being gay?'

'Don't be daft. It's not *us* I was ashamed of.'

It was everything else. His heart broke every time he left the house. There was no end to the torture of it, no end to the ways life could have been so different for all of them if he could just change a few of

317

the tiny, hurried decisions that had led them all there; to the killings.

'Kellock! Martinez! Bring the boat to shore, immediately.'

There were more sirens now, more slamming doors. Dave could make out the bulk of a police van on the harbour, knew how it felt to be bundled into that windowless cage with a jacket hiding your face from the flash of cameras and glares of a crowd who wished you an unhappy ending; remembered only too well the loneliness of it, how the enormity of regret left so little space for breathing. Dave had spent half his life trying to be a hero just to prove he wasn't the opposite. But it always came back to the blood on his hands and his conscience, the two lives he'd snuffed out between one agonisingly ordinary moment and the next.

Rafa's hand twitched. His thumb hovered over the button on the lighter. One push, one flicker, and they'd both be gone. Could Dave save two lives now? And if he did, would anyone thank him for it? He pushed all thoughts out of his brain except this one. *Amy.*

Then, with all the strength left in him, Dave hurled himself forward.

CHAPTER 41

*N*ice *try*, chiquito.

But for eighteen years I've been waiting for today; for me and you and her to come together as a family. If the three of us were broken down to cells and chemicals and the pieces of us were spread out on a little glass plate and gazed at by scientists wearing white coats and goggles they'd nod and tick boxes and say yes, yes, yes even though the lawyers and judges probably think they know better and would tell me no, no, no. But we don't need laboratories or courtrooms to prove anything.

All we need is to clear the way for the part that comes next.

My dictionary describes family like this: 'a group of one or more parents and their children living together as a unit'. That's it. That's us. There's nothing complicated or surprising about it, and it never changed no matter how often I read it. In jail I'd sneak to the library when my tasks were done and tug the hardback dictionary down from the high shelf and flick *through its flimsy pages until I found the only word worth reading.* Family. *There's a greasy mark on the page now from all the times I circled that word with the fleshy part of my fingers and read the definition over and over like a prayer that would come true if I repeated it often enough. Now, finally, it has.*

Suddenly you're here and I'm here and she's here and you say we're over but I'm sure that's because you're nervous. I know it didn't end well between us but that's because it didn't really end, did it? A love like ours doesn't just fade away or disappear because of a change in circumstances. But now your face has become a big fat no, a refusal, a rejection of me and the life I've come here to offer. When you say it can't happen you're pointing to the rulebook instead of using both your hands to rip open your chest and see what it tells you. You won't meet my eyes now and I know it's because you'll never want to look away. You're shaking your head and keep opening your mouth as if you're going to speak, then you don't. A string of saliva links your lips, trembling in time with your inhale and exhale. But it's the space between breaths that really matters, isn't it? That's the part where life makes a choice.

To be, or not to be. To live or let go.

I stretch out one hand, reach softly for your mouth.

I break the string of saliva with my fingertips, smile as part of you dries on my skin and becomes part of me. That's enough, *you say, and you're right. That's good enough.*

Blood is thicker than water, *I tell you. And then I flick the lighter.*

CHAPTER 42

Next thing Dave knows he's under the waves and his chest hurts and he's looking at the night sky through freezing water that blurs the world, gives everything a soft edge. Even the pain and the panic of it. His eyes sting but he keeps them open, sees his own hands pass in front of him again and again as he tries to push himself upwards. When he bursts through the surface his mouth springs open and he sucks in all the air his body can hold. The next swell catches him in the face and he drinks in the sea instead. Then he's spitting and gasping at the same time, trying to force his breath in two directions at once. Close to his ears there are slaps and thuds and whooshes and whispers and sirens and shouts and he's so cold he knows he must be in danger now but his body won't do what he tells it: won't swim, won't relax and just float. There's terror and panic and relief that it's finally happening; that the waiting is over.

Dave had always known that, eventually, life would settle the balance sheet. It was simple maths; the killer's equation. If nature is in charge then there has to be equilibrium. That's the rule. Energy is always met with energy of an equal force. Translation: fuck up and you're fucked, sooner or later.

Another wave pushes his head under and then Carmen's there, with him, and he knows it's the end; that this is what death feels like. She looks different now, without blood on her face. She's as beautiful as he remembers and within touching distance. Guilt flushes through him for the two lives he ended and he knows now that he'll die with the weight of it still in him.

It's impossible to think that the world continues as normal on the other side of the waves; that the good people of the city are up on a stage, collecting medals and applause; that nosy locals are edging towards the police gathering on the harbour. In moments of death birds should fall and skies should split and everyone should stop and bow their heads the way they do in films when a loaded hearse drives past. *Her* hearse was silver instead of black.

Now, underwater, their eyes meet. There's no place for words here but his brain churns them out anyway. 'You can't be here,' it says and he closes his eyes, praying she'll be gone by the time he opens them. But she's still there, still looking right at him with an expression he can't quite place. Her long hair moves gently in the water, like swaying sea grass. But her movements are sharp, strong, sudden as they can be with the force of the sea upon them.

For twenty years, he's imagined this: her return. He wants to reach out and touch her, wonders if his hand would pass right through what seems solid. He knows every detail of that face, has spent hours of his life staring at the newspaper articles reporting the killing; staring into eyes that had been inches from his before they stilled.

'You can't be here.'

She's gripping him by the shoulder now, harder than before. Dave's eyes blur, remove the tiny differences between this face and Carmen's. She's right here, and breathing. For a few moments there's a lightness in Dave's chest that has been lacking for years. In, out, in, out. He can hear her breath; feel it. Or is it his?

It's then that he realises he's lying on something solid and dry. When he opens his eyes all he sees is a dark September sky. He tries to sit up but his body is lead. Then he vomits sea water and hands are on him and he's a carpet, rolled. A siren gets closer and then there's a man above him, dressed in green, smiling. He says his name is Andy, tells Dave he'll be OK. Dave wants to tell him he's never been OK; that he Just Doesn't Get It; that he does not deserve this easy kindness; the gentle squeeze on his arm. From here he can see the little boat, burning. Officers holding powerful spotlights, scanning the surface of the sea. Shouts, splashes, sobs. Farida McPherson, running towards a set of steps at the other side of the harbour.

He can't see Suzanne or Amy or Rafa, and when he asks the paramedic if there's anyone else in the water, he glances at his colleague, and that's enough of an answer. Dave heaves himself into a sitting position, tugs free from the hands that are holding him back. Then he's on his knees, dragging himself to his feet and to the water's edge. Farida is caught in the spotlight, thundering along the far side of the harbour. She throws herself down the steps, hands outstretched to someone or something that Dave can't yet see. The spotlight drops to the surface of the sea and they're in it, the two of them. Suzanne's on her back, kicking hard. One arm is hooked around Rafa's neck and his head lies loose on her shoulder. She's kicking hard with her legs and little by little they move across the harbour, towards the steps and Farida's outstretched hand. But where's Amy?

Dave wobbles, stretches out a hand to steady himself against the harbour wall, but his fingers find the paramedic's hand instead. Andy. Smiling. Sympathetic. A good man. His hands are smooth, made to heal instead of hurt. 'You need to come with me, pal.' He nods to the ambulance behind him, to bright lights and open doors and drugs that will heal only part of it.

Dave stands firm, resists. 'We need to find her, save her. I don't know how she got here or why she was there but . . . she was in the water.'

'Who was?'

'Amy,' says Dave. 'My . . . *daughter*.'

Andy leans in, smiling; softly says a few words that close something in Dave's chest, and open something else. 'She's fine. Warming up.' He smiles. 'The police only brought her here to be reunited with her mum, didn't expect the pair of them to throw themselves into that freezing water. But there was no stopping them. And aye, before you ask, Amy saved *you*.'

CHAPTER 43

The strip lights on the ward were so bright they could probably be seen from space. Dave blinked his eyes open when he heard her voice, smiled when she paused at the end of his bed.

'Nice day for it,' said Crystal, dragging the chair closer to him.

'You look . . . pretty.'

'That'll be the concussion.'

'Maybe.' But it wasn't that. For the first time since he'd met her, Crystal wasn't wearing any make-up. She had no fresh bruises.

'I went to the wee shop to get you grapes but they only had chocolate.' She handed over a Yorkie bar, missing one piece.

'You're too kind.'

'Peace offering,' she said. 'I'm sorry for . . . doubting you.'

'Same.'

'I wish you'd told *me* the full story. I'd have understood, Dave.'

'Probably wouldn't have wanted me driving your buses, though, would you?'

'Nonsense. You were done for *careless* driving, Dave. Not dangerous. You passed your advanced test when the ban was over. You've had no trouble since then and you had none before it. Other than that one incident, you've got an impeccable driving record. Saying that, nobody would have blamed you if you'd changed careers, stayed as far away from cars and buses and roads as possible. Why did you stick with it?'

'I've asked myself the same thing often enough,' said Dave, then he blushed. 'It probably sounds silly but I suppose I'm trying to prove to myself that I can. For every passenger I safely carry, and every pedestrian I slow down to avoid, I kid myself that I'm cancelling out all the bad stuff.'

'Makes sense.'

'But will it change things between us? Now that you know?'

She shook her head. 'I've known for ages, Dave.'

'What? How?'

'A journalist told me, by accident. When the award was announced I wanted to do something special, decided to make you one of those glossy photo books, as a present to mark the occasion. I was keen to get pictures from your past as well, assumed I'd find some on your social media. But, of course, you don't use it.

Then I had a brainwave. I got in touch with that news photographer who came to the depot for your interview. She said she'd have a look on the newspaper's photo database, in case you'd been featured before. She found some pictures from way back and sent them over. I printed them off, ready to use. But then—'

'Hang on – are those the photos you kept in a box in your office?'

Crystal screwed up her face. 'Yes. And how do *you* know that? Was it *you* who was sneaking around in my office after dark? I assumed it was Colin, searching for evidence of my many torrid affairs.'

'Of that, he's innocent,' said Dave. 'It was me. But it's a long story. Finish yours first.'

She frowned at him, but her eyes were pure love. 'So the photographer sent me those photos and a few hours later she called me back. She said the images had been swiped from an old Facebook account, that I really shouldn't use them. I was confused, told her you don't use social media. So then she told me the account had belonged to a dead woman. Someone at the paper had downloaded photos from her page before her grieving family had closed it. Your photo was among them. The lassie wouldn't give any more details about that story so I did some digging, found out what had happened. I've tried to raise it with you a few times but you closed me down every time. And actually, that's partly why I've come. There's . . . something I need to tell you.'

'That I'm still suspended? For good this time?'

She shook her head. 'I'm here to tell you I understand. Because . . . I've stood in your shoes.'

She took another piece of chocolate from his bar, popped it in her mouth. When she opened her mouth to speak again he could smell it. But his focus shifted when the words came.

'You remember the minibus crash near the airport, few years before your accident? Just before the Millennium party?'

'Vaguely,' he said. 'Why? What's it got to do with you?'

She blinked a few times then and looked away from him. 'It happened at four minutes past two in the afternoon. I remember because, once my airbag inflated, my face ended up an inch from the digital clock. Bright red on black, 14:04 and those two dots in the middle flashing away as if nothing had happened. It was just time, just seconds passing. I couldn't see what was happening behind me. But I could feel them move, struggling against belts and bent metal and glass that wouldn't break. I could hear them too. They sounded like a group of rowdy drunks, snorting and spitting and talking over each other, crying one minute and raging the next. I kept trying to count the different voices, hoping the total would reach eight.'

Dave stared at Crystal but her eyes were fixed on the pale green lino floor.

'All they were doing was trying to go on holiday. Croatia. One of the islands. And all I was doing was my job. Airport transfers in one of those posh minivans, all black leather and LED lights and tinted windows. You know the kind I'm talking about. Big but easy to drive. I must have done that route a thousand times, used to joke I could do it with my eyes closed.'

'Hang on – *you* were the *driver*?'

She took one of those deep breaths that made her whole chest rise and, with it, her jewellery. Her necklace slipped inside the neckline of her blouse when she exhaled. It had heard this story before, didn't want a re-run.

'Five injured. Three dead.'

Dave opened his mouth to speak but she'd already made her hand a stop sign, held it up to shush him. 'Not guilty, according to the courts. My pals expected me to celebrate. No jail time. No conviction to blacken my name or *future prospects*, whatever the hell that means. I could just walk out of court and carry on, carry on, carry on.'

She leaned forward and dropped her head to her hands, bangles jangling as she massaged her temples.

'My sister had even bought champagne, left it chilling when she went to court.' Crystal puffed out the scrap of a laugh when she said it. 'She told me later that if I'd got jailed she'd have kept it for my homecoming instead. We clinked glasses when I got home from court, and for the rest of the world that was that. All I heard were words like *relief* and *justice* and the suggestions that the verdict meant it was finally over. But what does *over* even mean in a situation like that one? *Over* doesn't apply. I was at my lowest point when I met Colin. He seemed to want to listen, so I talked and talked, bared my soul in a way I hadn't been able to do with anybody else. It helped that he was a stranger, that he never knew me before the accident so he couldn't compare the two versions of Crystal and be disappointed with the one he'd got. He didn't try to fob me off like everybody else, giving advice or nonsense about time and healing. But, looking back now, I can see he thought *he'd* be the one to heal me, all by himself. I was a project, something broken he thought he could fix. When he realised he couldn't . . .' She sighed, a wave shifting under her skin. 'I suppose he started using my confessions as ammunition instead. He knows my weak points better than anyone.'

'Leave him.'

'I'm going to. I've been looking at wee studio flats. *That's* what I was doing on Sunday afternoon, when I told Colin I was at yours. I didn't go anywhere near your house but I couldn't risk Colin knowing I was viewing properties; that I was really leaving this time. And by the way, he told me he attacked you. I'm sorry you had to deal with that.'

'Not your fault.'

'But it *is* my fault he knew about your accident. He's always snatching my phone off me so he can scour my messages and search history. If he suspects I'm *up to anything* he confiscates it. Unfortunately I did my research into your accident on the main phone and he found it. He was delighted, and I knew he'd use it against you. I was kicking myself. That's precisely why I've got two phones. One's for Colin's viewing pleasure and the other's for me – for emergencies, and for private stuff he can't know about.'

'Like calling estate agents?'

'Exactly,' said Crystal. 'And the good news is, I've rented a place, just for me. Move in this week. In the meantime, I've got a hotel.'

'Good move. And good riddance.'

'End of an era. I'm not defending him but it's not been easy for Colin either. He couldn't understand why I was still dwelling on the accident after so many years; why he couldn't be the one thing that made me happy. *It's not your fault*, he'd say, over and over. And in some ways he was right. But that doesn't mean those deaths are not my responsibility. *That's* what hurts. *That's* what never changes.'

'Aye,' said Dave, and that was enough.

Crystal straightened up, back flat against the plastic chair. 'I've got some good news for you as well, by the way: the harassment complaint has been officially withdrawn so you're no longer suspended. Amy's scrawny pal came in to see me – he's the one who'd called in to complain about you. Said the pair of them were freaked out after Suzanne told Amy about the hoax call, especially after *some old guy* had been stalking her in the street and asking for her number in the pub. His words, not mine.' She winked, got away with it. 'He told me Amy went to hide out at his flat in case *the old guy* came after her. Switched off her phone as well so she could properly lie low. Didn't realise how much it would worry her mum. Anyway, the lad practically begged me to reinstate you, said he felt awful once Amy told him the full story. He was just looking out for his pal.'

'Aye, and that's how Rafa tried to depict him.'

'They knew each other?'

'No, but Rafa pretended to *be* him so that he could set up a meeting between us. He overheard me give the lad my number at the MOB Bar, warned him off then texted me himself. Long story but . . . I was stupid enough to fall for it.'

'Stupid my arse, Dave. You were manipulated. And I know better than most how it feels when the person you love most lets you down.'

She reached for Dave's hands and squeezed. He squeezed back.

'Peas in a pod, me and you,' he said.

'We are,' she said. 'And . . . we're not the only ones.'

'Meaning?'

'I'd like to introduce you to some friends of mine, when you're back on your feet.'

'Sounds ominous.'

'Quite the opposite. Me and a few others run a support group for . . . accidental killers. That's what we all are, even though most of us struggle with that second word. *Killer.* But it helps, somehow, to say it out loud. You should join; tell your story and try to work through it.'

'Maybe I will,' said Dave.

Killer. For twenty years he'd dreaded others calling him by that name. His mind would rattle through endless practice runs of how he'd feel when the truth of it was finally exposed. Dave Kellock, held up to the light so all the rot in him could be seen. He'd always imagined the moment would be accompanied with panic, fear, self-pity, shame. But what was real and happening now was something else altogether. What filled him now was relief; that the hiding part was finally ending, almost over.

CHAPTER 44

And then they were all there, at last: the four of them, plus Dave. Suzanne and her baby, Carmen and hers.

Suzanne held the urn close to her chest, one arm wrapped around its sleek metal sides. Dave had only held it once but he'd been surprised by how little it weighed, how two lives could be held so easily in one hand. Suzanne's other arm was wrapped around Amy's shoulders and they sat together on the brand-new bench that still smelled of varnish and polished brass. Rafa's bench for Carmen had now been removed.

And what of his life?

Dave stared out to the horizon, to a place where the sea bed would be too far out of reach for toes, outstretched. Suzanne had risked her own life to save him. Despite what he'd done to her, she hadn't been able to stand by and watch a man drown. He'd died later in hospital, was gone before Dave even knew he was there. The little boat he'd burned had sunk and aye, the grief would as well.

'Dave?'

He shifted his gaze to Suzanne as she stood up and stepped forward. 'You're family. You should be here, with us.'

She held out her hand and the whole world seemed to hold itself still. Gone was the gentle tap-tap-tap of the flag ropes against the metal poles that held them in place. Gone was the chugging motor of fishing boats as they headed out to deeper water. Gone was the whisper and rush of the tide as it swallowed the beach behind them. Gone was the hiss of bus brakes from the High Street. Gone was the conviction that pain and grief were things to be avoided, swallowed down like ragged glass for fear of upsetting anyone else. Gone was the guilt that squeezed Dave's throat so tightly that for years he'd feared he'd choke on it, eventually. It had left no room for any of the goodness to pass through, for words or confessions or apologies or simple acceptance. Gone was the belief that blame and responsibility were the same things. Gone were the lies and the desperate need to prove, over and over, that, actually, he was a good man after all.

Suzanne held out the urn and loosened the lid that had been shut tight two decades before. She took another step forward, curled the toes of her bare feet around the damp stone edge of the harbour. Surely tides would rise to meet the remains of them, waves would swell and curl to carry them off. Surely the seas would split wide open. But for now, silence.

Suzanne stared into the open neck of the urn, whispering; then slowly straightened her arms out over the edge. The ashes slid out, fell fast. There was no breeze to carry them back to the ones letting them fall, no gull swooping down to gobble up the dust of them. If there were fish beneath they held their breath and if there were crabs they bowed their head and left by the side door.

The whole world was just them and the sea.

When tears came Amy turned to Dave, held out two hands that looked just like his – but younger, softer. She was wearing that yellow jacket again. She'd left it at Dave's when she'd run from Rafa, but had come back to collect it herself. He'd offered tea, and she'd accepted. He'd met with Suzanne a couple of times as well. They'd sat together in one of the beachfront cafés in Portobello, sipping coffee and staring out to sea when the silences felt awkward.

It'd all take time; and who knew where it would lead them.

But right now they stood together on Musselburgh Harbour as gentle, endless waves broke then remade themselves below them.

Amy squeezed Dave's hand. He let her.

And then, when he was ready, he let go.

Acknowledgements

This book was mostly written and edited in my campervan as I travelled Europe and the Balkans with my girlfriend, Mari. So first and foremost I'd like to say a big massive *gracias* to Mari for her unwavering patience and understanding. And thank you, life, for bringing us together.

I'd never have got this far without the support and loyalty of my agent, Caroline Hardman. I'm endlessly grateful for your support and good humour and no-nonsense guidance.

This book would mainly have told the story of a dead dog had it not been for the wizardry and gentle nudging of editor Sophie Wilson. I'm blessed to have found an editor who understands me and my writing – and, with each book, helps me improve.

Delighted to be reunited with copy-editor Linda McQueen for this book. Never have I witnessed a sharper eye.

To all the team at my publisher – thank you for getting my books out into the world, even in difficult

times. Joe at Black Sheep designed the brilliantly atmos-
pheric cover.

As ever, early readers have been a great source
of insight. Huge thank you to my sister Claire for
being the world's fastest and most willing reader.
You can do hard things, big sis! Thanks also to
my brother Stevie and his wife Julie for late-night
chats on Harris, which helped shape some of the
key characters.

Huge shout out to a few fellow writers: to Liv
Matthews, thanks for always being there, and for
always listening to my 9-minute voice notes. You're
the best. To Fran Quinn, thank you for the music (plus
the faster-than-light read and much-needed reassurance). To the Chemical Detective, aka Fiona Erskine –
thanks for reading so quickly and spotting some key
plot problems. To Philippa East – thanks for always
being on hand for messages and Zoom calls. Our
chats take us to dark places but are always illuminat-
ing! To Nikki Smith – our idea exchanges are always
so appreciated. Thanks due as ever to the D20 authors
and the fiercely loyal Caledonia Crime Collective:
good humour and good advice on tap!

I suffered something suspiciously like writers' block
between the first and second draft of this book. It was
a new and fairly bleak experience, and not one I'm
keen to repeat. Thankfully my creativity was unclogged
by a chance encounter with master storyteller Turan

Ali. His passion for telling brilliant, authentic stories is contagious and, thankfully, I stood close enough to catch the bug! Thank you, Turan, for helping me rediscover my voice.

To all the bus drivers I've ever worked and travelled with – thanks for looking after us. And to Charlie, whose death inspired this story. I only knew you briefly but you're not forgotten.

To Mum, Dad and all the family: I'm often far from home but you're always on my mind. Thank you for the love, the support, and the best cups of tea on the planet.

Finally – a huge round of applause, please, for all the book bloggers who've shouted about my novels. Your support is priceless. And to *everyone* who's read, enjoyed and helped spread the word about my novels: every time you buy a book you make an author's day. Even more so if you leave a review online! Takes one minute and really makes a difference. Sincere thanks to each and every one of you.

For the latest news on my books and travels, please sign up to my newsletter at emmachristiewriter.com.

About the Author

Emma Christie writes psychological thrillers set in Portobello, Edinburgh's thriving seaside neighbourhood. Her debut novel *The Silent Daughter* was shortlisted for the McIlvanney Prize for Scottish Crime Book of the Year 2021, shortlisted for the Scottish Crime Debut of the Year 2021 and longlisted for the Crime Writers' Association John Creasey (New Blood) Dagger Award 2021. It was followed in 2022 by her highly acclaimed second novel *Find Her First*. When she's not travelling in her campervan, Emma lives in Barcelona with her girlfriend Mari and far too many plants.

Find her online at www.emmachristiewriter.com or across social media @theemmachristie.